MARY KELIIKOA

DEADLY TIDES

A Misty Pines Mystery

LEVEL
BEST BOOKS

This is an unrevised and unpublished Advanced Reader Copy. This copy is not for distribution to the public. This is an advanced reader's edition created from uncorrected proofs and is not for sale. Typos and errors will be corrected for the final released edition of the book. | www.LevelBestBooks.us | Cover Art: Christian Storm | Review/Publicity Contact: Lisa Daily at lisadaily@mac.com | Release October 24, 2023 | 292 pgs | 978-1-68512-279-9 (pb) $16.95 & 978-1-68512-280-5 (eb) $5.99

First edition

ISBN: 978-1-68512-279-9

Cover art by Christian Storm

This book was professionally typeset on Reedsy.
Find out more at reedsy.com

CHAPTER 1

Abby Kanekoa rolled through town in her Prius, scanning the empty streets and worrying her bottom lip with her teeth. Stonebridge Assisted Living Center had called an hour ago to let her know her mother, Dora Michaels, had walked away. Again.

It was early January on the Oregon coast. There'd been no substantial rainfall for several days. The chilly mist-filled winds had come through that morning though, and the home couldn't say exactly when her mother had slipped out their door. Time to put a better lock on that damn thing. Mom might not be drenched to the bone, but she'd be cold.

Thankfully, this was Abby's scheduled day off. Not that the FBI didn't work with her regardless. After her daughter, Lulu, died of leukemia, they'd brought her back to the team as if she'd never left. They understood her *bad* days. Same since her divorce. Despite what Jax thought about how she'd handled her grief, burying herself in her work and having the support of the Bureau had saved her more than once.

Especially the flex schedule. With her mother's early onset of Alzheimer's, it allowed for these occasional searches.

Or not so occasional, as it were. Mom had escaped three times this month.

Greenery and garland from the holidays still clung to the streetlamps on Misty Pines' main strip. But she had yet to catch a glimmer of her mother's fiery red hair. At a crawl, Abby glanced inside each of the storefronts. Last time, she'd found her mother at the donut counter picking out an apple fritter.

"Honey's favorite," she'd repeated all the way to the car, her hand gripping a white bag full of them.

Abby's Hawaiian father—"Honey" as her mother had called him—had treated the family to fritters every Saturday morning since Abby could remember. He'd died twenty years ago, but Abby had continued the tradition with her own family until Lulu died and it became too painful. Today, the donut shop's seats and barstools were empty.

On Scholls Ferry Road, kids played on the swings and monkey bars of the elementary school. The time before the donut shop, Abby had found Mom by the cyclone fence, her fingers clenching the metal lattice, watching the kindergarten class play kickball. They both cried as Abby drove her back to the facility. Alzheimer's had been brutal to her mother, stealing much of her mind. But memories of Lulu were engrained, even deeper than those of Abby; Dora often gazed at her like they'd never met.

Abby pulled in front of the bookstore, ignoring the pang in her chest. Emily Krueger greeted her from behind the counter sorting a new shipment of novels with bare-chested men and women in flowing gowns on their covers.

Abby explained the situation.

"I haven't seen your mom. But I'll call if I do." Emily reached a hand across the counter and squeezed Abby's forearm. Emily had endured the disappearance of her own daughter a few months ago. If anyone understood Abby's concern, Emily did.

"Thank you. I'm sure she's just out picking flowers or..." Or what? Where did a sixty-four-year-old woman wander to? What was she looking for when she left the warm confines of the assisted living home into the cool and murky outdoors?

"Maybe she's folding laundry," Emily said.

Abby chuckled, despite her worry. During the summer, Dora had wandered into the laundromat down the road to fold a stranger's tighty-whities. But that's also why fear prickled up Abby's spine now. Dora normally stuck to the downtown area when she walked off.

Why not this time?

Abby slid back into the car and dialed Trudy at the sheriff's station.

"No reports of any wandering women today," Trudy said.

"You'll call if one comes through?"

"Certainly will, hon," Trudy said. "And I'll let Jax know."

Jax. Abby took a breath. "Don't bother him. If needed, I'll call him later."

"Uh oh. I thought you two had decided to work on your relationship."

"We've been so busy and…" Abby trailed off. She didn't have a good reason for why things hadn't progressed between them, only that she was to blame.

"It'll work itself out," Trudy said. "You've both been through a lot."

Abby gnawed on her thumbnail. "Yeah. You're right."

"Have you checked the ocean parks?" Trudy said.

"Next on my list."

Abby accelerated out of town, tension growing in her shoulders. It shouldn't be so easy for residents to walk out of an assisted living center. In truth, she was more annoyed with herself for having to put Dora there in the first place.

But she had to work, which meant she couldn't give her mom the full-time care she needed. Better facilities could be found in Portland, those focused on memory diseases, but they were a couple-hour drive. At least when her mom walked off from Stonebridge, she couldn't get too far. If Abby placed her in a home further away, she would still walk; when Dora's Irish blood had her flaring at a nurse, or at the day's menu, nothing stopped her. Only she wouldn't be close enough for Abby to hop in her car to search. She'd been in law enforcement long enough to know those thirty to sixty minutes could make all the difference.

She was being reminded of that today, another source of frustration. Abby hadn't caught the call on her phone when the staff at Stonebridge first reached out this morning. It had taken three attempts. She'd been in the shower shaving her legs, of all things. As if anyone would notice.

Abby turned into the boat basin. She cruised through, noting the fishing boats rocking dockside. She scanned each of them, spotting a crew of fishermen getting ready to brave the bar, but no redheads traversed the area.

She left the basin and headed down Ocean Drive, taking a right onto Meddle Road a couple of miles later. The route led to the ocean and the cliffs, and was miles from the facility. Too far for Dora to wander? She'd been gone for at least half a day. If motivated, she could have made it this far. Abby's hands tightened on the wheel. Heavier mist had started to roll in and hung in the sky. The temperature had dipped.

She swung her car into an abandoned beach parking lot and got out. Wind whistled past her as she crested the top of the lot and scanned the shore. The sand blasted against her pant legs with hollow pops and stung her face. She lowered the sunglasses from the top of her head onto her eyes and wrapped her jacket tighter as the cool air bit through the thin fabric.

Where are you, Mom?

Seagulls squawked overhead, catching the drafts. A few landed near the surf, arguing over an empty Styrofoam container. Aside from birds though, the beach was empty. Only rocks stood sentinel offshore, water eddying around them. This was too far south of one of the surfing beaches, and too far north of the other. No place to crab or fish here either. Summer had long passed for tourists to visit, except for the random one or two that had lost their way and stumbled upon the place. Most didn't realize the coast could be pleasant during the winter months. The locals knew, but the morning beachcombers had already come and gone, likely sipping coffee in front of a warm fire by now.

Up on the hill, tall trees lined the cliffs above the beach. Some had fallen catapult and hapless along the cliff lines.

And that's when she saw the splash of red rising from a row of logs near the sandy ridge. Whatever was there was hunkered down. Hiding?

Mom. Abby raced down the hill, the soft white sand sucking at her practical flats. She gave up and kicked them aside. Fifty yards further she hit the hardpack and sprinted, the wind at her back. As she drew closer, another flash of red gave her certainty that it was hair flapping in the wind.

"Mom, is that you?" Abby hollered.

She dropped to a walk as she approached. The woman was hunched like a turtle with only her back showing. Dressed in a nightgown. Shaking. Her red hair, streaked in gray, whipped upward. *My god.* She was whimpering.

Abby's heart pounded. Her mother must be freezing.

She almost ran again but forced herself to take it slow. Always best to approach Dora in the same manner she'd approach a small child. Or a suspect.

"Mom?" she said again. No answer, but if she was deep in her illness, the word might not register. "Dora. Are you okay?"

Her mother lifted her head. "It's mine."

Abby blew out a long tension-filled sigh. She'd found Dora—alive and talking. That's what mattered. Abby pulled off her jacket and draped it over her mom before sitting on the log next to her.

"You sure came a long way." Abby gazed out at the water. Relief at finding her mother unharmed whooshed through her like the breeze around them. Her heartbeat found its steady rhythm. "How about we get some place warm and dry. Pancakes sound good, don't they? Let's find some hot pancakes. With real maple syrup. You love that, right?"

"Okay. But I want to take it with me. I found it."

Abby tilted her head. Probably some shells. Driftwood. Whatever her mother found, she could have. Abby would help her put the item on display in her room. "Sure, Mom."

Dora straightened, and Abby's stomach twisted at the sight of the blood saturating the front of her white gown.

"Are you okay?" Abby said, her voice inching up.

Then she saw her mother wasn't hurt at all.

In her hands she held a tennis shoe containing a severed foot.

CHAPTER 2

Three Hours Earlier

Sheriff Jax Turner bent forward, sweat trickling down his back from the three miles he'd put in to get to the beach park. *The ocean is a fickle keeper of secrets. Some it holds deep in its belly like a pirate's treasure; others, it spits out like they're an insult to its delicate palate.* The words of his former Lieutenant Commander flitted through his mind as he scanned the hard-packed sand littered with water bottles, fishing line and random junk on the ocean shore below.

He hadn't thought of that son-of-a-bitch Grady, or his pithy comments, in years. And didn't appreciate thinking of him now. After Jax's father had died, his friend Grady stepped into the role of taskmaster. He'd gone so far as to have Jax assigned to his ship so he could make his life a continuation of the hell he'd lived with the old man. Jax had never been good enough for either of them.

Maybe that's why Grady invaded his thoughts now. His last case had had too many secrets, costing him the ability to trust. Not only those around him, but worse. Himself. Grady and his old man might have been right about him.

But not entirely. Not long ago he'd driven out onto a similar stretch of beach and contemplated ending his life. A call about a missing teenager had forced him to put off the decision, and the urge hadn't come up since. He'd even managed to let go of some of the debilitating pain of losing his only daughter that had caused the temptation in the first place.

Let go. Huh. Hardly the right words. But the pain had moved from excruciating to tolerable some days.

Jax stretched. His emblazoned Navy-issued sweatshirt rode up and exposed his skin, sending a shiver through him. He might as well get a move on. Running was new. An idea from the counselor he'd finally relented to see at his ex-wife Abby's insistence. Something about exercise being good for the soul, and a place to work out the demons. Except he'd grown accustomed to hanging out with those red pointy-tailed friends.

Green-gray waves ebbed and flowed as tires on the gravel sounded behind him. Jax turned toward the parking lot and tracked a minivan. A slew of surfers tumbled out, their wet suits rolled down to their waists as they made quick work of unstrapping their boards from the top, giving Jax no heed. The scent of weed wafted out with them. The surf had been better earlier. These guys had probably slept in. Most youth didn't realize the gift. What would old Grady or his father have had to say about that?

The young men gathered their surf gear, tucked their boards under their arms, and made their way down to the sandy pathway leading to the beach. Jax took off running, the sounds of his own breath and his feet on the pavement filling his ears.

An hour later, he was home and ready for the day, dressed in his khaki uniform. On his way out, he passed Lulu's pink room. Her disassembled canopy bed sat in the middle, a canvas drop cloth tossed over the top. Three one-gallon cans of sandy beige paint were stacked next to that. He hadn't brought himself to change the color yet. Another exercise the counselor had suggested; he was turning out to have all sorts of pithy ideas like Grady.

Outside, Jax ducked into his patrol rig at the same moment his radio crackled to life.

His assistant Trudy's voice came across the mic. "Sheriff Turner, you there?"

"Just coming on duty. What's up?"

"Welfare check. Matt's on duty, but a fender bender at the four-way in front of City Hall has him occupied."

"Say no more." Commissioner Troy Marks liked feeling important, so he'd demand Matt stay on scene until every scrap of vehicle was accounted for.

"How about Brody? He's supposed to put some time in this morning." His cruiser window down, Jax backed out of his drive. His phone buzzed with an incoming call. His former partner at the Portland Police Department, Jameson. He'd just seen him and Gayle at Thanksgiving. He'd call him back.

"Kid has an interview at Len's Auto. He'll be on later. Before you ask, Garrett isn't on for another hour. But I have good news for you."

"Brody leaving me?"

"You'd consider that good news?"

He clicked his tongue. "No. Is that why he's interviewing?"

"Not that he's said. They all have livings to make. The Commissioner's short-term increase in budget for your deputies is, well, short term."

Jax ground his teeth. He could bring Brody on full-time and fill the vacant deputy position. *He* hadn't lost his trust, but it took more than loving the thrill to be a good cop. And to stick.

Looked like it was on Jax. "So, what's the good news?" he asked.

"You have an applicant for the deputy position."

His shoulders inched up. "Not interested."

"Don't have a choice. Commissioner Marks is adamant you get another full-timer in here. Preferably one who'll 'keep your department on budget.'"

Like they had much of a budget to spend. Other than his and Trudy's salary, a couple officers who worked jail duty, and the normal operating costs, Brody and the boys were volunteer reserve deputies. "Screw him."

Trudy cleared her throat.

"I'm serious. Assisting me on one case doesn't grant him permission to shove his agenda down my department's throat."

"This is only a theory, hon, but maybe he's looking out for you. You're not superman."

"Hell, I'm not." Jax ran a hand through his graying sandy hair, feeling old. He didn't need a mirror to know bags had taken up residence under his eyes. They used to be worse when he spent the sleeping hours working on Lulu's dollhouse. "Probably some damn newbie looking to surf on the weekends. Who else would apply down here?" This morning's mist had already permeated his regulation khaki shirt and any good mood he'd woken with.

"According to the resume, she's been a cop for a couple of years."

"How old?"

"Twenty-seven. Name's Rachel Killian."

Great. A wet behind the ears recruit with plenty of investigative skills to learn. He already had that on his team. "I'm telling you, Trudy—not happening."

"I've scheduled the interview for three o'clock this afternoon."

Jax rubbed his hand over his face. He'd worry about the interview later. "Where am I going?"

"Terry Chesney's place on Bull Mountain. He owns the Surfrider Shop on the outskirts of town."

"I'm familiar." A bit of a loner. Good looking by most people's standards with shoulder-length graying blonde hair he kept tied back. An aging beach bum, but one that did good business. Jax had seen the logos from his shop on the boards of both local and out-of-town surfers. One of the boys he'd seen at the beach that morning had had one tucked under his arm.

"His brother Gerard says he and Terry were talking last night when Terry heard sounds in the garage," Trudy said. "He went to investigate, but never called his brother back. Gerard hasn't been able to get a hold of him since."

"What time was that?"

"About eight."

Well past sunset. If he'd had a beer or two, Mr. Chesney might have gotten distracted when he came back in and fallen asleep in front of the TV. He also could have gone out into his garage and gotten hurt. Encountered someone or something. Any illusion he had that Misty Pines was free from crime had disappeared last year, although bears and cougars had been spotted in the area this past year too.

Signing off with Trudy, Jax made the twenty-minute drive to the other side of town and hit the winding forest-lined road of Bull Mountain.

Terry Chesney lived at the halfway point, and near a tree-filled ravine. The ocean lay somewhere behind that. A surfboard mailbox marked Terry's dirt driveway. Jax made the right and followed it fifty yards back to Chesney's timber-style house built sometime in the '70s. Plywood surfboard frames littered the front yard. The garage door was up, and the lights were on.

Jax pulled in behind Terry's Surfrider van in the driveway and got out. He glanced inside the van's windows. The back seats had been removed and replaced by a couple of old tires. The added weight would come in handy when the streets were slick, but it likely made it easier to transport boards too. Up front, a sweatshirt had been flung onto the passenger side. No keys in the ignition. Door locked. He placed his hand on the hood. Cold.

Jax strode into the double-car garage, scanning the space that served as a workshop. Two plywood surfboard frames laid side-by-side on waist-high wooden horses. Jax had expected foam and fiberglass, items often associated with surfboards, but found none of that. Terry was a wood craftsman. By the sleek curves and light wood inlays of the boards hanging above Jax's head, a damn good one.

The smell of cedar permeated the space. Wood pieces filled a bin in the corner. Sawdust littered the ground beneath a band saw against the wall. A rack of chisels, shaper planes, and lathes hung from hooks. A tray of clamps on top of a cabinet below that. A few scattered tools on the floor near the workbench looked like they might be out of place. A toolbox on its side. Not necessarily a sign of foul play—Terry might not have had time to do anything about it—but tools were everything to a craftsman.

Jax knocked on the access door leading into the house, noting the one jacket hanging on a hook next to the solid door and the pair of boots against the wall under that. He knocked again. No answer.

Outside, he rang the front doorbell twice. After a few minutes, he made his way across the backyard that fed into the forest behind it. He stood at the edge of the property as a slight wind rustled through the limbs. A couple of obvious trails snaked through the tree line. A mountain biker's dream. He hadn't noticed a bike inside Terry's garage, though. Only an empty wall rack and a helmet.

"Terry Chesney. It's Sheriff Turner. You out there?" His voice was lost to the foliage.

Jax returned to the garage. This time he cracked the unlocked access door into the house. "This is Sheriff Turner, Mr. Chesney. I'm entering your home."

When a response didn't come, he lifted the strap securing his gun. While Terry could be out on one of those back trails hiking or even biking, he didn't know for certain. And with a brother concerned something might be off, Jax wouldn't let his guard down.

Jax stepped into a warm mud room. The scent of rotting organic matter hit his nose. A humming sound came from the other side of the closed door leading into the house.

His jaw tightened as he pushed open the door to reveal the kitchen. He braced himself, expecting the worst. Instead, an open package of steak warmed on the counter. Flies buzzed around the rotting meat. A wallet, cell phone, and a home-baked pie in a ceramic dish sat near the sink.

A grocery bag on the opposite counter contained chips, a gallon of milk, and a quart of melted ice cream that had seeped through the paper. It sat next to a wood block filled with steak knives—one missing.

Jax placed his hand on the gun. "Mr. Chesney, are you injured?"

He listened for movement, breath, murmurs.

Nothing came back. He made quick strides through the small house. Empty, like the hole forming in his stomach.

Jax jogged outside and dropped back into his patrol car. Stared at the towering firs behind the house as he radioed Trudy. "All deputies to Bull Mountain Road stat," he said. "Brody needs to cut that interview short."

CHAPTER 3

The hum of the patrol car accelerating up Bull Mountain caught Jax's attention before it turned into the drive. The crunch of gravel followed until the car pulled in behind Jax's SUV. Garrett's crew cut and linebacker-sized body filled the driver's seat. He was the only one of Jax's deputies that applied regularly to law enforcement positions outside of Misty Pines, but downsized department budgets meant the list was long, and the wait longer. He was an asset in the meantime. He and Matt climbed out.

"What's up, Chief?" Matt said, wiping his forehead, his face red with anticipation. A little twitchy. He'd shown that nervous side during their last case. Being a volunteer deputy was about his speed. When he wasn't under Jax's direction, the twenty-two-year-old could be found stocking soup cans on aisle five at the IGA. Or flirting with the newest coffee barista at the Dutch Brothers in West Shore—the other girls had his number by his second visit. But with the boy's blue eyes and beach vibe, Jax suspected catching one of those girls' attention wasn't too far off.

"Men." Jax nodded at them in acknowledgement, refraining from saying *boys*. After what they'd gone through in recent months, they'd grown—and they'd bonded. Trauma was a tight glue. "As soon as Brody gets here, we need to fan out and search these back woods."

As if on cue, a motorcycle flew down the driveway. Brody was the most zealous of the crew, but the motorcycle was a new development.

He yanked off his helmet, leaving his usually wispy brown hair standing on end. He had a *Here's Waldo* paleness to his face and a scrawny body. He jogged their direction. "Here for you, Sheriff," he said, winded by the time he got to them. "What's happening with Chesney?"

"You know him?" Jax said.

"He gave a woodworking class my senior year. Good guy. He okay?"

"That's what we're about to find out." Jax filled them in on what he'd seen inside the house.

"Not good," Brody said.

"Agreed. But we don't know anything yet." He gave them a quick summary of Gerard's call. "It might be as simple as he's fallen or encountered one of our animal residents." The forest behind Chesney's place was full of dense underbrush that gave way to sinkholes and unseen drop-offs, along with coyotes, bears, cougars, and the innocuous deer and elk. The ocean was about a mile or two in and would be a far drop below as well. "What we do know is Terry might have been out there eighteen hours now. Temps dipped into the forties last night. Depending on what Mr. Chesney had on, he could be unconscious from hypothermia, not to mention injuries."

They all nodded.

"Going alone, or in teams?" Garrett asked. His baby face scanned Jax's expression. One of these days, he'd grow some facial hair and his looks would catch up with his brute body.

"Teams," Jax said. "And you'll be with me. We'll cover less ground, but we won't miss anything." He couldn't let that happen again. "The trails look well-used, making traversing them easier. Unless Terry went off the path. We need to be prepared for that."

Jax gathered his men at the back of his patrol car. Standard issue in these parts included anchors, climbing ropes and harnesses, although none of them were skilled outdoorsmen. West Shore had a bigger department and more expertise, but time was a factor.

They headed out with bear spray and walkie-talkies hooked onto their gun belts, and climbing gear looped around their shoulders.

"Radio check." Jax tested their communication a few minutes in.

"10-4," came the reply, but neither party had found anything aside from some long-discarded trash.

A while later, Garrett stopped along the gnarled path. "Got something," he said. Jax, ahead twenty yards, hustled back to where Garrett pointed to a bike tire barely sticking out from the underbrush.

Jax inspected the site and motioned Garrett to step out of the trail. The foliage around the tire hadn't been stepped on. Jax found a clear spot for his foot and reached in for the tire. It came out easy, not attached to a bike, its spokes rusted. "It's been here a while."

Garrett nodded and Jax took lead again as they went back to the main trail and resumed their search. Moss hung off the fir trees, giving it an other-worldly effect. Birds darted above in the canopy. Shots of light filtered through. No clues jumped out about where Terry Chesney had gone.

If someone had been in his garage and tried to steal something, he may have taken chase after them. If he was scaring off a predatory animal, though, Jax wouldn't expect him to venture out into their domain. A predator could have gotten to Terry first and dragged him out here, but Jax would have expected blood in that case, and he hadn't seen any sign of it.

The sound of the ocean played off the cliffs below and wafted the steady roar into the air. The farther they went into the forest, the farther downward the trail led. Slices of cobalt sky peeked through the thinning trees. If Brody and Matt had followed a similar westerly route, they'd be coming to the same end.

"Check in," Jax said into the walkie. "You men finding anything on your side?"

"Negative." Brody's voice crackled through the bad reception. "We've been fighting ferns for days. Matt about lost his boot in a sinkhole. I fell into a poison oak patch and I'm already itching."

Previous case or not, youth and inexperience surrounded Jax. He'd never miss Portland politics, but he did miss the seasoned team he'd had there. His three o'clock interview would be one of the inexperienced, but without the benefit of history. He didn't need to meet her. The answer was no.

"You approaching ocean front?" Jax said.

"We see a clearing; no water," Brody said.

Jax came to a fern-covered edge with more trees. Looking over, he found more of the same. The ocean would be past the foliage, and a sharp drop from there. Using a tree for balance, he stepped into the ferns and his feet slipped in the slick underbrush. He scrambled to get his footing and dropped his radio.

"Watch it, boss," Garrett said from the pathway. "You okay?"

He would be as soon as he retrieved his heart out of his stomach. "Fine."

The glimmer of metal caught his eye halfway down the cliff as he pulled himself up. A bike maybe. He situated himself sideways and took one side step. His feet flew out from under him again, dropping him onto his hip.

His heart plummeted once more as he slid down the embankment until his foot lodged on a branch, stopping him. Wet and cold soaked through his shirt. *Son-of-a-bitch.* He rolled to his hands and knees and then forced himself upright, shooting a look at Garrett that said *don't say it.* But said or not, he'd be unable to make the climb down without a harness and security rope.

He took the moment to sweep the area with his flashlight. Nothing caught his eye but the bike.

"Terry Chesney. This is Sheriff Turner. Are you out here?" He projected his voice down the ravine and strained to listen.

A breeze whistled through the leaves and limbs. Birds answered with a few high shrills.

"Call Brody and Matt to our location. We need to retrieve that bike," Jax hollered to Garrett.

"If Terry crashed and went flying off the end...."

Garrett didn't need to finish the thought. If Terry had enough momentum, he could be anywhere on this hillside—and that was the best case scenario with that edge looming so close. "And get that rope ready."

Jax climbed the embankment and caught his breath once he reached the top. While they waited for Brody and Matt to join them, Jax strapped into the harness and pulled on gloves.

"Sure you don't want me going down, Chief?" Brody said as he and Matt arrived.

"Positive."

Brody, as the lightest, might have been the obvious choice. But if he found an injured Terry in the ravine, he wouldn't have the strength to assist him.

Of course, they had to find him first. The bike might've only belonged to the rusted tire they'd found earlier. It might've also belonged to that empty hook in Terry's garage.

His deputies laid the anchor and monitored the rope as Jax moved along the ravine's edge. Any dip or sudden drop-off could send him to the bottom. They'd best be paying attention. With only more forest down below, he didn't want to find out where it ended and the cliff began.

Jax zig-zagged his way down to the bike. The dampness continued to make the incline slippery. He stayed steady, not intending to land on his side again. He eased down, catching himself twice and stumbling once before reaching his destination.

Unholstering his flashlight again, he inspected the bike. It was a hybrid. Older, but rust-free. The tires were inflated and intact. Couldn't have been out in the elements too long.

Jax cast the beam under the dense brush and along the nearby tree line. No obvious marks on the trunks indicating a crash. No blood. No tire marks or skids dug into the dirt beneath. No compressed foliage where a body would have landed had it crashed or indicating someone had walked away from the wreckage.

No Terry.

An uneasiness settled in Jax's shoulders as he pulled the bike onto its tires. The bike had been thrown out here.

"Coming up," Jax yelled. He rolled the bike to his men, grateful for their assist as he drew closer, and shared his suspicion.

"So where's the rider?" Garrett said.

That's what I'd like to know. "You and Matt keep looking. Brody, you're with me. Time to see if the neighbors heard anything last night."

CHAPTER 4

Jax set orange cones on the road in front of Terry's driveway, while Brody ran down the hill with a couple of others to warn approaching vehicles. He'd just rejoined Jax when a fully-loaded rock truck rumbled up the hill and rolled to a stop, spitting black exhaust. The man was pleasant enough but offered no help. He'd made a delivery yesterday morning to a neighbor off to the west and hadn't been back until now.

When the truck moved past, Brody caught Jax's eye. "What do you think's happened out there?"

"Too soon to tell," Jax said. "I'm not certain the bike belonged to Chesney, but people don't leave groceries to rot on a counter." *Or leave their phone behind when they go to investigate strange noises.*

"Good point."

Something had taken Terry away from his home, and quickly. And nothing at this point suggested he'd made it back.

Jax lifted his phone out of his back pocket. While he'd been retrieving the bike, Abby had called. They hadn't spoken since their last therapy session when she'd made some crack about him acting infallible. What a crock. On those rare occasions he thought he might be on the right track, he only needed to think of his dad or Grady... or his last case.

Besides, infallible was Abby's title with her locked down emotions and propensity to think she had all the answers. He winced. Maybe they were both full of it. Either way, the session hadn't ended well. They'd gotten into their respective cars and driven home. That was two weeks ago.

Maybe she wanted to try again. His finger hovered over her icon—a picture of her and Lulu taken the day their daughter was born. Reconciliation on the edge or not, that icon would never change.

A beat-up Chevy sputtered up the road before he could send the call through. Jax joined Brody as the old truck approached, the window rolling down at a snail's pace.

"What's the problem officers?" The driver, in his early seventies, had a day-old growth of gray beard and could use a dental hygienist. A hound dog, probably the equivalent in dog years, stood on the passenger seat, drool hanging from his jowls. A bath would do them both good.

"Trying to locate one of your neighbors, sir," Brody said.

"Whereabouts do you live, mister?" Jax eyed the fast-food wrappers on the floorboard and the shotgun strapped in a rack behind the man's head.

"McDonald. Old McDonald they call me. That's a shame. I assume since you're standing in front of Chesney's place here that he's the one who's up and disappeared?"

Disappeared was a strong word.

"Yes, sir," Brody said. "You see anything suspicious around here the last day or so?"

The man scratched his face. "Nah. Haven't seen or heard a thing. Course I live off Cumberland Road."

"Fair enough," Jax said. Cumberland was three miles further, across the ravine and facing the opposite direction from where they stood. "We think he might have been injured. If he's dazed or hurt, as you know…"

Mr. McDonald sucked in a breath through his teeth, creating a whistle. "Don't have to tell me. I grew up in these woods. It's a quagmire out there. You get off those paths, and something that looks innocent enough can send you reeling down the slope—or drop you to the base of a fifty-foot fir."

All things Jax knew. "Appreciate that. You see anyone milling around on your treks back and forth who doesn't belong up here?"

The man huffed. "Always. Things have changed last few years. The young ones race up and down these streets like they're Mario, and I mean the racer not that stupid video game." He sniffed. "Although maybe like him too. Anyways, some idiots nearly took me out a few days ago. Now that's something your department should be taking care of before someone gets killed."

Misty Pines had its share of bored teenagers who tagged buildings or found ways to entertain themselves. "They can be a problem. Any of those kids on the road yesterday?"

"Don't know. Ate something that didn't agree and never even got out to get the paper."

"Hope you're feeling better now, Mr. McDonald," Brody said.

"Much." He sniffed again. "Well, hope you find him."

"Thank you." Jax handed him a card. "You call if you hear anything?"

"Will do."

This roadblock approach might not get him the information he'd hoped for. Jax and Brody stepped back and waved the old man on as another small sedan approached. "You got this?" Jax said, as he grabbed his phone out again to call Abby.

"You bet, boss."

He'd just gotten the number on the screen when Brody motioned him over. "Lady says she knows you."

Jax made his way to the car and the smiling forty-something woman whose long lashes framed deep-set blue eyes. She wore blue scrubs, and the heat blasting from the air vents fluttered the big blonde curls that fell at her shoulders.

The combination of the cool outside air and the warmth from the car sent a shudder through Jax, as did the realization that he *did* know her. Though the last they'd spoken her hair had been swept in a bun.

And she'd been consoling him and Abby after Lulu had taken her last breath.

"Nurse Coleman?"

"Please, it's Margot. After all our time together."

Jax's chest tightened. "You live in the neighborhood?"

"Do now. Moved here from West Shore for a change of scenery."

He'd left Portland for similar reasons. "Misty Pines is definitely that. You still at the hospital?"

"I am. They gave us so much when our son Joey died, I can't imagine ever leaving there. But when I found the place up the road, even with the commute, I couldn't resist. The ocean and forest have always called my name. How's Abby?"

He hadn't realized Margot had lost a child to cancer. It didn't seem right to ask when, but she'd said *us*. Another relationship that didn't withstand the stress no doubt. She'd been kind to him and Abby—and more importantly, cared for Lulu like she was her own.

"Abby's good. We've been divorced for a while now, but we're in touch." Why had he said that? They'd been more than in touch. They were in counseling. Trying to reconcile.

She frowned. "I'm sorry. Too many of my patients' families don't make it when there's a loss."

Jax nodded and ignored Brody's intense gaze on them. Jax hadn't intended to get into his personal life or to rehash losing Lulu on the side of the mountain road. He preferred those feelings be stuffed down deep and far away. Especially when he had a job to do.

Hell with what the therapist suggested.

But Margot had seen him and Abby at their lowest. There was connection and solidarity in that. "Well, welcome to Misty Pines."

"Thanks. So, what's happening here?"

Brody gave her the rundown. "Do you know him?"

"Oh sure. Made it a point to meet my neighbors right away. Very nice man. I hope he's okay."

"That's what we're here to find out," Jax said. "Anything stand out as unusual last night? People that didn't belong here? Sounds perhaps?"

She shook her head. "No one. And only a few coyotes yipping was all."

"Close by?" Yipping often happened when one of the family made a kill to share. But coyotes didn't generally cause problems—they were more afraid of humans.

"Not in my backyard, and of course I live a few miles past here, but close enough that it woke me."

"Remember the timeframe?"

She furrowed her sculpted brows. "Probably around midnight."

"Anything else come to mind?" Brody said. The kid at least was proactive. Jax would miss him if he got that job at Len's Auto and left the team.

"No," she said. "I had an early start-time at work this morning and didn't see anything unusual then either."

Jax handed her a card. "If you do, or if you think of anything else that might be relevant, please give me a shout."

"Absolutely." She smiled and placed his card on her dashboard.

Jax's radio crackled to life. "Sheriff Turner, please report?" Trudy said.

He walked across the road and stood in Chesney's driveway as Margot accelerated away. "Turner here."

"Abby called, hon."

His heart leapt. She wouldn't call the station unless…. "Is she okay?"

"She's fine, but…"

He blew out a breath, annoyed that he'd felt concern. "Then she'll have to wait. We haven't found Chesney."

"Jax, stop for a second. Someone needs to meet her off Meddle Road. Unless you want her calling in the FBI."

His hand gripped the phone. They had their place with their resources. But they could also muck up a case for local law enforcement. "What's so important it can't wait?"

"A foot's washed ashore."

He rubbed his forehead. Another pithy wisdom from his former commander flitted through his mind. *When it rains it pours—and you best be wearing a jacket.*

"Tell her I'm on the way."

CHAPTER 5

Jax radioed Trudy his location when he spotted Abby's Prius parked near the sand's edge. His ex-mother-in-law, Dora, slept in the passenger seat, a wool blanket pulled under her chin and strands of her red hair falling across her face. Just as well. Even when he and Abby were married, and Dora functioned at one hundred percent, she hadn't liked him. Abby's father, Kaveka—or David as most knew him—had been a police detective and Jax suspected any resentment Dora held against her husband simply transferred to Jax. Even though Jax and Mr. Kanekoa had never met, Jax would never be husband enough for Abby. Losing Lulu had cemented that fact in Dora's eyes.

Abby stood at the overlook dressed in a blue track suit, her arms crossed over her chest. It must be her day off. Her black hair blew behind her. She should be wearing a warmer jacket, but she didn't look cold. Her regal silhouette made his heart squeeze nearly every time—even when she was mad at him.

"Trudy said you found something," Jax said, coming up beside her.

She didn't turn to meet his gaze, her eyes locked onto the ocean. "Tried to tell you myself, if you'd bothered to answer."

Her tone suggested her time and job held more weight than his sheriff position. An old argument. But he'd give her some leeway. "Terry Chesney, the owner of Surfrider, is missing." He gave her the brief version of what he knew so far—which wasn't much.

She closed her eyes. "Sorry. It's been a day."

"I imagine. Trudy gave me some indication, but what did you find exactly?"

She opened the large plastic-lined evidence bag on the ground in front of her.

Jax squatted next to the bag and visually inspected the severed foot inside. It was still wearing a Converse tennis shoe, the translucent skin frayed at the ankle. Hard telling what the state of the foot was inside the shoe, but it hadn't been out in the elements for too long. "Appreciate you calling Trudy and not your buddies at the Bureau."

"Your jurisdiction."

That didn't always stop the FBI and its profilers from attempting a power grab. But this was Abby. Not just some FBI agent. "You out walking the beach this morning and came across it?"

"No. Mom did."

"She wandered off again?"

"Yeah. No biggie." Abby frowned.

Jax shook his head. That had to be traumatic. And Abby's roughed-up thumb from consistent gnawing was a tell that Dora's frequent walkaways had begun to wear on her. Not that she'd told him about those. Trudy had let it slip. "Where did she find it?"

Abby pointed down the beach in front of the hillside. "Behind that log. It's where I found them both."

"I'm sorry her condition is getting worse."

"Is what it is. Right?"

He nodded. His father had died of a heart attack the day Jax enlisted in the Navy. His mother had run out on both of them years before that. He didn't know where she was at this point, or if she was even still alive.

His parents had never been close to their families, so for all intents and purposes, he was an orphan. Seeing what Abby went through, he only regretted that fact on rare occasions. Being alone with no one to care for had its advantages. He gazed at Abby and what they'd once had flashed before him. And its sorrows.

"Did you scan the area for additional evidence?" he said to move her onto another subject.

"Not as well as I could have. She refused to give up the foot, and it was a struggle to get her to the car. Then I had to wait until she fell asleep before I could bag it." Abby grimaced.

He hoped his brain would never betray him like that. "Did she say anything about how she found the foot? Or if anyone was nearby?"

"It was all I could do to negotiate with her to leave the beach. I haven't been able to ask. Although these feet washing ashore haven't amounted to much. There was a report earlier in the month about another one in West Shore."

He'd heard about that. Finding feet wasn't a new phenomenon in the Pacific Northwest, but in the ten years he'd been in Misty Pines, he'd never encountered one. In fact, out of the fifteen recovered over the last decade, many farther north than here, none had been due to foul play.

But he wouldn't be lax about it when he had a missing surf shop owner.

She lifted the bag to him. "I need to get my mom back to the assisted living center."

"I appreciate your doing this much. I'll take it from here."

Abby nodded. "Maybe when she's awake, she can offer more. It'll be better if I ask her, though."

"Agreed. Let me know what you find out."

"I will." She headed to her car.

"And about our last counseling session…," Jax said.

"Later, okay?"

He sighed. "Yeah. Of course."

He watched Abby slide into the driver's side and ease her door closed. Dora didn't stir, thankfully. She might not like the fact that the foot had been taken from her. Or that he was the one taking it. She'd accused him a few times of taking what was hers. Like Abby. But Abby was as headstrong as her mother and hadn't listened when Dora tried to convince her not to marry Jax that autumn day in the Rose Gardens above Portland.

Despite how she felt about him, she'd been a wonderful grandmother. She'd gone downhill soon after Lulu died. Something she and he had in common.

He set the evidence bag in the back seat of his rig and made his way down to the beach where Abby had pointed. The log she referenced rested about thirty yards from the surf. High tide would have brought the foot in because the buoyancy of the tennis shoe would have kept it from sinking to the bottom of the sea.

The ocean is a fickle keeper of secrets. Grady's words drifted through his mind. Clearly, body parts were an insult to the sea's palate. And if the surf had pushed the foot onto the other side of the log, it would have lodged, explaining why it hadn't been pulled back out. Or that the elements hadn't made it a skeleton already.

Jax trotted partway up the cliff side for a better view of the stretch of beach. Large rocks with water eddying around them blocked half of the shore about a hundred yards down. Closer to where he stood, a used diaper had been partially buried in the sand. Plastic rings from milk cartons and six-packs littered the ground. A gillnet had found its way onto the bank, along with candy and fast-food wrappers. General signs of kids and families not cleaning up. The disregard of the environment wedged under his skin.

Nothing looked relevant, but he couldn't leave the trash there either. He gathered it in a pile and wrapped it together to take back with him.

He scanned the beach one more time for anyone who might've witnessed something and found no one. The wind had picked up, swirling the sand. He'd get back to the station and turn in the evidence before returning to his men who he hoped had come up with a solid lead for where Chesney had gone.

Because he now had a missing person and a severed foot. Misty Pines had woken again, and not in a good way.

CHAPTER 6

Abby drove around the asphalt drive of Stonebridge Assisted Living, a one-story sprawling gray building nestled into a cluster of towering evergreens. Craftsman beams framed the entry, along with black wrought-iron railings that lined the ramps and walkway to the double wood and glass front doors. During spring, flowers and trees would be in full bloom. At least the grass was lush and green with the winter rain they'd had.

She parked in the guest designation. It was beautiful here, but it didn't decrease the twinge of guilt in her gut that she had to bring her mother here at all.

"Where am I?" Dora said, rousing from the passenger seat of Abby's car. She untucked her arm from under the wool blanket and swept her heavy bangs away from her eyes.

Abby placed her hand on her mother's leg. "Home."

Awake and talking were good signs because Dora had to have been exhausted from her ordeal of wandering. The beach where Abby had found her was miles away. All that time in the elements until she'd been found must have been horrible as well.

Abby ached thinking about what her mother had endured the past few hours. The confusion. The disorientation. What was her memory doing to her that hovering over a severed foot made any sense at all?

Dora looked down at her nightgown and back at Abby with her eyes wide. "Am I hurt?"

"No, Mom."

Her mother appeared lucid, a fact that could change without warning.

The disease had a way of stripping away the person underneath and all the sensors. In the late stages, it would revert its victim to early childhood and first words. And tantrums. She'd been a target of her mother's rants more than once, as had Jax after Lulu died, but it was still better that she ask the questions Jax wanted to know.

"What took you out to Meddle Beach?" Abby said, keeping her voice gentle.

Her mother's face scrunched. Thinking. "Was I there?"

"You were."

Dora turned her head toward her window. "It's pretty at the ocean. But I don't know." She frowned. "I hate this place."

Meddle Beach was beautiful, but she'd never heard her mother say she hated the center. "Why, Mom? Don't they do well by you?"

She didn't answer.

Abby turned toward her mom. "Do they hurt you?"

Dora shook her head.

Thank God. "You've told me you like that they play bunko on Thursdays, and the food is decent, right?"

Dora clicked her tongue. "The potatoes taste like paste."

With everyone's varying diets, it couldn't be easy to cook for all the residents. "Most of the time though?"

Dora shrugged.

Abby unclenched her hands. Every time she prepared to hear the worst—and relief flowed through her when she didn't. Dora could be upset at the mere thought of assisted living. Abby had heard that complaint before. But she couldn't do anything based on her mother's sadness about having to be there. Dora couldn't be at home any longer, and it was safer for Dora to be around people—when she wasn't escaping.

Dora hung her head. "It's all fine," she finally said.

Abby nodded, but her mother's words didn't ease the guilt. She appraised Dora. Deep lines framed her eyes. Her red hair stuck out in odd directions. Her mother could use a warm bath and a long nap.

She made a move to get out but hesitated. Dora had no memory of walking to the beach—facts often flowed in and out. They could show up unexpectedly. "How did you find the foot, Mom?"

"It's mine. Where is it?" she said, looking at the floorboard, in the side pocket of the passenger door, whipping her head around to check the backseat.

Abby's chest clutched again, wishing her mother was whole. "It's safe and sound."

Dora let out a long sigh and nodded.

"I was hoping you could tell me how you came across it though." She'd try one last time. "Did you see it wash ashore?"

"No."

"You just came across it then?"

Her eyes narrowed. "I wanted to give it back."

The depth of her sickness stung Abby's eyes. "Give it back to who, Mom?"

"The person it belonged to, of course."

"Of course. Was there someone out on the beach that you thought it belonged to?" Abby held her breath. Some with memory disease believed a stuffed toy was alive and needed caring for. Had she seen the foot as something along those lines?

Dora's eyes flitted back and forth like she was searching the databanks of her brain. She frowned and barely shook her head.

"Were you by yourself?"

"No."

Abby's hand slid off the door handle. "You weren't alone? Was someone else trying to get to the foot?"

"I'm hungry. Can we eat? I don't want to be late. The food is cold if you're not there on time. I hate cold food."

"I know you do, Mom." Abby shifted in her seat. "But can you answer the question first? Who was with you?"

Dora looked out the window. "Huh?"

"You said you weren't alone."

"I'm hungry, Abby. I'm hungry." Her tone had turned to frustration.

Pushing wouldn't get them anywhere. Dora might have misspoken and now the questions were confusing her.

When the test results came back, the foot would probably end up having been attached to an individual who'd walked off and drowned hundreds of miles away. The other found feet had had similar stories.

Jax would be disappointed at the lack of information from Dora, but no more than she was every day at the situation. Abby got out and rounded the car, assisted her mother to the front door.

Inside, a large woman in scrubs, wearing a name tag that read *Bernice,* rushed towards them. "Is she hurt?"

"No. Just dirty," Abby said.

"Ms. Michaels, so glad to see you're back with us." Bernice rested her hand on Dora's arm. "May I help you to your room? I bet we can find you something much more comfortable to wear."

Dora looked back at Abby. "You coming?"

"Yes," she said. But Mrs. Vernon, the administrator of Stonebridge, appeared behind the reception desk and held up her index finger. "I'll be right behind you."

Dora didn't respond and let Bernice guide her down the long hall to her room.

Once Dora had disappeared, Abby turned her attention to Mrs. Vernon. "Why'd she get out this time?"

Mrs. Vernon huffed. "She's a real Houdini that one."

"No, I mean, did someone upset her? Was there a problem?"

She shifted on her feet. "Mrs. Turner…"

"It's Ms. Kanekoa."

"My apologies. I wasn't aware."

It's not like she'd advertised her divorce from Jax. But she'd changed the information on her contact sheet last year. What else did Mrs. Vernon not pay attention to? "It's fine. But my mother doesn't just walk out. Something must have happened to upset her."

The administrator squared her shoulders. "There's been nothing brought to my attention. But Ms. Kanekoa, her disease is progressive. Her wanting to leave, act out, yell at us, these are traits that will only worsen over time as her condition deteriorates. We're not equipped for that level of care. You understood that when you placed her here, and we only agreed to try it out. But it's not working. Have you considered…?"

Abby put her hand up. She knew the alternatives and she couldn't hear it. "No, I haven't. But you care for the elderly for God sakes. It should be a basic responsibility to keep the patients inside."

Mrs. Vernon stiffened and straightened her suit jacket. "This is a low-risk facility. They are not patients. Your mother needs to be in a place with more security, and more direct care."

The thought of putting her mother into a locked facility where she might feel like a trapped animal sent a violent ripple down Abby's arms. The guilt of having to leave her here with people who couldn't watch their own front door was hard enough. If her mother was miles away and essentially imprisoned, Abby might never sleep again. Not that she'd ever slept well after Lulu.

Maybe she wasn't equipped to make decisions for her mother—for anyone. She'd lost Lulu. All the love and care in the world hadn't saved her little girl then. She'd done no better for her own mother. What if she failed again?

The answer was, she couldn't. Dora was all Abby had. "Thank you, Mrs. Vernon. I'll take that under advisement. In the meantime, could you please be more *aware*?"

Mrs. Vernon gave her a small smile. "Next time, I'll have to call the police."

"I am the police." An exaggeration. Jax was the local authority even if Dora wouldn't appreciate his involvement. But being FBI should mean something.

Abby turned away and strode toward her mother's room. Before she reached the door, a man in his late eighties, his pale eyes sunken, stepped through another doorway and in front of her. "Don't let them fool you."

Abby hopped back. His gaze darted from her to the hallway walls. To the fire extinguisher. To the ceiling. "Mr. Casey. How are you?"

"Don't let them fool you. They don't watch."

"The door?"

"Anything. Anyone. We're all pawns. They're going to kill us."

CHAPTER 6

"Mr. Casey." Mrs. Vernon's shrill voice came from behind. "Please go back into your room."

"But I love her," he yelled down the hall. "And you're not taking care of her. Where was she last night?"

"I'm sorry, Ms. Kanekoa." Mrs. Vernon approached quickly, two nursing assistants with her. "He has a vivid imagination."

"I know." He jutted his chin out in defiance. "I know."

Abby stepped out of the mix as the aides assisted Mr. Casey back into the room. Mrs. Vernon accompanied them and shut the door behind her.

Abby gathered herself. Mr. Casey often yelled out accusations or even directions to anyone who'd listen. The list was long: they turned off the heat at night, the food in the Korean War was better than the slop they served here, or sometimes a step-by-step tutorial on how to mop the floor. His military background made him a man Jax could connect with. Next time she saw Jax, she'd ask if he'd come visit Mr. Casey. He didn't appear to have other family that took the time. It might help in the long run.

But today, while agitated, he was succinct in his concerns. Was the fact that Dora had gotten out the reason for his outburst? The reason they weren't taking care of her? One way to find out.

Abby opened the door to her mother's room. Dora perched on the edge of the bed, her bare feet dangling over. Her shoulders slumped.

"Oh dear, where are my slippers?" she asked Bernice before landing her gaze on Abby. "Do you have my slippers young lady?"

Her mother had slipped away. Tears pushed into Abby's eyes. The shifting winds kept her off-balance. Mrs. Vernon was right. Dora needed more care than this facility or she alone could give her. "No, Ms. Michaels, I don't," Abby said, then turned to Bernice. "Can you make sure she has pancakes for dinner? I promised her pancakes."

Bernice gave her a small smile. "You bet. I've got this ma'am."

Abby closed the door behind her, wiping her eyes. It never got any easier. It never would.

Her phone buzzed with a text. Her partner, Olek. She opened the message. *So much for a day off. Chief wants us to report. Sounds like the foot that washed*

31

up in West Shore last week was attached to a local.

CHAPTER 7

Jax passed a Toyota Rav-4, a black lab hanging its block head out of the passenger side window, on his way into the sheriff's station. The department was housed in a standalone building near the courthouse and located a few blocks from where Commissioner Marks and the city council conducted business to keep the city progressing "into the future." Not that many around here wanted that. The lack of tourists and the homegrown values of the town had always grounded the community—it's why he and Abby had come here to raise a family.

Only recently had the status quo been upended when an old case had reared its head.

And now Terry Chesney.

He'd radioed his men on his way back from the beach, with no response. Reception in the woods behind Chesney's place would account for that. They must still be out searching.

Trudy, her gray pixie cut smoothed perfectly, leaned back in her chair and was filing her nails when Jax came inside. The headset wrapped around her head made her look like she could be conducting air traffic, or fielding a call from a concerned citizen as she was now. He brought in the evidence bag containing the foot and set it on her desk.

Her eyes went wide as she finished up. "Mr. Courtney, I have no doubt that's what happened. Have you looked in the freezer yet? I've been known to put my keys in there a time or two."

"Hey, real quick," Jax whispered, but Trudy whipped her hand up to shush him. Whether air traffic or the sheriff's department, she had total control in her world. They got along best if he didn't push his own agenda.

"You found them, hon. Excellent. Glad I could help." Trudy pointed to the waiting room as she clicked off. "Your three o'clock is waiting."

Jax followed her gaze. A young woman, her long blonde hair pulled into a ponytail, sat in a corner chair, a magazine covering part of her face. From the side, he noted her mock turtleneck with a Nike white running jacket matched with blue jeans. She read "cop" from a distance. And partially covered or not, he'd recognize that face from miles away, since he'd been at the hospital the day she came into the world.

"Rachel?" he said, approaching with arms wide.

She jumped up like she had when she was a kid. But without running into him and bouncing off his stomach. "Uncle Jax."

He gathered her into a bear hug. "Don't tell me you're the one applying for this job?"

"One and the same."

Jax turned to Trudy. "You said her last name was Killian?"

"That's what it reads on her resume." Trudy popped her index finger up as another call came through her headset.

Rachel smiled. "It is Killian. I took my mom's maiden name when I graduated from the Academy."

"What's wrong with Jameson? Your dad's well respected."

"Right, leaving me no room to make or break it on my own."

He pushed her to arm's length, wondering what his former partner thought of the name change. "Good for you. Always hated those brownnosers who ride in on their parents' reputations and think they're owed the keys to the kingdom." He'd seen it far too often in the force, but it wasn't isolated to those situations. His thoughts turned to Commissioner Marks and his son, Dylan. Nepotism could be found everywhere. He stiffened. "I hope you don't think our connection will make a difference in my hiring decision."

She chuckled. She had Gayle's laugh. Jameson's chin and height. She stood nearly eye to eye with Jax. "The only reason I applied here is because I knew you wouldn't let that happen."

He punched her shoulder. "You got that right. So, what's going on up north that you'd want to cut and run from the Portland Police Department anyway? Can't imagine Misty Pines being much of a draw for a twenty-something like you."

"Cut is the word. Budget, to be precise. As newer hires, we were the first to go. Koa and me are about to be homeless and I've always loved the ocean. But I've got experience, uncle. I spent two years in Vancouver PD before Portland."

"Uh-huh." He wasn't sure he believed that was the only reason she'd apply a hundred miles from her dad. Although Portland had a few heavy issues, and plenty of politics running through the precincts these days. Even more so than when he'd left. Still, he wouldn't let emotion get the best of him. "You mentioned Koa. Is that the dog out in your car?"

"Yeah. My police dog dropout."

"Couldn't find the suspect?"

She laughed. "It's what happens when she does find them. She won't touch them or bring them to the ground—unless they want to play." Rachel's face lit with a smile. "I fell in love with her and started her on nose work. She excelled, and of course she isn't required to be aggressive once she finds her target."

"Some just don't have the heart for it."

"Nope. We do search and rescue on our off days. It helps me unwind. Keeps my humanity intact."

"A good thing. It can certainly be tested." Her and Koa's skills could come in handy around here.

"Damn straight," she said. She was a chip off her dad's block for sure. He was a good man. A good friend.

Jax had let the friendship slide after Lulu died, but they'd reconnected this past year. Rachel could be a continued link, if he could get past the fact that she'd fallen asleep on his shoulder once when he'd babysat on her parent's anniversary. Could he work alongside someone he instinctively wanted to protect like a daughter? Or could that give them a stronger bond since she would feel the same about him? Trust didn't come as easily as it once did…and he couldn't get a read on whether it would be good or bad with her in the mix.

"What's your dad think about your applying? He called earlier, but I haven't had a chance to call him back." Jax raised his brow, having a hunch what his old partner might have to say about it.

"You know Dad. He's totally up for anything." She kept her eyes on Jax, but her right eye twitched. Her tell from the first time she'd told an untruth—she'd denied running her scooter into the back of his truck.

"Hmmm." Jameson's earlier call might be about putting in a good word and she didn't want his help. Or not.

He'd feign belief for the moment. Rachel could work it out with her dad if she got the job. Search and rescue experience in his own office could prove helpful in the deep woods surrounding the coast range. Like now, with Terry missing. But he wasn't ready to commit and he wouldn't make decisions based on his manpower shortage or the fact he and Rachel had history.

"How are your parents anyway? I haven't seen them since Thanksgiving."

"Yeah, I was sorry to miss you, but duty called." She cleared her throat. "They're hanging in. Cold cases keep Dad up at night. From what he says, you know all about that kind of thing."

He did. They both grabbed onto cases like meaty bones and didn't relent until that bone was clean. That didn't always bode well for resting...or relationships. "When do you have to be back?"

"I don't. Planning to stick around for a few days. If you'd prefer to push off the interview until tomorrow, that's not a problem."

"Might be good," he said. "I'm on a case and need to get out to my men." He leaned in, about to give her a hug goodbye.

"Hold up," Trudy said to Jax and then returned to her call. "I understand. Sheriff Turner will meet you at the shop."

"What's that about?" Jax said as Trudy took off her headset.

"That was Brandon, Terry Chesney's employee. He just arrived at the shop to find it ransacked."

His men would have to wait. "On my way."

Trudy nodded and stared at Rachel, her meaning clear.

36

It wasn't orthodox, and he wouldn't do it for anyone else. Oh hell. What better way to know if Rachel was qualified than to test her out. "How about your interview starts now?"

"With or without Koa?"

"She could come in handy I suppose. Bring her along."

"Great."

If Rachel joined the team, he'd be surrounded by women. Much like when Abby and Lulu filled his life. Kept him on his toes. "Hope she doesn't mind the back seat."

"She's happy anywhere the action is."

He smirked. He and Koa might have that in common.

CHAPTER 8

The Surfrider Surf Shop sat on the eastside of town. Its cobalt blue siding and purple trim made it hard to miss. Jax got out, followed by Rachel who left Koa in the backseat. But Koa's attention remained locked onto Jax until he'd walked away. If her look and Abby's resistance to getting back to counseling were indicators, he was always making some woman in his world unhappy. Story of his life.

"You the one that called?" Jax said to the twenty-something kid standing in the garage, a splotchy beard covering his dimpled chin. Several wood surfboards in various stages of build were laid out behind him.

"Yeah. I'm Brandon," he said with no urgency, as he flicked back his greasy hair that rested on his sloped shoulders.

Brandon's hands were scarred with tiny scratches, a gauze bandage wrapped around his index and middle fingers on his left hand. Jax nodded at the injury. "What happened?"

He lifted his bandaged hand in the air. "Cut it when I was cleaning the mess. Come see for yourself."

Jax glanced at Rachel, who scanned the shop and followed them inside. When he'd worked with her father, Jameson had been the senior man. Jax followed like a fresh puppy. That was not an apt description of Rachel. Standing shoulder to shoulder, the little girl he'd once known presented as a capable officer.

Inside the eight-by-eight office, a coffee cup—once filled with souring cream given the stench in the room—had crashed to the floor, a smattering of fresh blood near the mug's handle.

38

Brandon followed Jax's gaze. "I hit the cup on my way to call you."

Jax nodded.

Diagrams, drawings, and sketches on blueprint paper were scattered on the desk. Trophies that might have once been on shelves were piled in a corner. Pictures of Terry Chesney during his surfing years either hung tilted on the wall or had crashed to the cement. His once chiseled and athletic body, swooped bangs and tan, qualified him to be on the cover of any California surf magazine. One such magazine had fallen to the floor. Shirtless, Terry posed in a pair of jeans, his thumbs hooked into his belt framing a custom-made surf belt buckle with its gold tones and diamond fin. Last time Jax had seen Terry, his belly protruded from a bit too much beer and gray hair had overtaken the blonde. Any tan he might have had would have long faded in this part of the state.

"Were you aware you had a surfing legend in town?" Rachel said, nodding to a picture of Terry receiving a trophy in the Eddie Aikau Competition held in Honolulu.

Jax shook his head. "Didn't, until now."

"They used to call him Yo-Yo. He could find the wave and ride it front and back right into the beach."

"Still do call him that, sometimes," Brandon said. "Although he gets mad when I do."

"Why's that?" Jax said.

Brandon shrugged. "Imagine he doesn't like to relive the past. A wave broke his ankle and after a few surgeries, ended his career. Maybe he's bitter about it."

Jax directed a question to Rachel. "You were a fan?"

"Graduated from DeVry University near Laguna Beach. You pick up things."

Jax hadn't known where she'd gone off to college. He'd missed too much of his old partner's world while he'd been checked out of life.

He continued his assessment of the office. Deep dents marred the desk. Best guess, a baseball bat given the width of the marks. Same for the filing cabinet. He pulled out his phone and took several pictures of the damaged office furniture, and of the broken cup. He turned to Brandon. "When was the last time you talked to your boss?"

"Yesterday when he left. Expected him to be here today. But sometimes he doesn't show."

"Tell me more about that," Jax said.

"He drinks some. Maybe too much. But he's a good guy. An artist. You seen his work?"

"I've seen his boards around town."

"They're freaking awesome. He's been getting a lot of interest lately from a major manufacturer too."

"To buy his business?"

Brandon busied himself picking up a few of the fallen pictures. "No. And I probably shouldn't talk about it."

"Understand." It wasn't relevant unless it factored into Terry's disappearance, and he could circle back. Brandon's sudden interest in cleaning up felt off though. "Was he interested in whatever they were offering?"

"Not that I could tell. But seriously, dude, none of my business."

"You've had no contact with Terry since yesterday then?"

He shook his head. "I mean, I texted him at noon when I got up and told him I was running behind. He didn't answer; nothing new. You know because of the drinking, or if he's deep in a project."

"I see. His brother hasn't been able to get a hold of him since their conversation last night. Do you know whether Terry bikes much out on the trails behind his house?"

"He knows those woods like the back of his hand, but I've never seen him bike them. Though he owns one. Some fancy white thing that looks new. I've given him shit about whether it was just for decoration or whatever."

The bike in the woods fit Brandon's description. Terry might have used it to get somewhere faster than his feet would take him.

Whatever sound Terry reported hearing to his brother must have had two legs attached to it—and Terry went after it. At some point he might have decided it was easier to go the rest of the way on foot. Or he wanted to be quieter in his approach to who or whatever he'd encountered. None of that explained why he'd tossed the bike...or why he hadn't come back for it.

"How did they get in?" Jax asked.

Brandon's face turned another shade of red. "Terry won't be happy about this, so, if you don't have to tell him, I'd sure appreciate it."

"Okay..."

"I forgot to lock one of the garage doors last night when I got distracted."

"By what?"

"My girl called."

Given the boy's age, not implausible. "Would anyone else have known the place was unlocked?"

"Nah. I mean, I usually remember."

"Why do you think this happened?" Jax said, nodding to the mess.

"Who knows. Could be someone unhappy with their board and thought this was more effective than a Yelp review. People do all kinds of weird shit."

Rachel took out a notepad and made some notes. Jax often worked the information after the fact, making his observations after absorbing the entire scene.

"Anyone in particular he have problems with?" Rachel asked, stepping directly into the investigation.

"No. I mean, it's just a theory."

Rachel tucked the pad in her coat pocket.

"Anything missing?" Jax asked.

"Just some plans for the surfboard design he's been working on. He probably took them home with him."

"How long have you worked for Terry?" Jax said.

"Couple of years."

"Good guy to work for?"

"Checks don't bounce."

Not a ringing endorsement. Did his own deputies think the same of him? Jax handed Brandon his card. "If you can think of anyone who might have done this, or if you hear from Terry, you give me a call."

"You check with his girlfriend?" Brandon asked.

"Who's that?"

"Lisa. She bartends at Castaways."

Rachel already had her pad out again and jotted down the information. They ducked in the car and Koa put her nose up to the glass partition.

"It's all right, girl," Rachel said, opening the slider. "A little longer."

"She need a break?"

"She's good. Where to now?"

Jax drew in a breath. "Back out to Chesney's house. See what the men have found. I'd also like to put hands on those blueprints that Terry might have brought home."

"You think they could be important?"

"Not sure. I'm not buying a disgruntled customer. There's no graffiti, and nothing but the office was touched. Whoever was angry enough to pummel the furniture must have been looking for something. If they didn't find what they were looking for there, they might have gone to Terry's place and…"

He didn't finish his sentence. But Rachel's nod said she'd been a cop long enough to get the gist.

CHAPTER 9

Jax had barely put his cruiser into park when a man, wearing a Yale sweatshirt pushed up to his elbows and a taut expression, emerged from Terry's house and started taking long strides in their direction.

"Wait here," Jax said to Rachel and got out.

"Where are you on finding my brother? Have you even started to look?" The man's precision razor cut hair and manicured nails suggested he was used to giving orders, not taking them.

Ivy league or not, Jax bristled. "You're Gerard Chesney?"

"Who else would I be? I called you people hours ago. Why are you just arriving? Where is everyone?"

Jax's shoulders inched towards his ears. "My men are in the woods looking for signs of your brother and have been for a while." He nodded toward the other cruiser and motor bike plainly parked in the driveway. "I've been working it from down below."

Gerard's jaw tightened. "I warned him about living out here in Podunk, USA."

Rachel got out of the vehicle. Perhaps she'd read the tension in Jax's body language.

Maybe Misty Pines was a small town that he often ran as a one-man show on any given day, but only locals got the privilege of insulting it. Not some outsider who didn't like the speed with which he worked. "It's not for everybody, I assure you," Jax said. "But we're doing what we can, given the information that was provided."

Gerard cleared his throat and nodded. Then he stepped back, perhaps checking himself.

Stress and worry could make a man do many things out of character. Jax would give him a little slack—very little. "Why don't you take a breath and start from the beginning?"

"Like from the day he was born? Because that could take a while."

Jax stretched his neck to dispel the grate this man had on his nerves. "How about we start with your conversation last night?"

"Already told your secretary what I knew."

Secretary? He'd do Gerard a favor and not tell Trudy. "Humor me. How was Terry when you spoke to him prior to his hearing the sound outside?"

Gerard folded his arms in front of him. "Fine. He's always fine. Does life to the beat of his own drum and sugarcoats the entire world, as far as I'm concerned. Guy never has a cross word about anything."

Terry might also be a saint, because a few minutes chatting with his big brother had a few choice words crossing Jax's mind. "From what I gathered on my first assessment, he'd just returned from shopping."

"Yeah, he'd mentioned that he'd stopped at the IGA. Had a pie and wanted some ice cream to go with it."

"Who brought him the pie?"

Gerard shrugged. "Probably baked it himself. He's domestic like that. His mom made sure to teach him those skills. I may have gotten all the brains and business sense in the family, but Terry can create things like nobody else."

"Not your mother?"

"Right. Terry's my half-brother."

Jax nodded. Gerard was right about one thing. Jax had seen the craftsmanship in Terry's boards. It wasn't easy making something out of a lump of wood—Jax knew that firsthand having spent five years designing and whittling on a doll house for his Lulu. Was Gerard jealous?

"How often did the two of you talk?"

Gerard shifted feet. "We hadn't talked for a while until yesterday morning when he left me a message. I was in meetings all day and only got back to him last night. He wanted some business advice from me, for a change."

"What kind of advice?"

"A company out of California wants to mass produce his board design. They're offering him a good amount of money."

Brandon had said something about a corporation—and that Terry didn't seem interested. He'd put a pin in that. "The sound that your brother heard, was it loud enough for you to hear?"

"No. But it concerned him enough to want to check it out."

"Did you urge him to wait or call the police?"

"Neither. I told him to take bear spray."

"Does he own a gun?"

"Yeah." Gerard's gaze darted around the yard. "His car is missing."

"He owns another car besides the van?" Jax didn't recall seeing him in anything else.

Gerard nodded. "A '72 VW Bug, with a pearly white paint job. He's been restoring it, but motor ran good. Thing was worth a penny. I guess he could have it in the shop somewhere, but he didn't mention that. And he would have. We share a love of cars. Probably the only thing we share."

An attempt to steal his car would've taken Terry outside. "Has anyone tried to steal the car before?"

"Not that he mentioned."

"What was his response when you told him he should take the bear spray?"

"He said the critters that had been bothering him lately weren't of the animal kingdom kind."

"Any idea what that meant?"

Gerard tilted his head to the side. "No, but it's why I thought you should come here and make sure he was okay."

"He ever talk of suicide?"

"God, no." Gerard's eyes narrowed. "You think that's a possibility?"

Everything was a possibility until it wasn't. "Just covering all the bases."

Jax thought back to his darkest day when ending his own misery had played out as an option, not to mention the numerous suicide scenes he'd been called to over the years. Some were methodical in their plans, right down to turning off the water in the house and canceling the utilities. Others went out in chaos, reflective of the life they'd left behind. Terry's last words to his brother didn't indicate either.

Rachel had stepped away from them and her attention was focused on one of the bushes about fifty yards from the house and closer to the road. She waved Jax over.

"One moment," he said to Gerard and joined her. "What is it?"

She pointed to a man's athletic shoe. Fairly new style, the kind a basketball player might choose, although it could belong to anyone for any reason these days. Jax crouched down to examine it.

It didn't match the shoe on the foot he'd checked into evidence. And there was no indication of how it got here. A hunter or camper could have left it behind anywhere on the mountain and an animal dragged it to this location. Those kids that old man McDonald had mentioned might be messing around up here. Downtown, there'd been more than a few times when the teenagers had tossed their shoes up onto power lines crossing the streets. But until they found Terry, he wouldn't ignore anything.

Jax strode to his car and slipped into the seat, grabbing the radio mike. "Trudy, Turner here."

"What's up, hon?"

He relayed the information about the VW Bug and directed her to put out an APB.

"You got it."

Next, he retrieved an evidence bag.

"You got something?" Gerard said, joining them near the bushes.

"Don't know." Jax picked up the shoe with gloved hands and placed it in the bag.

The sound of footfalls came from the back of Terry's house. Jax straightened. Brody emerged from around the side. "Sheriff," he hollered. "We got something."

"You found him?" Gerard said.

"I…" Brody eyed Gerard, who had an odd look on his face and stiffened, like he was expecting the worst. "Can we speak in private?" Brody said to Jax.

Jax nodded and Brody spoke in a low voice. "We've found something you should see."

Without a word, Jax strode to the trunk and exchanged the bag of evidence with his collection kit and camera.

"Well, what is it?" Gerard demanded. "Is he alive? Where is he?"

"Stay here," Jax said. "Officer Killian, please make sure he doesn't follow."

"Yes, sir."

Jax tossed Rachel the walkie-talkie. "Hell of an interview, huh?" He didn't wait for a reply. "We'll be in touch."

She caught it and turned to Gerard. "How about you make us some coffee?"

Gerard nodded and Jax followed Brody out onto the trail. As he went further, he could hear Rachel taking control of the situation.

"You like dogs? Koa's a good listener."

"Yeah, they're okay."

"Great, I'll get her."

CHAPTER 10

Abby was dwarfed by Olek Lasko's six-three height and long lean body. Up until a few months ago, she'd flown solo. The SAC, or special agent in charge, of her regional branch had assigned her a partner after a drug investigation she'd been working turned south. She'd done solid work since, but that didn't count for much. Apparently.

The Bureau had been supportive of her personal situation, but assigning her a babysitter might be their insurance. She should be thankful she was investigating at all. She could be stuck behind a desk, pushing paper and answering phones.

Besides, she didn't have a problem with Lasko, who dished out the Polish jokes as good as he got them. His sense of humor was an asset, and he didn't seem to mind he'd been given the nickname Laska, which meant walking stick. But babysitter or not, she had seniority and had been with the Bureau for fifteen years to his five.

"What's bothering you?" Olek said, as they made their way to West Shore. Their SAC had directed them to meet with an officer there and to examine some evidence. In particular, the foot that had washed ashore a few weeks ago.

"Nothing."

"Your mom, again?"

Olek's background was in psychology. Get them talking. Analyze them to death. She did enough of that in her counseling sessions with Jax and the doc who'd helped her through Lulu's death. She didn't need a passenger seat session. "No."

Olek looked out the window and tapped the glass with his knuckle. A sign he didn't believe her. In their short time together, he'd learned not to push, but his rapping put her nerves on edge.

Fine. "It's more something she found today. Until we get to where we're going and see what the detective at West Shore has to offer, I can't say more."

Olek was gung-ho. Last thing she needed was to play referee between her partner and her ex-husband about jurisdictional issues. They might present themselves anyway depending on the next hour.

Inside the West Shore Police Department, Abby looked around as they waited. Unlike Misty Pines, a two-man operation with a handful of volunteers, West Shore buzzed with activity. Receptionists. Document clerks. Detectives meeting in conference rooms. The halls filled with the clomp of patrol officers' boots. Laughter erupted from the lunchroom. In the main room, chatter floated up from the cubicles. Despite her love of the small-town vibe, the hustle of the bigger city precinct had her feeling right at home.

When they were settled in one of those conference rooms, cups of stale coffee in front of them, West Shore's chief of police joined them. Balding and round, he was a man who spent too much time on administrative duties and not enough in the field. It wasn't fair to compare him to Jax, who always filled out his uniform...well, nicely.

"Thanks for coming," he said, carrying his own coffee. He set it down and extended his hand. "I'm Chief Albertine."

Abby and Olek introduced themselves and shook his hand. "What brings us here?"

He pulled out a file that he'd tucked under his arm. "I'm sure you're aware of the phenomenon where feet detach from drowning victims, whatnot, and wash ashore. Been a thing for the past decade up in Washington or on the Canadian side."

"We are," Lasko said.

"Well, a couple of weeks ago, we had one of our own come up in the bay."

"We're aware of that too," Abby said.

"You federal boys don't miss much."

She ignored the jab. Their assistance wasn't always appreciated. But he'd called them. "Last we heard, you were having it tested."

"Yes. And it was expected to come back tied to some poor chump a thousand miles away who'd wandered off, fell off a boat...maybe offed themselves. The one found last January was tied to a guy swept from the deck of a Canadian troller over a year ago."

Abby nodded. "The fact we're here makes me think it's not that simple this time?"

"Right-o." Albertine tossed a picture onto the table of a man in his early forties. Handsome in a rugged outdoorsman kind of way. Dark hair, with a salt and pepper streak. "Jonathan Lilly. Lives across the bay in Washington and was last seen a month ago when he went for a run. Never came back."

"Family?"

"Single. A bit of a lady's man from some accounts. Worked for the Bonneville Power Administration as an outside consultant. No one knew he was missing for a few days as he often worked off-site. An older neighbor noticed the Amazon package at his door was never picked up and reported it."

"Sounds like simple jurisdiction. Why are we here?"

"Because of the BPA connection. Don't want to rule out he was targeted because he worked for a federal employer."

But he only consulted. Oftentimes local jurisdictions were adamant about keeping cases to themselves regardless of the connection. "Anything else?"

"We're a big group around here, Agent Kanekoa, but we don't have psychologists on staff. You FBI are good at profiling."

"Right. Profiling when a serial killer is suspected. Is that what you think this is about?"

He shrugged.

Abby sensed Albertine was holding back. "You know about the other foot that washed ashore this morning, don't you?" She ignored Olek's raised eyebrow.

"When it was logged into the lab I was notified. The results haven't come back on that one yet of course, but it seems a bit coincidental."

Abby started to chew on her thumb, then caught herself. Jax wouldn't like that there was about to be interest in his small-town find—her mother's find. "Seems premature. You know as well as I do, to date, none of the feet found have been connected to foul play."

"Perhaps. But I didn't get to the top of my game by playing catch-up."

There was no use in arguing. Bureau chief had sent them in and Albertine seemed happy to be rid of the case. She was too low on the ladder to have any sway one direction or another. Maybe if they handled this one quickly, she could move herself up and get some traction again with the bureau. "Noted. How do you know he didn't go out for a jog and decide to kill himself?"

"He may have."

Olek shot her a look. He caught it too. Albertine's department had done little on the case, and if they had, they didn't intend to share info. Local cops often treated them like they were the enemy. Nothing could be further from the truth. And they certainly didn't need local cases to stay busy. Anti-terrorist and civil rights issues along the Oregon coast, the ever-present and growing drug or human trafficking concerns, racketeering and mob activity. That was more than enough. But Albertine appeared to have his mind made up about the Bureau, so she'd save her breath. "I'll be checking out your file then. If the new foot that turned up this morning has a local connection, however, you can break that one to Sheriff Turner yourself."

The police chief eyed Abby. "Afraid of your ex?"

Of course, he knew they'd been married. Who didn't? "We have a history of stepping on each other's toes. I'd prefer someone else be the bearer of bad news."

"Let's cross that bridge if needed."

"Agreed." Being on a lateral case wouldn't do much for their counseling sessions—and she'd already begged off the last couple of them. She'd hoped the sessions would help her figure out what she wanted. Instead, they'd brought confusion. Having to deal with her mom might've been part of that, but...

She rubbed her fingers together and noted the roughness of her thumb.

Fought the urge to chew on it again.

Being afraid to lose another person in her life might play an even bigger part.

Back in the car, Olek was too quiet. "Spill it," she finally said.

"This is a waste of time," he said.

Perhaps, but the senior agent part of her took over. "We don't know that. We'll work it like we do any case. What's the file say?"

Olek flipped it open, a scowl on his face. "No body found. Only recent credit card activity was at a florist shop the day before he was last seen. His job at BPA consisted of consulting on when the fish were running."

"Doesn't sound like that would be a factor in someone wanting to hurt him…unless it was another employee I suppose."

"People at work said he was a little full of himself when he'd drop in, but generally a nice guy. They reported him as single, as Albertine mentioned, and the elderly neighbor didn't have much to say."

Abby nodded. The local police had at least done a little preliminary work. Given the facts just relayed to her, the neighbor might be the best place to begin since she'd seen Mr. Lilly last. And having a mother with dementia, Abby knew memory could come in waves. "What's his address?"

Olek reeled it off and Abby turned her car toward the Megler Bridge, which would take them over the river to Washington.

CHAPTER 11

Jax hovered over a smattering of congealed blood on a pile of broad leaves. Not fresh, but the moisture in the forest was a factor, making it hard to tell how long it had been there and possibly messing with its DNA profile. The crime lab would determine that. He took a couple of pictures, then swabbed the droplets with a Q-tip and placed it in a sealed pouch.

"You find anything else?" Jax asked his men.

"There's an abandoned campsite around the corner," Brody said.

"Show me," he said to Brody before turning to Garrett and Matt. "You two stay behind and look for any other evidence."

They nodded.

"Sorry about your interview," Jax said as he fell in behind Brody. "Heard you're applying at Len's Auto."

"Yeah. But he knows this job is priority, Sheriff."

"Appreciate that. With us being short-handed."

"I get it. Who's the chick?"

Jax raised an eyebrow. "The chick's name is Rachel. She's applying for the deputy position."

"Oh," Brody said. "Us guys figured Garrett would get the job when you were ready."

Jax did a double take. "Since when has Garrett wanted to stay in Misty Pines? He's been verbal about being a Portland Police officer from the beginning."

"Right. But he's well past the age to go and hasn't made a move. Says a lot to me about what he's thinking."

Maybe it did, and Jax had missed it. What else had he missed since his last case? He'd been wallowing a bit…not trusting his own gut. His father had told him more than once he was self-absorbed. A sentiment Abby echoed in their recent counseling sessions. Is that why she hadn't wanted to come with him the last few times?

Jax had gone anyway hoping to show his commitment to the process. But counseling would do no good if he was unfixable. Unlovable. His own mother had left a ten-year-old Jax and a cantankerous father to fend for themselves. When he'd joined the force, he'd searched for her once and found her living on the other side of the country with a new husband and his ready-made family. He'd contacted her when Lulu was born…and when she died. Neither event had drawn her back. What did it say about Evelyn Turner that she couldn't be bothered to mourn the only grandchild of her only son?

What did it say about Jax?

Maybe his dad had been right that he'd never get it together. But he had before. He had to again for Mr. Chesney. As for unlovable, Abby had loved him once and he'd known Lulu's love. He'd hold onto that.

The bushes turned into trees that towered past his head, thick as a hedge. He and Brody rounded them into a makeshift campsite—possibly abandoned. Rain had pelted the plastic tarp into the ground. No signs of food or a recent fire. He could see why the men had dismissed it. But in this terrain, deterioration of any scene didn't take long.

He entered the tent, a musty mixture of dirt and human filth in the stifling space. Under the bedding was a slew of candy wrappers. A nail file, wipes, and fingernail polish were tucked under one of the pillows. A crossword puzzle, a razor kit, more wrappers under the other. A couple had lived here perhaps.

He stepped out of the tent and stood in the middle of the campsite, turning in all directions. A bent trail of ferns led away from the camp. He followed them, Brody on his heels. Within twenty yards, the flat forest floor ended and dropped straight down. The roar of the ocean echoed off the trees. Birds took flight from the tops. He peered over the edge.

A man's body, dressed in layers of flannel, sprawled at the base of the rock ledge. The light dropped towards the west, but he still recognized the figure below—not Terry Chesney. Walter, a homeless man who he'd had to shoo off Main Street a couple of times over the last year. Jax often wondered where he'd go when he'd disappear for days at a time. He had his answer.

Walter was inseparable from Lois, who loved colored hats and bright pink nails, the fragrance of cheap rose perfume mixed with the need for a shower wafting wherever she went.

Had she gone to get help? Had she fallen too and wasn't visible from here? When a team went down for recovery, they'd be able to send back a full report. Jax wasn't equipped for that, however. Regardless, the instability of the cliff meant it was far too dangerous to ask Rachel to bring Koa into the area.

He'd have to make the trek back to the house to get better reception and get the coroner and recovery team up here. With the direction Walter's body lay, he was dead. Given the skid marks down the side, it could be as simple as a bathroom break gone wrong. But with a missing man not far from this location, he wouldn't put money on that until he knew whose blood was on those leaves.

Jax made his way back through the camp toward Brody and nearly stumbled on something stuck in the ground. He caught himself and stepped off the trail. He stopped short of a pool of blood that he'd missed on his way into the camp. The item he'd stumbled on had been covered by fern, but the wood handle was clear. He yanked on a pair of latex gloves before picking it up. A knife.

No blood on the blade, so not what created the pool. But the handle looked like the missing steak knife from the set in Terry's kitchen.

Jax's stomach tightened. Terry might have heeded his brother's advice to take something out with him when he heard the crash in his garage. He might have used it as a weapon to protect himself. But you didn't bring a knife to a gun fight, and by the amount of blood that had not absorbed into the dirt, that was his best guess. Jax bagged the knife and stood upright. From the evidence kit, he tossed Brody some yellow crime tape.

"Watch where you step and give me a perimeter. We have a body down below so take it up to the cliff line...but be careful."

"Terry's?" Brody's voice tightened.

"No. Walter, the likely inhabitant of this camp."

Brody nodded and set to work. Jax took pictures and more blood swabs before the forest further deteriorated the evidence. The light continued to fade beneath the tree canopy. The rush of the ocean reverberated in the background like elevator music. Always present.

Morning light would show more, but he wasn't seeing an obvious trail of blood or drag marks.

He looked around to the firs and pines in proximity. No obvious lodged bullets or ricochets. He didn't know what he had.

But every scene had a secret—if only the trees could talk. Something tragic had happened here. He just had to figure out what and where Chesney had gone in the aftermath.

CHAPTER 12

Gerard hunched in the chair, his face buried in his hands, as Jax updated him on his brother's status. Jax had waited until the medical examiner and the Oregon State Police crime investigators were en route. Even though it was sundown, they'd have that area of the forest lit like an international airport soon as they set to work on recovering Walter and gathering evidence.

"So, Terry could still be out there. Alive?" Gerard said.

"It's possible," Jax said, not convinced that was the case. "And the search will continue even as they process the area."

"What have you got so far? You must have something at this point."

"We found evidence to suggest that Terry was out there."

"What kind of evidence?"

"A utensil from his kitchen."

"Must be more than that if you have a crime lab coming."

Jax nodded. "Blood was discovered on the trail, but until we have additional information on how it got there and who it belonged to, I can't say more on that." He went on to explain the forensic team's role. "I'll be waiting on a full report from them to know which direction we go next."

Gerard straightened. "Basically, you know nothing."

"We know plenty."

"You should be using that dog of hers." He pointed at Rachel. Koa looked up in expectation. "Maybe the dog could do better police work than you're doing right now."

Rachel looked more than willing to put Koa into action, but this wasn't a simple missing person case any longer. Jax gave her a slight shake of his head.

Rachel placed a hand on Gerard's arm. "Mr. Chesney, I understand this is upsetting. Given the evidence so far, the best way for us to move forward is to get as much information as we can. This is a potential crime scene. Koa isn't a police dog." She rested her other hand on Koa's head as if to reassure Koa that fact didn't matter to her.

Jax observed Rachel's mannerisms and soft tone. He'd worked with plenty of female officers before and seen Abby in action. They had a way that he'd never master. "She's right. You mentioned his VW Bug is missing. Let's start there."

"But the blood..." Gerard said.

"Could belong to someone that we don't know about yet. Or perhaps Terry met up with whoever was in his garage, they had an altercation, and Terry left. Maybe to get help for his own injuries. Maybe to get away."

"My brother wouldn't do that."

"Not saying he would. But things happen when one is defending themselves."

Gerard waved him off.

Jax's gut agreed. If Terry had been hurt, there would've been a blood trail all the way back to the house. And other than Walter, there were no signs of another victim.

There was also enough blood to suggest whoever lost it wouldn't be able to run.

"Can you think of anyone who'd want to cause Terry harm? You said he'd mentioned that the critters he'd been dealing with weren't from the animal kingdom. Anything more specific would be helpful."

Gerard pushed the heels of his hands into his eyes. "He worked with troubled kids. On occasion, he mentioned they caused him grief."

"What kind of grief?"

"He didn't say. But you know kids. They have tempers. Don't take direction. He was teaching them how to smooth a board, get the balance just right. Working with wood is different than fiberglass. It's a goddamn art form. Any kid should feel privileged that Terry would take time to show him the craft. Some can't see a gift when it's wrapped and put at their feet."

"Was he working with local boys?"

He shrugged. "You'd have to talk to the rest of the group that helped with that."

"You know any names?"

Gerard thought about it. "He mentioned a Troy a couple of times."

Jax closed his eyes. "Troy Marks?"

"Sounds right. Has a kid in the program. Or did."

"What's the name of the program?"

"No idea. He might have written it down." Gerard hopped up and went to a stack of papers on Terry's desk next to a new computer and an industrial-sized printer with a roll of paper threaded through sufficient to handle a blueprint.

Jax followed him. "Nice set up."

"It was for his design work."

"Terry's employee Brandon mentioned Terry might have brought home some blueprints last night and you'd mentioned a corporation interested in his work earlier. You happen to see those prints here?"

Gerard stopped scanning the flat surfaces. "You've already been to the shop?"

"Yes. Someone tore Terry's office apart sometime after close. Perhaps they were looking for that blueprint Brandon mentioned."

Gerard shook his head, his face red. "I wouldn't know."

The man might just be responding to the stress of the situation, but Jax didn't buy that. "If you have information on who broke in or who might have an interest in Terry's designs, it's a place for me to start."

"Like I said, wouldn't know."

Jax nodded. "Brandon also mentioned that whatever was happening with that corporation, Terry wasn't interested."

"Now that's not true."

"How so?"

Gerard sighed. "In Terry's last competition, he rode the wave in with a broken ankle. Granted, it wasn't the largest wave of the set, but it was impressive." Gerard gave a small smile at the memory before he frowned. "But the stunt cost the fool his career. Adrenaline had taken over and he didn't even know that he'd messed up his ankle. By the time he came into shore, it was obvious he had a compound fracture. He had multiple surgeries, even put in a couple of pins, but no matter what they did, he wouldn't surf again."

"Tough break."

"Yeah. But Terry's resilient and when he couldn't surf, he channeled his knowledge into design. That's when he came up with a concept that improved stability. It's that design that has caught the interest of a large manufacturer."

"Interest that Terry didn't care about."

"Again, not true."

"Why would Brandon believe otherwise?"

Gerard cleared his throat. "Who knows. But I'm his brother. Terry wouldn't have spoken to any employee about his true feelings."

"Except by your own admission, you hadn't spoken recently."

"I said not often, as in not for long conversations. If he'd changed his mind, though, he would've told me." Gerard swooped up a set of keys on the desk. "I'm going to check his van to see if the prints are in there."

Jax followed him out the door and watched as Gerard stuck his head in the van. The dome light lit enough to reveal that the van was empty of any blueprints.

"Could he have put it in the VW?" Jax asked.

"He wouldn't have driven that to work. And you said his employee thought he'd brought the prints home."

"Perhaps his routine changed?"

Gerard's shoulders slumped. "It's possible."

Rachel appeared in the doorway. "I'll confirm with Brandon?" she said to Jax.

"Please." He turned to Gerard. "Out of curiosity, what would a design like Terry's be worth?"

Gerard scoffed, like Jax had asked a dumb question. "Surfing is a multimillion, no, make that a billion-dollar, industry. You can't recognize it from here with the cold weather and limited waves, but in California, Hawaii, Australia.... People pay big bucks for a competitive edge. Terry was one of the best and he poured that experience and passion into his chunks of wood."

A lot then. A surfboard design could be at the root of what happened here. When big money was in play, people got greedy. Greedy enough to murder? He couldn't discount that. People killed for less.

CHAPTER 13

Jax sent Garrett and Brody home to sleep sometime after nine. They'd reconvene first thing in the morning for a briefing and to get their marching orders. Matt would take the night shift and stay apprised of what was happening at the crime scene. The deputy DA from Oregon State was also on site, and he'd call Jax direct if something came up.

What Jax did know was Walter's body did not show initial signs of being riddled with bullets or knife wounds. Walter appeared to have died from injuries sustained in the fall. Which meant the blood pool likely belonged to Terry Chesney, bolstered by the location of the steak knife that matched the others in Terry's kitchen. Although Walter's other half, Lois, was unaccounted for so he couldn't be certain what he had yet.

With the Oregon State forensics techs scouring the area for clues that they'd report on in the morning, Jax, Rachel, and her sidekick headed back, pulling in shortly to the department's parking lot next to Rachel's SUV.

"Welcome to Misty Pines," he said, as he popped the gear into park. "We don't always spend time wandering the woods, but you showed up on an interesting day. Has it scared you off from applying for the job?"

Rachel leaned her head back on the headrest. "Not at all. In fact, I could see where Koa and I would come in handy around here."

"About Koa." On cue, Koa sat up and stretched in the back seat, then dropped her head between them. She put her chin on Rachel's shoulder and side-eyed Jax.

Rachel massaged the fur between Koa's eyes. "She knows when you talk about her."

Did all the women in his life have an issue with him? He cleared his throat. "I haven't worked with K-9 much, and I'm not sure how we'd work her in."

"She's search and rescue, Uncle. That's all. She might have surprised you if you'd have let her out in the woods with you. Might have found that blood faster. And certainly would have tracked the body over the cliff." She shifted in her seat. "What do you think happened out there?"

"Gerard's certain that Terry said he heard something, and that could have been Walter. Maybe the old man came looking for food, or to steal something he could sell. I detained him for that once, although the shopkeeper didn't press charges."

"And what? He chases him out into the forest?"

"Possibly. Terry could have caught up with him near Walter's camp, and it was simply an altercation gone bad."

"Except Walter fell off a cliff."

"That's one assumption. We won't know until morning whether Walter has blood or injuries on his hands. It's possible if he did stab Terry, he panicked, dropped the knife and ran himself off. He could also have been pushed. Only problem with these scenarios is where's Terry? Other than the puddle of blood, which may or may not belong to him, that's it. Where'd he go?" Jax stretched his neck, fatigue setting in.

"So definitely a murder investigation?" Rachel said.

"Is from my perspective, and we'll be working the leads we've gathered thus far." Koa nudged Jax and he reached out his hand and put it on her snout. "Good girl."

"She is and she could be an asset here. She has great instincts. I hope you'll consider us both for the job."

It had been an unorthodox interview, and she'd done better than he expected. But what if he got it wrong? He wasn't sure he could trust himself to know.

"Speaking of instincts," he said. "Koa sat close to you in Terry's house. I figured being search and rescue, she'd try to comfort Gerard."

"That's more therapy dog, but I would've expected her to sit at his feet. You caught that too?"

Jax nodded.

"It was strange. Gerard said he loved dogs, that's why I brought her out. But she didn't think much of him, and he never moved to pet her. Although she could have been feeding off my vibe because I couldn't get a read on him."

"He seemed like a concerned big brother to me at first, aside from the demanding and cocky side," Jax said. "But the more he talked, I got the sense he's a businessman trying to make a buck off his little brother's fame."

"Like a stage mom?" Rachel said.

"Just like."

"The kind that wants to shine in the light of their daughter's successes?"

Jax rocked his head back and forth. "Maybe. I don't want to get tunnel vision. I plan to stop by and see someone else first."

Rachel pulled out her notebook and flipped to her notes. "Troy Marks?"

"Yeah." Jax said the word with a little too much force.

Rachel raised an eyebrow. "Must be a story behind that tone."

"It's Commissioner Troy Marks, and our paths have crossed a few times. Not always in great ways. His boy, while better, has a history of being an entitled prick just like his father. Which explains why he'd be in a program for wayward youth." Although Jax hadn't known about it. If five years of his life hadn't been a complete blur after Lulu died, he might have. But he was tired of beating that drum—the skins were about wore through.

She nodded. "You know, if you put me on as a reserve, at least until you decide whether to make it permanent, I can help with the investigation. Your boys seem like they mean well, but I have more experience."

Jax folded his arms over his chest. His boys did have the same training Rachel had, but there just wasn't enough crime in Misty Pines to give any of them the diverse experience she'd had. "Let me think on that."

"Fair enough." She put her hand on the door handle.

"Rachel, why do you want to come to Misty Pines?"

She loosened her grip. "I told you."

"You did. Is there more?"

Her hand slipped off the handle. "Remember when I was a little kid how I would spend hours listening to the police scanner?"

"I do." He'd gone into Jameson's house countless times to find Rachel curled in a ball, sleeping next to the radio.

"You know I did that for years because I was afraid my dad wouldn't come home. Mom too. That's why we kept it on all the time. Do you know what it's like to worry about someone never coming home?"

"Only in the case of my daughter." And Abby. Although in many ways, Jax didn't worry about her. She'd shown she could take care of herself far better than he had.

Rachel closed her eyes. "Of course. But I mean, afraid that someone will shoot them. That they'll be taken from you before you have a chance to say all the things…" Her voice clouded. "You know?"

He did know. It was a risk they all took every day on the force. But it wouldn't help Rachel to hear that. "Your dad's a good cop. And he's smart."

"Right—and I still grew up afraid. Even so, I wanted to be a cop. After getting my degree, I jumped at the first opening to become one. To be just like him."

Jax shook his head. "Your mom must love that."

"Exactly how you'd expect. One day I drop over to find her listening to the CB again. Come to find out, she'd been doing that since I got my first assignment."

"So, moving away is for her?"

"Yes. So she can't listen anymore."

Jax shook his head. "You think that makes it easier on a parent?"

Rachel looked out the window, resting her hand on Koa's scruff. "I guess not. But somewhere along the way I realized it's better to create a separate life. Especially when everyone is used to watching each other. Less worrying all the time. Less judgment. Less feedback. Less opinions on how you're doing."

That he understood. The authority structure in Portland was part of why he wanted out of there.

"Understood. Do you have a place to stay for the night?"

"A friend of mine moved here recently and I'm staying with her. I'll make that indefinite when you say the word. I want this job, Sheriff. I need this job."

No Uncle Jax this time. Koa lifted her head. They both stared at him.

But he owed his ex-partner Jameson a phone call. He didn't feel right about moving forward with Rachel until they'd talked. It was a formality, like asking a father for his blessing.

"Give me until morning."

* * *

Jax ripped off his uniform the moment the front door of his house slammed shut. Traipsing around the woods had left his clothes layered in filth and him in need of a hot shower. After emptying the hot water tank, he pulled on a pair of sweats and slipped his gray Navy-embossed sweatshirt over his head.

In the kitchen, he started a pot of coffee and opened his fridge. He hadn't eaten since breakfast; he felt it in his legs. Three slices of left-over pepperoni pizza from the grocery store looked less appetizing by the day. With nothing else in the house to eat, it would do.

He folded a cold slice down the middle, stuffing half of it into his mouth, and grabbed a beer before heading to Lulu's room.

The door remained open now. He and Abby had spent a day a few months back packing up the remainder of their daughter's belongings. It had taken him five years to put her stuffed toys into a box. The stack of boxes remained in the closet.

"They need to go too," Abby had said. "Let's make another trip to the hospital and take them to the kids."

"I'm not ready," he'd said. He could only do so much at one time.

She'd looked at him that day. "We need to go to counseling if this has a chance to work." Her hands were firm on her hips, her jaw tight.

"A shrink? I already told you…"

"You're either ready to let go or you're not. Just remember, you called me this morning."

He'd stared back. Uncompromising.

"You decide."

He gazed at the still-pink walls surrounding him and the boxes. He'd relented and gone. But no amount of counseling had propelled him to donate the boxes. Or Lulu's canopy bed that he'd disassembled, but still waited under the tarp for a new little girl to love it. He finished the other half of the pizza slice as the coffee maker dinged.

He poured a cup and grabbed his phone. Jameson. Not only had he called earlier, but three more times, each time going to voicemail. He'd left no messages—only a hang-up indicating he'd thought about it.

Jax had promised himself he'd call him back before he went to bed. He perched on the couch and hit send.

"Hey buddy," Jax said. "Sorry I missed your calls."

"No worries. Things hopping down there?"

"Yeah. A local business owner gone missing. Signs point to a bad ending."

"Not related to any cold cases, I hope."

A wry chuckle escaped Jax. "I think we're safe this time."

"Good to know."

"So, what had you blowing up my phone?" Jax asked, although he suspected the reason.

"Heard my daughter applied to be your new deputy."

Just as he'd thought. "She said you knew."

Jameson sniffed, followed by silence.

Jax had heard that combination before. His ex-partner was a thoughtful man who measured his words. But measured words were only needed when he struggled with his emotions. "I take it you're not happy about it."

"She's so damn independent. I don't get it."

"Hmmm. Sounds like someone else I know. What's not to get? She wants to make it on her own."

"In Misty Pines? That's hardly a place a career goes to thrive."

Jax stiffened. "Tell me how you really feel."

"You know what I mean."

He didn't. "There's nothing wrong with training in a small town where you're forced to rely on your own instincts and skills. We don't get to call in an entire team every time a blood droplet hits the floor. If I'd started here and ended in Portland, I might have been happier myself."

"Quit selling it. Any place there's authority would be a problem for you. But what are you saying about Rachel?" Jameson said.

What was he saying? He didn't want to get between his old partner and his daughter. He'd only recently set that cart upright between him and his old friend. Twelve hours ago, he told Trudy he didn't even want a new deputy. "Look, Rachel wants to get out of your shadow, cut her own path. Obviously, since she changed her last name."

He huffed. "She only did that so she wouldn't embarrass me."

Embarrass? "I don't see how she'd manage to do that. In the short time she's been here I've found Rachel to be smart and capable. She'd make a great right hand."

"She's gay," Jameson said.

Jax had suspected that ever since he'd seen how she looked at the girl she'd gone to prom with. Had Jameson not seen that as well? "And?"

"Did you hear me?"

"Clear as day. What's that have to do with anything?"

Jameson sniffed again, followed by more silence.

"Don't tell me you have a problem with that."

"It's Gayle."

If his ex-partner could see his face, he would have backpedaled fast. "Right, Gayle." Gayle's own sister was gay—a sister Jax had sat next to at Thanksgiving.

"Look. I can hear that condescending bullshit tone you throw around," Jameson said. "You have no idea what it's like to have hopes and dreams for someone and they're snapped away in an instant."

"Are you kidding?" Jax said, his voice tight.

"Shit," Jameson said.

"Shit is right. Your daughter's alive, a privilege that was *snapped away* from me as you put it. Whatever issue you have about Rachel's sexuality, get over it. We don't get to choose for our children. We get to love them. If we're lucky, they outlive us. At least you still can make it right with her."

Jameson took in a long breath. "I don't want you to hire her."

"Because she's gay?"

"No. Look, it's a big ask, but I'm hoping our friendship still means something. Friend to friend, I want her back in Portland."

"She's twenty-seven, Jameson. Time to let go."

"You'll hire her then, regardless of my feelings?"

"I didn't say that."

Jameson sighed. "Thank you. I appreciate that. Gayle and I want her home to talk some sense into her."

Jax cleared his throat. "I didn't say I wouldn't either. She's only just applied. There will be other applicants to go through."

"Good. That's good. Then it won't look like I asked for a favor."

Jax had to stretch his neck side to side to disperse the tension. How could he have been Jameson's partner all those years and not seen this bias running through him? They'd worked with people from all walks of life. All races. All sexualities. He'd never seen the slightest bit of prejudice. Did it change everything when it hit close to home and affected one's own hopes and dreams? When it was personal? It shouldn't matter. This had better just be an adjustment period.

"When did you find out?" Jax asked.

"I didn't know she applied until I tried to call her sarge this morning and learned she'd been part of the recent layoffs."

Rachel had lied about that. Clearly, she had her reasons for not wanting her father in her business. "I meant that she was gay."

"We've known for a while. But we only learned she had someone special in her life when she told her mother a few days ago."

Jameson should be celebrating the fact Rachel had a chance at happiness. Who gave a shit who it was with? He shook his head to clear it. "Bye, Jameson."

Jax clicked off. He didn't like this turn of events and Rachel wanting to come to Misty Pines made more sense now. He also didn't want to jump one way or another based on Jameson's reactions or Rachel's desires before he was ready.

And trusting someone again—that was a big ask.

He flopped back on the couch. Reservations aside, he could use the help. Whether she got the job or not would be based on how much he could rely on her. He'd treat her like anyone else because that was only fair. Friendship be damned.

He'd have Trudy do the required screening particulars in the morning, but he already knew Rachel's record would be spotless. He shot off a text. *Deputy Killian, be ready for temporary reserve duty at seven a.m.*

He tossed the phone on the table and finished his coffee.

CHAPTER 14

Abby waited for Olek to pull curbside in front of her house. They'd set out to visit Jonathan Lilly's neighbor yesterday and were immediately sidelined. An accident on the bridge shut it down for hours. They'd U-turned the Bureau's putrid-brown Chrysler for home. With confirmation that the bridge had reopened, they'd try again this morning.

Abby ducked into the car, and nearly sat on a box of pastries.

"Not again?"

He chuckled. "If I'm going down, I'm taking you with me."

"Your mom in the baking mood again?" she said, popping the lid.

"You know it." He pulled out into traffic.

Abby eyed the glaze-drizzled diet-busters with jelly or what appeared to be a cream cheese filling sitting in the well. They reminded her of open crust pies, but without the fussiness. "What are they, besides two hundred calories each?"

"Kolachkes. Grandma's recipe."

Abby pulled one out and took a bite, savoring the flaky dough melting in her mouth. "Your mama's a good cook." Her own mom had never grasped the skill. Abby had usually pulled together dinner, especially after her father died, and it often consisted of mac and cheese or a sandwich. She stared out the window, remembering. They'd survived, although Jax had never been impressed by her repertoire and done most of the cooking. She grabbed another Kolachke.

"She is," Olek said. "But full disclosure. They're only partially for us. I took the liberty to find out more about Jonathan's neighbor, Eleanor Baka."

He pointed his chin toward the file he had tucked between the two seats.

Abby laid the file West Shore had provided onto her lap and flipped it open. "And in here you found she likes sweets?" She thumbed through the reports.

"Baka is a good Czech name. Figured it wouldn't hurt to bring the lady something from the old country to get her talking."

Abby gave him a sideways look. "You think pastries will do that?" She popped the Kolachke she'd taken a moment ago into her mouth and nearly sighed. "Okay, maybe your buttering up skills are getting better."

He smiled.

Abby wondered if the pastries truly were for Ms. Baka, or for her. Olek always wanted to talk and listen to her thoughts. Like Jax, though it was different with him. He was like a comfy pair of sweats. Too comfy perhaps. They had shared pain, but that seemed their dominant common ground. Olek had never tried to date her—nor would she mix business with pleasure—but a little attention couldn't hurt.

They made the rest of the drive in silence.

The town of Long Beach was home to an annual Rod Run that drew in over a thousand classic cars and roadsters every September. A parade would come right down the main strip. Now that strip was desolate. The tourists had long gone from this and every other coastal town, driven away by the cool and the winter mist.

Olek took a right on Beach Drive and a few minutes later pulled in behind a small blue sedan at the appropriate duplex. Eleanor Baka's side, according to the black numbers screwed to the vertical beige siding. The residence on the right was listed as Jonathan Lilly's address.

Abby took lead to Ms. Baka's front door, knocking on the screen's wood frame. Olek stood next to her with the box balanced like a tray on his hand.

A yapping sound came from the other side, and the shadow of a woman brushed past the side window panel.

"Who is it?" an elderly voice said.

"Ms. Baka. I'm agent Kanekoa and this is my partner, Agent Lasko. We're with the FBI and we'd like to ask you a few questions about your neighbor."

"My tenant, you mean," she said through the closed door.

"Yes, Mr. Lilly."

Another beat before the door cracked. Ms. Baka's bulbous nose was the most visible and she couldn't be more than four-foot-ten. "What do you have there, young man?"

"Kalochkes, ma'am. My mother baked them last night and it would be a crime not to share." He winked.

A brief smile passed her face before she frowned. "You have ID?"

Abby had her badge ready.

The woman scanned the badge and Abby several times before she sniffed and opened the door. She was slight and stooped, with soft wrinkles hanging off her thin face. She had to be north of eighty by a year or two, but her eyes were bright, and they went to the small box in Olek's hand.

"Come in." A toy-size dog sat at her feet, eyeing them warily as they entered.

Big dogs could take you down fast, but Abby watched out for the little guys. They were often the first to bite, and that behavior didn't only apply to dogs. "Appreciate it. We won't take a lot of your time."

"Sweetie, time is all I have these days. But I can't be too careful. I put an ad on Craig's List for people to call if interested in the rental, to be proactive, you understand, and they are randomly showing up. Damn newspaper put Johnny's name on the second page and it's not like Long Beach is a metropolis."

"Who's been coming by?" Abby asked.

"Looky-loos. Everyone wants to know where he is. Good rentals close to the water are hard to come by too. I assume you found him if you're here?" She hung her head.

Abby wouldn't get graphic—and they hadn't found him. Exactly. "We know enough at this point to believe he's deceased."

She nodded, frowning. "When can I get his things out of there so I can rent the place?"

Abby masked her surprise with a matching frown. Usually, people wanted to know what happened—or how they'd determined the victim was dead.

Ms. Baka had a business side to her and a little chill. Not wanting details could be a protective shield. The less one knew the better. Or maybe at her age, hearing about a death was all too common.

"Can we sit?" Olek asked.

Ms. Baka smiled. "Of course. Let me get us coffee."

"No need…" Abby said.

"That would be wonderful," Olek said, cutting her off. "Thank you so much."

Ms. Baka beamed as she shuffled into the kitchen at the speed of molasses. The little dog stayed behind and glared at them.

Abby rolled her eyes. She had an all-business side herself and it landed her in trouble sometimes. Jax had accused her of that on more than one occasion. Olek had more experience in being the "good son" that Ms. Baka apparently viewed him as. If it ultimately helped them wrap this case up sooner, she'd go with it.

The desire to get closer to her mom in case she ran off again niggled at her. As did the foot that had washed ashore on Jax's beach. She couldn't discount the possibility of a connection to her present case. She dropped onto the sofa and took a breath, tucking her personal stuff aside.

A few minutes later, Ms. Baka returned with a tray of coffee and set it on the table in front of them.

Olek leaned forward and poured them all a cup. "When was the last time you saw Mr. Lilly?" he asked, handing her and then Abby a coffee.

"I already told the officers when I'd called that it was about three weeks ago. He took his garbage out to the street, and mine too. He was a good man. Very helpful."

"Did he ever give you the impression that he was depressed? Concerned about any events happening in his life? Or at work, perhaps?" Abby asked.

The woman took a sip of coffee. "No. Johnny was always happy. Always. And he seemed to like his job."

"Did he have many visitors?"

She shook her head. "He worked a lot of hours. If I saw him, it was in the evening, and only on occasion. Most of the time I only knew he'd been around because he'd do little things."

"Like the garbage?" Olek said.

"Yes."

"The morning he disappeared," Abby said, "he went out jogging. When was the first time you noticed he hadn't returned?"

"When I came out later in the day and my trashcan was still at the street. On his way back from a jog, he'd pull mine back under the eaves."

"But you didn't call the authorities at that point?" Olek said.

"No. There'd been times in the past when he didn't get in a jog because he didn't feel well or had to leave earlier than normal. I didn't want to sound an alarm right away. I had bunko all day with my lady friends at the senior center, so I didn't think much about it until the next morning when it was still there."

"Did he normally tell you if he'd be out of town?" Abby said.

"He would, yes." The little dog stretched and laid at Ms. Baka's feet. She bent to run a calming hand down his back and his tail wiggled in reply.

"Did you ever hear Mr. Lilly arguing with anyone through the walls?"

"I'm no busybody." She straightened and lifted her chin.

Olek gave her a knowing smile. "It's okay, Ms. Baka. You can tell us."

She sniffed. "Well, there might have been a couple of times when I heard him cuss. But I didn't know what that was about."

"Was he on the phone perhaps?"

"I wouldn't know. It's not like I ran out to see if someone had come by or not."

Olek tilted his head but gave her a reassuring nod.

"Okay, I did do that." She placed a hand on her chest. "But no one was there that time."

Olek had a way of settling in with a witness that seemed to work. She might have to take notes. "Could we take a look at his home?"

"The boys from the West Shore have gone through already. And if he comes back..."

She understood the land lady's discomfort, but "the boys" wouldn't have been as thorough in their search at that point. "The status of the case has

333

changed some, so it's important we get in. If you prefer, we can get a warrant," Abby said.

Jonathan wasn't coming back. His foot had been found. Had it been accidental, they'd have found him in a hospital, or nearby. They hadn't found his body yet. It could be at the bottom of the ocean.

And while the report wasn't in, the pictures suggested the foot didn't come off by natural progression in the water. She hadn't said it out loud because she wasn't the coroner. Best to leave those determinations to the experts and do what she did best—investigate.

"We won't be long," Olek said. "And we won't take anything that isn't relevant to finding Jonathan." Ms. Baka's face wrinkled. "Please?"

She reached out and patted Olek's arm. "For you, I guess that would be fine." She got up and found a key in a nearby writing table and handed it to Olek.

"You have a way," Abby said after they'd left the older woman's home and stepped into Jonathan's open layout. The heat hummed in the cozy space. Johnny, as Ms. Baka had referred to him, must have had it set to run on auto. The front door led into the living room which reflected Jonathan's modern and minimalist style. Low-slung white leather furniture, sleek lines, abstract art on the walls.

"It's easy when someone reminds you of your grandmother. Besides, I'm not always this charming."

She didn't take the bait. They needed to gather any clues and keep moving.

An eating bar defined the kitchen space that contained stainless steel appliances, black granite with flecks of gold and green, and a basic gray tile floor. Inside the cupboards, whey protein powder, an array of vitamins, and trail mix and fruit and nut bars for snacks.

A man who took care of himself.

At least he had food in the house. Abby barely did more than pop something in the microwave anymore. Not much fun cooking for one. And too many memories were tied to the mac and cheese Lulu had begged for.

Jonathan's refrigerator contained soymilk and salad fixings that were slimy and well past expiration. The freezer overflowed with chicken breasts and fish filets ready to go. The counters were clear, except for a plate of stale cookies. An out-of-place addition to the health food she'd found, but everyone had a vice. Perhaps Ms. Baka liked to give him goodies in exchange for garbage detail.

There were two rooms off the living space. Abby took his personal bedroom and Olek disappeared into the office, featuring a wall of trophies.

"The man loved his running events," Olek hollered. "And there's some papers on the desk I'll photograph."

"Sounds good."

The bed in the master bedroom was made. Not much in the way of pictures on the walls, only a silver-framed one with a woman and a little girl on the nightstand. Mother and daughter, given the shapes of their noses and smiles. Could be an ex-wife and their daughter. She turned the frame over and slipped the picture out. *To Uncle John. We love you!* She slipped the picture back in the frame and joined Olek.

"Anything?" she asked.

"Looks like he was dealing with insurance on something. We can make a call on that. But other than that, no. He did marathons. Lots of them. And placed in more than a few."

"I knew a marathon runner years ago in the academy. Training consumed a lot of his life."

"I bet. You don't get to a competitive level on weekend jogs alone."

"I'd imagine he'd have a set routine too. If someone was out to get him, they'd only need to lay in wait for him."

"Right. That's if it wasn't random," Olek said.

Abby looked around one last time. The DNA results on the foot her mother had found might tell a bigger story. "Or if it was foul play at all. You've read the stories of the other feet. People who kill themselves by drowning are sometimes found feet first." She winced at the way that must have sounded.

"True," Olek said.

Except Mr. Lilly seemed to have a solid and, according to Ms. Baka, happy life. "He's got a picture of what appears to be his sister and niece in a photo. Let's find out the sister's name and see what she knows," Abby said. "And let's get those phone records. If he was arguing with someone, it might be a factor."

"Will do."

"One more thing," Abby said, taking a final look.

"What's that?"

"You said the last credit card purchase was at a florist the day before he went missing and I didn't see any flowers. Let's find out who he sent them to. It might tell us a bit more about Jonathan Lilly."

CHAPTER 15

"I want you to welcome Reserve Deputy Rachel Killian," Jax said to most of his team. They'd gathered in the conference room for a morning briefing, and to plan out their action for the day.

A small murmur of greetings came up from Garrett and Brody.

"Hi, guys," Rachel said. She was dressed in khakis, her long hair pulled into a bun. She looked every bit law enforcement in her bullet proof vest. It wasn't something they wore routinely, but she'd come from the city. Jax had been like that in the beginning as well. Koa didn't accompany her today.

"I think we can do better than that." Jax frowned at the men. Whether he had pride and defensiveness over Rachel from their shared history made no difference. Rudeness wouldn't be tolerated.

"Hi, Rachel," they said with a little more enthusiasm.

"Good to have you part of the team," Garrett said, meeting her eye too long. Jax recognized a stare off when he saw one, and Rachel's cocked eyebrow meant *it was on.* Brody had been right about Garrett.

"Thanks," Rachel said.

The door to the conference room swung open and Matt rushed in. "Sorry I'm late. There was an injured owl out on 101 that I had to get to Wildlife."

Being law enforcement in Misty Pines meant you did a little of everything. "The little guy going to make it?" Jax said.

"Think so. He wasn't too happy when I threw the blanket over him and put him in a box, but he'll recover. Broken wing."

"Anything on the case during the night?" Jax said.

"Forensic team wrapped up around three and headed out. The Deputy

DA said they'd be in touch with results." Matt slid into the chair next to Rachel with a smile. His cheeks flushed when Rachel smiled back.

Lord. The room was filled with a bunch of hormonal high schoolers. One figured he had a chance with Rachel; the other would personally drive her to the county line. Jax hadn't thought of the implications of adding a female into the mix. Trudy was like a mother to them. But Rachel—she could handle herself without a doubt. His men would have to grow up and deal with it if he chose her for the job.

"All right. Here's what we got," Jax said. "I received that report first thing in my email. The blood is being tested, but some early results suggest it's human and a match to Terry. How it got there is what we need to find out. No additional fibers or bullets have been found yet. There were some beer bottles close by, but they've been there a bit and don't appear to be related to the scene. They were collected for prints, just in case."

"Could be kids out partying," Brody said.

"Or Walter's," Jax said. "The preliminary post suggests that he died from the fall, with no obvious signs of foul play, or foreign blood on his hands."

"Why was he on ledge in the first place?" Garrett asked.

"Are they doing a toxicology report on him?" Rachel said.

Brody stared at them. Matt sipped his coffee, clueless.

"Yes, to the toxicology," Jax said, "and perhaps that report will explain if his physical state contributed to his lack of balance near the edge. But with Terry's blood nearby, we can't discount that he might've witnessed an altercation and been driven over that edge. That's why we need to find Lois, a woman he was known to spend time with."

"Lois has been gone for a while now." Trudy had appeared in the doorway with the stealth of a stalking cat. She often popped in on briefings when the phone lines were slow.

"When did she leave?" Jax said.

"I put her on a bus to Portland a month ago. Or our church group did, I should say. There's a homeless shelter in the city that helps women get educated on a skill, and then transitions them into the workforce."

"Wasn't she old?" Brody said.

"Forty-seven, but the street ages a person. You can't possibly think that's old." Trudy's tone had the bite of a challenge.

"No, ma'am."

She nodded. "Walter was older, late sixties, and a father figure to her. Her departure is why he took to the woods in the first place."

"That means he's been out there for a few weeks living about a mile out from Terry Chesney's place. I saw a few women's items when I inspected the tent area. No chance she came back into town?"

"Haven't heard that she returned. He might have been holding out hope though."

"Possibly." Jax had kept everything of Abby's she'd left behind after moving out. Didn't touch her side of the bed like she was about to crawl in next to him at any moment. Bought her favorite coffee creamer and kept it in the door of the fridge for their shared breakfast. It went on that way for months before he realized she wasn't coming back. She still hadn't, although the creamer was back in the fridge door and had been used a couple of times—but only after a counseling session.

Brody coughed. "Do you want me to confirm Lois hasn't returned?"

"Actually, Trudy, would you do some of the preliminary on that?" Jax said. "It's possible she snuck back in without us knowing. Maybe someone from your church has heard different."

"That does happen," Trudy said. "I'll check."

Trudy didn't agree with him often. Jax would take that as a win. "Appreciate it. Any word back yet on the foot?" he asked her.

"Not yet," Trudy said. "But we should have something this afternoon."

"What foot?" Garrett asked.

He briefed them on the appendage found on Meddle Beach yesterday.

"Sick," Matt said, yawning.

"Very." Jax gave them the short version of the past instances and how shoes made great floatation devices that brought the feet ashore. "But with Terry missing, and blood in the woods, I won't be writing it off as accidental yet. And I don't want to make too much of it. Last thing we need is reporters getting wind and trying to make it something it's not."

"Got it," they all said.

He stood. "Let's get this day going. Until we have a body or confirmation otherwise, we'll be referring to Chesney as a missing persons case to anyone you interview. The APB is out on Chesney's VW Bug. There's been no sightings, but everyone is to keep their eyes open. Brody and Rachel, you're together. Rachel was part of the conversation with Terry's brother last night about the blueprints. Get back to Surfrider and see if there's anything more to know about that." They both nodded and headed to the door. "Garrett, I want you to have a chat with Lucy, the bartender at Castaways, when she comes on duty. Unless you can find her beforehand. She was dating Terry. Let's see if she has any insights. Matt, go home and get some rest. You can catch up with me this afternoon."

Matt straightened in his chair. "I'd rather not go home, Sheriff. I'm fine."

"Don't argue. You're no good to me if you're exhausted."

Matt nodded, his shoulders sagging.

"How about you?" Garrett asked. "I can ride shotgun and we can cover more ground."

He suspected that Rachel's presence had sparked his desire for that deputy job, but they both knew he wouldn't stay. He wanted a bigger town, and he should have it. But right now, Jax had other plans. "I gave you the lightest duty so you're available to answer any other calls the good people of Misty Pines might make. I'm counting on you."

Garrett frowned at first, but then stood a little taller. "Yes, sir."

Now it was time to fly solo. Jax had a stop to make, and he wasn't looking forward to it.

CHAPTER 16

Commissioner Marks' office was in City Hall, which consisted of a reception area, a few offices, and a meeting hall. It housed the water district and planning department as well. Council meetings were held there, and the town residents hashed out the impact of tourists on their small community, the annual summer barbeque, and tax assessments for the businesses that tried to make it through the winter.

Jax found the commissioner in black track pants and a Nike sweatshirt, feet propped on his desk, thumbing through a pile of reports.

"Didn't entirely expect to find you here so early," Jax said from the doorway.

"Council meeting is coming up and they'll want the budget. You hiring that young deputy that applied?"

Jax's mouth twitched. He didn't like having to answer to Troy Marks, but the man had appointed him to this position of sheriff in the first place. Like it or not, his department's budget ran right through this train station. "It's a definite maybe."

"Good. The faster you decide, the faster we can get this town back on track."

"Agreed." They didn't talk about what had happened a few months back, but they'd both been affected. Their trust had been broken and they'd both lost that day. How did one do that, win and lose at the same time?

"What brings you here?" Troy asked, interrupting Jax's thoughts.

"Terry Chesney."

"What's up with that son-of-a-bitch? I haven't talked with him for over a year."

Jax came in and plunked down in the chair in front of Troy's desk. "He's missing."

"Missing? You sure? He's a bit of a naturalist. Likes to hike. He could be out on an extended one."

Jax shook his head.

Troy picked up the signal and the usual tightness in his face faded, diminishing his cheeks to soft jowls. "What happened?"

Jax gave him the run down.

"But no body yet?"

"Correct. Plenty of blood though." Jax envisioned the pool. "Too much blood."

Troy drew in a measured breath. Even he understood that the body could only lose so much. That the forest of the coastline was thick and treacherous. That a person could be lost for days out there, too injured to protect themselves, and a cougar could have gotten to them first.

If Terry was out there, they'd eventually find him. Unless he did fall down the ravine or off the cliffs into the ocean. Then the body would only be found if the ocean decided to let it go, like the foot that Abby's mother found.

Jax stifled the urge to check his phone and see how the results were coming on that. The appendage was found on Meddle Road… "You have a map of the coastline?"

"Of course. You do too?"

"Save me a trip back to my office."

Troy got up. "Follow me."

Troy led Jax into a meeting room with drafting tables and bar height chairs. The walls were covered in maps of Misty Pines and the jurisdictional lines that made up their territory. Outside the hard black lines were red dashes. And blocks of spaces slotted for development on much of the empty ground.

"You've been busy," Jax said.

"We can't stay small forever."

"Why not?"

Troy cleared his throat. "Because if you're not growing, you're dying."

Jax had heard that said about business. But a town? "Seems the people of Misty Pines might have a different view of that. People come here for the size, the pace, and the obscurity." He and Abby had embraced it, not missing the city's hustle.

"People often must be pushed into the future, Sheriff. They elected me to be the person who shines the light on what that path is."

"A future with more money coming in?"

"More businesses. More people. More money, not only from the economy but from the state. You could soon have the equipment and the department that most sheriffs dream of."

"I'll need it because what you describe will bring more crime. More drugs moving through here. More theft. You're not doing me or this town any favors by attracting that." It sounded like a power grab to Jax. "If Misty Pines isn't enough kingdom for you, you can always move."

Troy drew in a breath but didn't respond. "There's your map." He pointed. It was secured to the wall by thumbtacks and reflected the entire town's boundaries and streets.

He and Troy could argue all day, and he didn't have time for it either. Jax scanned the map, fingertip tracing the coastline until he found Bull Mountain Road. It was located three fingers from the ocean, which according to the key indicated a mile. He searched for Meddle Road. It was about the distance of one of his hands to the left. Walter's body had been found in the ravine that was four fingers in on his hand.

Dora had found the foot down on the beach, north, and about a quarter-mile from Meddle Road itself. He'd stood at the spot where the foot had been and looked up into the forest wall. Up the cliffs. Had he been looking up to where Walter's encampment was? Or at least near it?

If an injured Terry had moved off in a western direction, the theory of him going off the cliff could hold merit. Except Jax hadn't seen any trails of blood leading that direction. If Terry had been attacked by someone out there, that person could have carried him to the cliff's edge though…

Troy cleared his throat. "Find what you're looking for?"

"Yes. Thanks," Jax said.

"Is that all you needed? To check a map you already have on your own walls?"

He might as well get right to it. "Dylan was in a program for boys, wasn't he?" Jax turned to Troy's stony face.

"There you go having a thing about my boy again. Goddamn it, Jax. You and I are going to have problems at this rate."

Had they ever stopped having problems? "Calm down," Jax said. "I'm more interested in the program itself. Isn't that how you knew Terry in the first place?"

Troy folded his arms over his chest. "Yes."

"How was Terry involved?" Jax said.

"Why?"

He didn't owe Troy an explanation, but the fastest way through a slog was a straight line. "His brother indicated that Terry might have been having some problems with one of the boys in the group. I want to know more about it."

"Then you should be talking to Shaun Evans who runs the thing."

"Shaun Evans?" He hadn't heard that name before.

"Yeah. Not sure what he does for a day job, but he's a great guy from West Shore. Really works to get the boys on the right path. He coordinated some skill building events with Terry, who essentially taught woodworking by way of surfboard crafting."

"Is this a new group?"

"Newer. Came about in the last couple of years."

He ignored the fact that he hadn't known of the group, and thankfully Troy didn't pounce on that fact either. But if Evans worked out of West Shore, he might not have any information. "The group do anything else?"

"Sure. Hiking. Surfing. Fishing. Camping. Anything to get the boys focused on something other than causing trouble."

"Did they happen to use the woods behind Chesney's place to do some of the outdoor activities?" He thought of the tennis shoe in his trunk.

"Not when Dylan was part of the program. But Dylan wasn't in it for long so I couldn't speak much on that."

"His choice or yours to be in it?"

"He straightened up fast when I told him this was step one of 'get on track or else.'"

It hadn't adjusted Dylan's attitude much. Or changed the fact he'd gone on to deal drugs at his own high school only six months ago. Troy's definition of *on track* and his were quite different.

Jax turned to go. "Thanks for the info."

Troy followed him to the front door. "Hope you find Terry's body, or whoever caused him harm. He was a good guy."

"Seems like," Jax said. "And an expert craftsman. Some big company has been after his designs for a board."

"Which he'd never sell."

Only one person didn't seem to agree on that. "Not according to his brother." Unless he was projecting, hoping he could get his little brother on the commercialism path.

"That doesn't sound like the Terry Chesney I knew. Now Riley Higgins, maybe."

"Who's that?"

"Another surf legend who set up shop in West Shore. I've met him a couple of times. Talk about an arrogant son-of-a-bitch. He hated Terry. They'd had problems years ago, but I hadn't heard anything lately."

"Did he hate him enough to be concerned about him selling a surfboard design?"

Troy shrugged. "Suppose when money's involved, anything's possible."

That had been his experience as well. "Is Riley's business suffering?"

"Don't imagine, but he's a designer too. If he thought his own work would get shoved aside for Terry's, that might not set well. Given their history, he probably wouldn't mind him out of the way altogether, although I've never met the guy. And that said, you'd have to be motivated to kill someone."

They met eyes. They both knew motivation was only part of it. Sometimes it was self-protection. Rage. Delusion.

He left Troy in the shadow of the dark city hall. If Riley Higgins had a killer competitive streak, it was time to find out. But his radio crackled before he had even settled into the driver's seat. Brody.

"Whatcha got?"

"Terry's VW Bug and a kid named Scott."

CHAPTER 17

Jax rolled up on the scene in Trillium Park. Brody's patrol car was parked behind a beige VW Bug that matched the description of the APB. Rachel had a young man in his late teens cuffed on the ground about thirty yards ahead on the side of the road, her hand placed firmly between his shoulder blades. The boy's cheek was flat against the gravel, and he wasn't resisting.

Jax got out.

Brody answered the unasked question. "He took off running."

"Didn't get far, I see."

"That girl can run and I..." Brody's face turned a light shade of pink.

"That girl is Rachel, or Deputy Killian. Doesn't matter who caught him, so long as someone did."

Brody shrugged. Rachel lifted the young man to his feet, her jaw tense, and walked him back their direction. His trembling chin had the beginnings of a sad excuse for a beard, and he needed to buy some decent jeans. The ones he wore were frayed at the knees.

Jax put on a pair of black latex gloves and opened the VW driver side. "Secure him in my cruiser and come see me," he said to Rachel as she walked by.

"Yes, sir," she said, panting. The knees of her khakis were scuffed, and perspiration had sprung across her red face. Adrenaline had to be surging through her veins, but the signs of anger were universal, and a good deputy kept it in check.

Jax slid his hand along the inside of the VW side pockets. Like Terry's other work, he'd done a nice job at restoring the car. The paint had a perfect gloss. The interior brown leather had been upgraded. He popped open the unlocked glove compartment. A box of bullets for a handgun.

"You checked him for weapons?" Jax called out to Rachel.

"Yes, sir. Nothing, sir," Rachel said.

He nodded and closed the compartment. He ran his hands along the cracks of both seats and peeked into the back. No backpacks or duffel bags. Two Rockstar cans, empty, tossed on the back floorboard. Probably belonged to the kid. A stash of pot wrapped in a baggie shoved into the space between the driver and passenger seats. With it being legalized now in the state, nothing he could do with that except confiscate it if the kid was under eighteen and evaluate whether he was under the influence. Although he didn't reek of it when he walked by.

Jax bent down and flashed his light under the passenger seat. Something in there, wedged sideways. He yanked it out. A tennis shoe. One. A pair of socks stuffed into it. He stood and strode to the back of his car and popped the trunk to confirm what he already knew. He had the match.

Once the young man was secured, Rachel and Brody approached Jax at the back of his car.

"What's the kid's story?" Jax said.

"Punk thought he could outrun us," she said.

Jax nodded. Rachel was pumped. He used to be overzealous in his twenties. Trying to make an impact. Trying to impress. But that's not the answer he'd been looking for. If Rachel planned to work well within the confines of Misty Pines, the slower pace, the small town, she'd have to learn balance. A trait he didn't always possess himself, as Trudy often reminded him.

"I recognized the car the minute I saw it coming up the main road," Brody said. "We ran the plates and it came back as Mr. Chesney's. We flashed our lights and the driver accelerated. When he couldn't lose us, he pulled over. Said he couldn't hear us and wasn't paying attention."

"You didn't believe him?"

"The minute we asked him to step out of the car, he took off running," Rachel said.

Jax appraised Rachel, whose pants on her hip and bottom were scuffed with dirt. "And he shoved you on your ass to get by you."

She straightened. "He's lucky I didn't shoot him."

Jax frowned.

"Sorry, Sheriff," she said.

He nodded. "What's his name?"

"Scott Heffernan," Brody said. "He's eighteen and lives in West Shore. He's unemployed and just happened to find the vehicle on the side of the road a couple of nights ago. With the keys in it, of course."

"Of course," Jax said. "Except I just found the mate to the shoe we found out on Chesney's property. It'll be interesting to see if they fit Mr. Heffernan."

"You think he's the kid that was causing Terry problems?" Rachel said.

"Can't rule it out yet." The wind had picked up. "I'll take him in and question him there. Call Trudy to get a tow truck to take the car back to the station. You head out to Surfriders and ask about those blueprints. I want to know if they're for the 'design' that Gerard thinks Terry was apparently famous for."

"But this kid might be the reason Terry didn't make it back to his house."

"He might be," Jax said. "Until we're sure, we work every angle."

"Yes, sir." Brody stepped away to make the call and Jax secured the shoe in an evidence bag, tagged it, and put it in the back of the trunk before sliding into the patrol car. He lowered his rearview mirror to look back at Scott and started the car. As he pulled out, he opened the window between them.

"Scott Heffernan. You sure are a distance from home."

The kid's jaw twitched in reply.

"What brings you here? Sure can't be the weather." Mist had begun to condense on the windshield.

Scott stared out the window.

"Want to tell me how you got here? You with someone? Can't imagine you just walked."

Silence.

"That's fine. You can talk to me at the station."

"I get to make a call, right?"

"After questioning, sure. You'll probably want to wait for that anyway.

Bail money and all."

The kid's face reddened, but they made the rest of the drive in silence.

Matt was at the precinct when they arrived and Jax directed him to take Scott to one of the interview rooms. So much for his deputy staying off work and resting. But Jax couldn't force the young man to sleep. When a case was hopping, the team wanted to be part of it. He couldn't blame them for that.

Trudy ripped off her headset and cocked an eyebrow at Jax. He ignored it and headed straight for the kitchen. Poured a tall cup of coffee, black. He'd expected to be driving to West Shore directly after seeing Troy, but he wanted to know more about how Scott Heffernan had come into possession of Terry's pride and joy. What he hadn't found in his brief search was any blueprints.

When Jax came back into the reception area, Trudy still eyed him. He rubbed his neck. "What did I do this time?"

"You tell me."

There were a dozen reasons on any given day that he and Trudy didn't mix. But he'd been legible with his reports and hadn't asked her to stay late. Hadn't wallowed recently, like in the past. Or as much. Insomnia was in check. He raised his hands in surrender. "I give."

Her lips pursed together. "After everything you and Abby have been going through, I thought you might have a chance. Guess you're determined to blow that, too."

He'd done nothing to sabotage Abby. Where had she gotten that idea? "What are you talking about, Trudy?"

She shot out of her chair and marched over to him with a plate of banana bread in her hand. It was covered in Saran wrap and nicely sliced. She set the plate down with a clank on the desk next to Jax and proceeded to fold her arms over her chest.

"Banana bread is the problem?"

She frowned.

"Seriously, you'll have to give me more than that," Jax said.

"How about the woman that brought it to you."

Jax's eyes widened. "What woman?"

"Margot Coleman. Ring a bell? Cute little curly haired blonde. Swung by right after you left and said she was so happy that you'd reconnected and went on and on about how handsome you were."

"Margot Coleman brought this?"

"You heard me the first time."

He unwrapped the bread, grabbing a piece. "I've known Margot for a long time. Abby knows her, too. She was the nurse who cared for Lulu at the hospital." He picked up the plate and held it in front of Trudy. "She's a nice lady. Moved here recently, sounds like after her marriage broke up. I'm sure she appreciated seeing a friendly face. That's all. We only chatted for a short time because she lives up past Chesney's place."

"Hmmm," Trudy said. "Well, I think she's viewing you as more than just a friendly face."

He took a bite of the banana bread. Trudy's loyalty to Abby was evident, and after what they'd gone through with Lulu, he didn't blame her. "It's not mutual. I promise."

He left Trudy with the plate and smiled as he sipped his coffee. He had no interest in Margot, but he couldn't lie: it tickled him that some women still found him desirable.

Except the only one he wanted wasn't giving him a lot of her time these days. How long would he wait?

He brushed off the thought along with the crumbs on his shirt and walked into the room with Scott Heffernan.

CHAPTER 18

Abby perched on the end of the chenille sofa, waiting for Tabitha Pickford to return from her kitchen. She'd welcomed Abby with a sad smile a few minutes before.

After leaving Jonathan's apartment, it only took a brief perusal of the file to find out the picture of the woman and little girl on his nightstand had indeed been his sister and niece. Tabitha lived only a few short miles away.

Olek had gone to the West Shore precinct to research the floral order that Jonathan Lilly had placed the day before he went missing. Tabitha might be able to narrow down that information, too. By hitting it from both angles, they'd cover more ground.

Tabitha offered Abby a glass of water and carried a Hydro Flask for herself when she returned. Her appearance—black running tights, a sweatshirt that ended at her trim waist, a high ponytail of jet black hair—suggested she might be a runner like her brother.

"Have you found Jonathan yet?" Her voice trembled. "I know about the foot, but…"

Knowing about the foot could only add fuel to her fear for her only sibling. "The local department just recently handed off the file so we're getting up to speed. I saw your picture in your brother's place, which is what prompted my call." Abby sipped the water. "I saw Jonathan had several ribbons for marathons. Are you a runner as well?"

Tabitha chose an armchair and sat on the edge, one leg tucked under, and set the flask on the wood coffee table. "Yeah." Her gaze drifted to the floor. "We were supposed to run the day he went missing until I bailed on him."

"Did he seem upset by that?"

She shook her head. "He never got upset. But he did seem quieter than usual on the phone. I asked if everything was okay, and he said of course, and then joked that I worried too much. Which he's right. But now I just feel horrible that I didn't go."

Abby had seen the sadness the minute the woman had opened the door. Sadness with a measure of guilt could be debilitating—something she knew plenty about. "Did you often run together?"

"Not all the time. I work part-time at a bakery, which is why I run, and with having my daughter, Angel. But I did when I could."

"Angel's a beautiful name."

Tabitha smiled. "She's a beautiful soul." Her eyes misted. "And she loved her Uncle Johnny. He was so good to her, and such a great brother."

Abby nodded. "Can you think of anyone who would have wanted to cause him harm?"

"The West Shore police asked me that before, and I've searched my brain. I can't think of anyone."

"How about when you were out running? Did Jonathan mention issues with another person on the road? Did you cross paths with anyone on the route who gave him a sideways glance, or who you sensed he had problems with?"

She bit her lower lip, thinking. "Nothing stands out. He was a competitive racer. Did other men want to keep pace with him when he was running? Sure. He didn't stop to answer questions about his training regimen or diet, but if they kept up, he'd chat with them. I never saw animosity or anything that led me to feel concern for his safety."

"How about his work?"

"He seemed happy doing what he did, but he didn't connect with the staff either. He consulted and that had him travelling or working from home." Tabitha jumped up and started to pace. "But his foot being washed ashore. That just freaks me out. I mean, how angry does someone have to be to take his foot off?"

Abby could read the pain and uncertainty in Tabitha's face. The woman wasn't saying the words, but the question in her mind was, *Did he suffer?*

"Maybe this will help. Because of the way our hands and feet are attached, when a body is in water, they often separate first. The shoes make it so they float." She wouldn't share her suspicion—that there appeared to be signs of removal—because there was no way of knowing it was right. Besides, a family didn't need to hear that at this stage.

Tabitha's body deflated with the breath she let out. The weight of that had been consuming her. "Thank God."

Abby nodded. Although until the report came in with certainty, she couldn't leave any angle untouched. "Was your brother suicidal?"

She shook her head. "Never. Our family has no history of depression, and he was as even-tempered as they come. He used exercise as his therapy when he was having a bad day. And he'd been up lately. Excited about something, but he said he wasn't ready to share the details."

The flowers. "We found a charge on his credit card indicating he'd ordered flowers for someone the day before he went missing. Do you think that could have contributed to his good mood?"

"It's possible, I guess."

"Any idea who they'd be for?"

"No. But the last time we'd run he'd said he found his happy place. Maybe he did find someone."

"Is it strange he wouldn't have told you who that was?"

She shook her head. "Not really. He was protective of Angel, so he wouldn't be introducing people into our world until he was sure about the person."

"It's not odd that he wouldn't at least talk about it on one of your runs?"

"We didn't do a lot of talking out there. The pace he keeps, I was lucky to keep my breath in check. We kept it to small talk. But I was happy to just hang out with my big brother. You know?"

She didn't. An only child, she'd stood in awe of large families, wishing she could be part of one. At one time, wanting to have one. But her career had taken precedence and she'd been enfolded into the family of the Bureau. And then after Lulu....

The door burst open, and a doe-eyed blonde came swirling in, dressed in her puffy pink jacket, fur lined hood, and a Dora the Explorer backpack. Abby put her at about seven.

"Hi, Mama," she said, running straight for Tabitha, who embraced her in a long hug.

Abby's chest squeezed. Lulu would be about nine, a little older. She could still see her soft curls. Her big brown eyes.

"How was your day?" Tabitha said to her daughter.

"Good."

The girl whipped around to Abby. "I'm Angel. Who are you?"

It was then Abby noticed the circles under the little girl's eyes. The paleness of her almost translucent skin. "I'm Abby." She squatted to meet her at eye level. "What grade are you in?"

"Second. You're pretty." She reached out her hand and Abby didn't flinch as she touched her long black hair. "Why are you here?"

Tabitha had a comforting hand on the little girl's shoulder. "So many questions. How about you get your stuff to your room, and we'll talk in the kitchen over a snack."

Abby stood and extended her hand. "Very nice to meet you, Angel."

Angel shook it, then ran to her room with a wide smile.

"Sorry about that," Tabitha said. "She doesn't have much of a filter anymore."

"Is that because of her illness?"

Tabitha's eyes flashed wide for just a second. "How did you know?"

"Mother's intuition. And my daughter, Lulu, had leukemia." She held back the details. She didn't want the sympathy...and Tabitha's child was still very much alive.

"My girl had non-Hodgkins. She made it through. Barely, but she's here. The people at the Children's Cancer Hospital are amazing."

"Here in West Shore?"

"Yeah. Is that where they treated Lulu?"

"It is. Small world," Abby said.

"Cancer makes it smaller. How's your girl now?"

Abby gave a small shake of her head.

Tabitha reached out her hand. "I'm sorry you didn't have a better outcome."

Not a day passed she'd wished that too. Abby nodded and cleared her throat. "What's Angel's prognosis?"

"If we can make it past the five-year mark, we should be home free. That's why I'm trying to stay strong. I don't want her feeling sad about her uncle until we know what's happened. Even then… She needs only positive vibes right now."

"Absolutely."

"And going back to that hospital, without Johnny there to cheer her up—it might kill us both. He was her cheerleader. He refused to let her feel down. I'm not sure I could do this again without him." Tears rimmed Tabitha's eyes.

"You would find it in you," Abby said. Even if it left her hollowed out inside, Abby knew a mother would spare nothing to save her child. She cleared her throat. "No father in the picture?"

She looked away. "He's alive, but the moment I got pregnant, he took a job in New York. We haven't seen him since. Wouldn't even know he existed except for the court-mandated child support that comes into my account every month."

Abby nodded. For whatever she deemed Jax's faults, he'd been a wonderful father. And before Lulu's death, a good husband. Like her, he'd given up every piece of himself to save their daughter, leaving nothing left. How did they come back from that? How did they trust each other again?

"Well, thank you for your time," Abby said. "I'll let you get to your daughter. If you think of anything else, please reach out." Abby handed her a card with her contact information.

Tabitha walked her to the door. "I hope you find my brother so I can bury him properly. I keep thinking I shouldn't be so resigned to knowing he's dead without his body. But truth is, I knew the day he disappeared. Even before his foot was found. We've had a connection from the time we were kids, and that day, I couldn't feel him anymore."

Abby didn't put much into telepathy herself, but she didn't doubt people's stories of it. She still heard Lulu in her mind. Her laughter. Could smell her fruity shampoo. Feel her arms around her neck. Despite the twinge of pain it caused every time, she would never choose to turn it off. It was all she had left. "I'm sorry. I'll be in touch with anything I find."

Abby trotted back to her car to get Olek and found him waiting at the curb. He climbed into the passenger side.

"How was it?" he asked.

"Jonathan Lilly had a great sister and a wonderful niece. We're not looking at suicide. How about you? What'd you find out?"

"Awaiting a call back for the insurance claim, and the call records will take a bit. But I did have a little success. The flowers were sent to a Margot Coleman at the Children's Cancer Hospital."

"Margot?"

"You know her?"

"She's the nurse who'd cared for Lulu. She must have been assigned to Angel as well."

"Angel?"

"Jonathan's niece. She had cancer and left treatment about a year ago."

"Small world."

"That's what I said. Perhaps he was saying thank you for the care she'd given Angel. Any way to check on what the card said?"

"Already done. *Can hardly wait for this weekend.* I think he was planning to thank her in a bunch of different ways."

CHAPTER 19

Scott Heffernan looked even smaller and younger in the large Formica-floored room than he did cuffed on the side of the road. Now those cuffs were linked to a hook on a heavy oak table and his chin touched his chest. Jax came in and put a bottled water in front of him, set his own coffee down, and stuffed the bag he'd brought in under his chair. The kid wasn't paying any attention.

Typical teenager. "Rise and shine," Jax said.

Scott looked up and yawned. He either didn't grasp the gravity of the situation, or he didn't care. With the slack in his jaw and the way he gazed at the ceiling, the latter seemed spot on.

Jax pulled out a chair and sat down.

Scott eyed the water. "Got some kind of truth serum in there?"

Jax sipped his coffee. "You read too many spy thrillers."

The kid shrugged and opened the bottle, taking a long drink. "When do I get my call?"

"Who you calling?"

He shrugged again.

"How about we chat for a bit first."

"I didn't do anything. I already told that to the chick that tackled me. I should be filing a complaint for abuse."

"Abuse?"

"Yeah, she ran me down."

"You ran."

"She scared me."

Rachel did have a presence. "From my experience, people only run when they're guilty."

"I was afraid she'd find my stash."

At one time, he would've believed that. "Pot's legal now. You're eighteen."

Scott stared at the ceiling without responding.

Enough games already. "Let's cut to the chase, shall we. I have places to be, and you have a cell to get to."

Scott's face flushed. "I didn't do anything."

"You were cruising around in a stolen vehicle."

"I didn't know it was stolen and I wasn't cruising."

"Where were you headed with said vehicle then?"

"Home."

"Where's that?"

"West Shore. I already told that chick all of this. The keys were in the car. I found it, and I was going to figure out what to do with it after I had time to think."

"Most people would not assume they can get in a car and take it. So cut the crap."

Scott jutted out his chin with defiance.

Jax pulled the bag out from under his chair, placed it on the table, and removed the shoe he'd found under the passenger's seat. He set it in front of Scott.

"This belong to you?" Jax said.

Scott barely glanced at it. "Never seen it before."

"Do you know a man by the name of Terry Chesney?"

"Yeah."

"How?"

"Everyone who hangs around the beach with a surfboard knows Terry. He's a surf legend, man."

"Have you met him, personally?"

He shrugged.

"Ever take any of his classes?"

Scott looked away. He might be weighing how much Jax knew. "Maybe."

"You part of the youth group he was affiliated with?"

Scott took another drink of water and leaned in on his forearms. "You can't hold my past against me. I know my rights. I'm sure you're running me right now. But I was a juvie at the time and the charges were dismissed."

"What'd they arrest you for?"

"I don't remember."

Did he think he couldn't find out? "No worries. My assistant will tell me in a minute."

He huffed. "Fine. Trespass and B and E. But it was innocent enough. I mean, I didn't take anything. It was just a joke."

"Breaking and entering is a joke? Is that how the youth of today view that?"

"All I'm saying is the charges were dropped and it was no big deal."

Except it could speak to a pattern. And why Scott had been in the youth program. "What was a West Shore boy doing in Misty Pines in the first place?" Jax asked.

"Hanging with my friend."

"Who's that friend?"

"Dylan Marks. And before you ask, we had a fight and I was walking home when I found the car. Beat hitching a ride."

Jax held back an eyeroll. He should have known Dylan was involved. He'd thought they'd come to an understanding. That he'd stay on the straight. "What were you and Dylan arguing about?"

"He's all gung-ho about getting out of here and going to college. When I lit up, he came unglued. Said he didn't need any issues with his dad who has a real stick up his—"

"I get the picture." Jax took a breath. Maybe he had made an impact. If not, at least his dad had. "How'd you meet Dylan? In that program?"

"Yeah. What time is it?"

"You need to be somewhere?"

"Just expecting someone."

Scott must have shot off a text before he'd been taken into custody since that phone call had yet to happen. Jax could hardly wait for an irate parent to arrive and give him the riot act about messing with their kid. Visions of Commissioner Marks flitted through his mind. Except Scott Heffernan was not a kid. In almost every legal sense, he was an adult.

"Terry Chesney is missing. What do you know about that?" Jax said.

Scott's arrogance slipped off his face like a mime's mask. "He is?"

"This shoe was found in the car you were driving. It's a match to one found on his property. So cut the crap that you only found the car. Why were you up at his house two nights ago?"

"I wasn't. We weren't." Scott sputtered.

"Then how did the shoe get there?"

"It was already there."

Did he look stupid? "You're trying to tell me the car you magically find just happens to belong to someone you know, but you weren't at his house and have no idea how a man's tennis shoe was tucked under your seat?"

"Exactly what I'm trying to tell you."

Jax had never liked merry-go-rounds. "Let's say that's true. Where exactly did you find the car?"

"Meddle Road."

A pang hit Jax's stomach. "Meddle Road?" That area had been too much in his radar in the last twenty-four hours. It lay below Chesney's property. Walter's body had been in a nearby ravine. A foot had been found off that beach. When he'd been out there, had he searched far enough?

Scott's head bobbed. "Maybe instead of harassing me, you could talk with the lady who was out there walking around like she was insane."

"When was that?"

"That first night I found the car."

Jax straightened. "What lady?"

"Some old woman with crazy red hair and wandering around in a nightgown. I asked if she was okay, but she ran."

Dora? Abby had made it sound like she'd escaped during morning hours. She would not be happy to hear otherwise. Scott of course could be mistaken, but doubtful. And Dora would have walked down Meddle Road to get to the beach where Abby had found her. Where she'd found the foot.

"Where'd she run to?" Jax asked.

"No idea. I didn't follow."

"What time was that?"

"Midnight, maybe. I don't remember."

"Try."

"Yeah, okay. Close anyway. That's when D and I had a fight."

"D is Dylan."

"Duh."

Had Dora been out of the center that long? If so, she might have seen who abandoned the VW—if Scott was telling the truth. What else had she seen?

"And you're telling me you found the car at midnight."

"Yeah."

"And what. You slept in it?"

He nodded. "Yeah. That night, I wanted to get high, you know. So, I climbed in and did, and then passed out. Woke up about mid-day. I went back to D's house then, but the gate was closed, and he didn't answer my call. So I've been hanging out at the beach and figured I'd try again today.'"

"Doesn't make sense you'd stay. Why not go home—back to West Shore?"

"Because I wasn't sure if I should take the car out of town or not." Scott shifted. "I mean, okay, I'll be honest."

Jax leaned back in his chair. "That would be nice."

"I liked driving it and thought it would be a shame to leave it on the road again. But I was heading back to Dylan's house. That's when I ran into your deputies."

"Where's the gun?"

"What gun?"

"The one that belonged to the bullets we pulled from the glove compartment."

He straightened. "No, sir. There was no gun. I swear."

He'd been reaching. But most people didn't secure bullets in a car unless they had the gun nearby. "Did you see anything the night you 'found' the car that seemed suspicious?"

"Nothing. I slept most of it. And I don't know what happened to the old

104

lady or anyone else." His face turned white. "Did something happen to her? I didn't do anything. I swear to that too."

Jax ignored the kid's ramblings. Scott was either stupid enough to climb into an abandoned vehicle and be a dumb teenager, or something sinister had gone down. He either had an accomplice or he was acting alone on a B and E at Chesney's house that had gone terribly wrong. Dora might be able to shed some light—if he could get Abby to facilitate that.

"Where did you take classes from Terry?" Jax asked.

"At his shop. I've never even been to his house. I didn't know that was his car. Honestly, it was just sitting on the side of the road."

"What size shoe do you wear?"

"Ten."

Jax looked under the table at Scott's sandaled feet. Crazy choice this time of year. But the tennis shoe in his possession was a size thirteen. At one glance, Jax didn't suspect Scott's feet were anywhere close to that. That didn't mean anything if Scott had an accomplice.

Trudy tapped on the door, breaking his thoughts.

"What do we know?" he asked, stepping out of the room.

"Mr. Heffernan had a trespass at the age of sixteen, and a break and enter."

"He mentioned those. Said the charges were dropped?"

"Not entirely. He got community service because of whose house he broke into. Someone named Shaun Evans."

"Shaun Evans." The leader of the youth group. "Wonder what that was about?" he said, although he had some clue.

"You can ask him yourself. He's in the reception area waiting to speak with you."

CHAPTER 20

Jax entered the reception area to find Shaun Evans pacing. He'd had the youth program director on his list, so appreciated that the man had saved him a few steps by popping in.

Shaun had bulky arms that stretched the fabric of his black T-shirt and legs like tree trunks under his camo pants. A sheath on his belt held an initialed leather-handled blade. His freshly shaved buzz cut suggested he could be ex-military—a common ground.

"Mr. Evans." Jax extended his hand. Shaun squeezed a little too tight; Jax squeezed back. "Let's go to my office."

Last night, after he'd left Gerard, he was convinced the direction he needed to investigate was toward the missing surfboard design blueprints—blueprints that had yet to show up. Even the conversation with Commissioner Marks had him believing he was on the right path.

But with Scott's history of breaking and entering, the theory of a burglary gone wrong could be in play.

"Hear you have one of my kids in custody," Shaun said, following Jax into his office.

Jax rounded his desk and shifted the plate of bread Margot had brought to the side. He sat down. "Word travels fast."

Shaun eyed the plate.

"Would you like a piece?" Jax offered.

"No. Thanks." Shaun's jaw twitched. "But it looks good."

He didn't seem the type to binge. More willpower than Jax had. "I assume Scott called you?"

Shaun nodded and Scott's claim of innocence dissipated. If he called for help before even talking to Rachel and Brody, he knew he was screwed.

"He had reason to be worried. The vehicle doesn't belong to him."

"He said he found it," Shaun said.

Youth often twisted facts to suit their situation. Jax had more hope for an adult who mentored them. "Right. You don't find vehicles, Mr. Evans. If they're parked on the side of the road, it should be assumed someone is coming back for it." Although given the blood, Terry wasn't coming back for anything.

"Scott has impulse issues," Shaun said.

Jax leaned back in his chair. "Obviously. I saw he broke into your house, and you were his community service."

"He did. It happens. And I took that as an opportunity to turn him around. Truth is, every one of the young men I work with, one way or another, has made bad decisions. But the program I run helps them through that."

Clearly not a foolproof system. That wasn't fair. No one could save them all. "I understand that you engaged Terry Chesney to help you with that."

"Yeah, Ter's a good guy. Heck of a woodworker. You surf?"

He had about as much grace as a monkey on the dance floor. "Tried it once. Wasn't my thing."

"Me either, to be honest. I'm more of an outdoorsman. Deep sea fishing. Hiking. But we found giving the kids a skill, like the focus needed in carving or shaving a surfboard, worked well at keeping their hands and minds busy."

"Terry ever mention any problems with the young men?"

He bristled. "We get a lot of cocky shits. But they understand who's in charge. Eventually."

Shaun had a quality about him like Jax's old commander, Grady, that set Jax on edge. Or maybe he reminded him of Troy Marks. "Anyone in particular that gave Terry a particularly hard time?"

He shrugged. "None that come to mind. They all challenge at first, but they come to respect us. Why all the questions about Terry? Did someone from the program harass him?"

"That's what we're trying to find out."

"Why not ask Terry himself?"

Jax held Shaun's gaze a few extra seconds.

"Oh shit. What happened?"

"Again, what we're trying to find out."

Shaun sank in his chair, which looked odd on a man with so much muscle. "It's not like we were buddies who spoke on the regular. We got together a few times a year and I'd send boys through a class with him. That's the extent of our paths crossing." Realization seemed to hit him. "That's whose car you think Scott stole?"

Jax nodded.

Shaun's focus turned toward the door like he was looking in Scott's direction. "Stupid kid."

"You think he knew it was Terry's?"

"Don't know how. He never took a class with Terry that I remember. Terry might have come in for a brief meet and greet once, but that would have been about it."

Scott had already admitted to taking a class at Terry's shop, but Mr. Evans, like everyone else, might be juggling too many things to remember every detail. "When was the last time you saw Terry?"

He shifted in his chair and leaned his elbow onto his knees. "A month ago. Maybe. But we only talked on the phone. Planning an upcoming class."

"Anything come up at that time that someone from the class had wanted to cause him harm?"

He shook his head, lips pursed in thought.

"You know about his design work?" It was a long shot, but men talked. Maybe Terry had brought up how people wanted a piece of him and his designs.

"I don't."

"You ever hiked out behind his place?"

"Don't know where he lives. Classes were held at his shop. Any hikes he joined us on were out of West Shore."

He hadn't asked the last question, but Shaun was proactive. "Well, appreciate your coming by. Unfortunately, Scott's next phone call should be to a lawyer. Or his parents."

He shook his head. "Doesn't have a dad. Mom's in and out of rehab. He lives on his own. That's why he called me. I'm the only one who believed in him. Still do."

That story was all too familiar. He'd heard it more often in Portland, but kids with little parental influence were becoming more the norm here too. "That's a shame. But it doesn't change the fact he was in possession of a vehicle belonging to a man that's presumed dead at this point. Until I get to the bottom of that, Scott Heffernan will remain in custody."

They both stood, the height disparity between them obvious when Jax tilted his head to look up at him. "Fair enough," Shaun said.

"Sorry you made the trip for nothing."

"It's never nothing when it comes to the boys. You win some, you lose some. But no man gets left behind." He drew in a breath. "You get that, right? You look former Army to me."

"Navy."

"Marine."

That much had been obvious from the minute Jax saw the haircut. "It's a nice thought. Sometimes you don't have a choice."

"Not me. Even when someone says they want to be left, you just don't."

Jax thought of Lulu. Of his friendship with Jameson, now in jeopardy since he hadn't dismissed Rachel as a candidate for the permanent deputy position. Of Abby. He'd gone back for her, and it might not have been enough. His gut twisted. "By the way, you know anything about a Riley Higgins?"

"Yeah, he's a jerk. Why?"

"Strong words."

"He's got some skills and you'd think as the only other surf pro in town, he'd be more giving to the community that supports his shop. But he'd rather use them to make money. He helped mentor the kids for about a second. Otherwise, only interested in helping himself."

"Interesting. Was he so money driven he might be willing to steal?"

"A guy like that? Wouldn't put it past him."

Jax walked Shaun out. "Does he have any connection to Scott?"

He thought about it for a second. "Scott wasn't in the program at that point. To be honest though, until today, I hadn't heard from Scott in a while. Guess you'd have to check with him." He shook Jax's hand and left.

"I don't know about that one," Trudy said, clicking her tongue.

"Not a fan?"

"Oh, he's nice enough. It's not what he says. It what he doesn't say."

He smiled. "I ever tell you you'd make a good cop?"

"Oh, hon. I could have told you that."

He scooped up his keys, glad "hon" was back in Trudy's vocabulary. He hadn't realized he'd missed it until it returned.

But Shaun wasn't for everyone. That military core ran deep and like his commander Grady, you either loved him or hated him. A rare person straddled the middle. He, however, had learned to both hate and respect the man at the same time. And Shaun Evans sparked that familiar feeling.

"Where you headed?" Trudy asked.

"Couple places, including Meddle Road. It's where that VW was found. I want to make sure I didn't miss something."

Trudy gave him a side look. "You have to quit second-guessing yourself."

"Easier said than done. By the way, you hear from Abby?"

She shook her head. "I'm worried about her too. The pressure of her mother failing. Her job. You."

"I'm not failing her. She's not telling me what I need to do."

"The 'not telling you' *is* telling you."

Women. What was that supposed to mean? No doubt to read between the lines. But right now, the only lines he needed to read between were the ones he may have missed out on Meddle Road. "If you hear from Abby, tell her we need to chat about Dora."

"That could be a touchy subject."

What wasn't these days?

His next interview was about to stir a hornet's nest.

CHAPTER 21

He found the Marks house miles from Meddle Road, surrounded with farm and rural land. Scott would have had to be fueled by a good amount of anger to make it that far on foot from here. Although at the age of fifteen, Jax had sprinted nearly three miles after his dad had slammed him against a wall. Only cold reality and a lack of cash had brought him back.

In Scott's situation, a falling out with Dylan didn't seem enough. But he had been in the Meddle Road area at some point because he'd crossed paths with a woman who matched Dora's description.

The Marks property had a gated entry. He'd expected to have to explain his arrival to Deanna, Dylan's mother and Commissioner Marks's wife, to get in, but the landscapers had left the gate open—their trailer was sitting at the edge of the property, where they were trimming the street side.

He took that as a good omen and eased up a paved road that led to a circular drive. A gaudy Roman water fountain in the middle spewed crystal clear water into the misty air. In the summer that might feel refreshing. Now Jax shuddered with the idea of the chill.

He rang the bell and Deanna opened the door. He'd half expected a maid to answer.

"Jax, what brings you here?" she said, smiling. Her graying blonde hair was swept into an elegant pile on her head, but a few strands fell to her shoulders and against her linen smock. She looked like money even when she puttered around her house.

"Was hoping I could come in and chat with Dylan for a moment."

She stiffened. They'd only had the occasional nod at the grocery store since the funeral they'd both attended last year. She'd always been pleasant. Her friendliness downshifted fast at Dylan's name.

"You're more than welcome to join," Jax added. "I have some questions about Scott Heffernan. I understand he stayed here the other night."

Her shoulders lowered an inch. "Of course. Scott. I'll get Dylan."

He followed her to the living room and stood at the edge, taking in the white sectional, lamb wool throws, and crystal accessories. He hadn't a clue where to sit.

Dylan shuffled in behind him dressed in dark gray sweatpants, black-socked feet, and a Seahawks' sweatshirt. His long frame was hunched slightly, like he'd just woken up or had been playing video games all night. "What do you want?"

Despite finding some common ground in recent months, Dylan was every bit a seventeen-year-old. Some things didn't change without the benefit of growing up some. "Thought we could chat a minute about your friend, Scott. Where were you two nights ago?"

He ran his hand over his hair a few times to make it lie flat. "Home."

"And Scott as well?"

"Yeah, so?"

Deanna navigated around Dylan and headed for a velour-covered chair. "Come in and sit, both of you. You look like you're about to have a pissing contest."

Jax nodded and took a seat on the white couch. Dylan dropped onto a fuzzy ottoman. He looked out of place. They both did. But Deanna was clearly used to dealing with testosterone in the house.

"What's this about Scott?" she asked.

"He was taken in this afternoon for possession of a stolen vehicle."

"Scott?" she said.

Dylan didn't seem fazed. "What an idiot."

"Explain that, please," Jax said.

"We had a fight that night and I told him to leave."

"What time was that?"

"Eleven. Maybe twelve. Didn't pay attention, except it was too late to wake up my dad to take him home."

"How'd he get here?"

"Uber. I figured he called another one to leave, but I have no idea. I went back to bed."

Dylan and Scott's version lined up so far. "Did he know Terry Chesney?"

Dylan shrugged but straightened a bit. "Why?"

"That's whose car he was driving. Says he came upon it, abandoned, and the keys were inside."

"Oh." He shifted, clearly holding back.

"Son, if you have something to tell me about that, you should do so."

Deanna's gaze locked onto her son and he in turn gazed at the floor. His mother wouldn't be shielding him from this—she was a far cry from his dad in that way. There might be hope for the kid yet.

Deanna was done waiting. "Dylan Douglas Marks. If you are hiding something."

"Mom."

Jax cleared his throat. "What size shoe do you wear?"

"Thirteen," Deanna said. "Why?"

Dylan's face flushed.

"Because we found a shoe in the VW Scott was driving."

"Don't tell me it was a red basketball shoe. Adidas," Deanna said.

Jax nodded.

Deanna leaned forward, putting her face in her hands. "I'm usually falling over them in the entry, and they were missing today." She focused on her son again. "You stole a car?"

"It's not what you think," Dylan said, stammering.

"Then by all means enlighten us," Jax said, "because the match to that shoe was found at the edge of Terry Chesney's property. The property where he has gone missing."

"Dylan." Deanna's voice shook.

"No, Mom. I don't know anything about that."

She glared at him. Jax appreciated the assist. Troy would have been so busy worrying about his own reputation that Jax would have been going around in circles trying to get two minutes with Dylan.

"Fine. It may have been a little different than I just said," Dylan said.

Jax waited and Deanna's face scrunched, clearly expecting the worst.

Dylan winced. Parental guilt could be a wonderful thing. "Scott and I went joyriding that night on my scooter after you and Dad went to bed," he said.

Deanna straightened but remained quiet.

Dylan stared at his hands. "If you go a quarter mile or so up from Mr. Chesney's place, you'll find that piece of junk in the ditch behind some bushes. It ran out of gas. Which was my fault, I guess, even though I was sure it had gas when we left."

"Why Bull Mountain Road? There are closer places to joyride," Jax said.

He shrugged. "Scott's idea. He said the ride down was a roller coaster. Except we didn't get to ride it back down on the scooter."

"Why didn't you call? We would have come and got you." Deanna shook her head, her jaw set in anger and disappointment.

"Right. And be subjected to Dad's lecture. No thanks."

"Continue." Jax didn't need to hear more on that subject. He'd been on the receiving end of Troy's tirades before.

"Anyway, we were hiking back down when Scott said he recognized where we were, which was near Mr. Chesney's place. I'd never been there, but I'd met the guy a couple of times through this thing my dad signed me up for. Anyway, we started up the driveway, I could see a light in the garage. We figured maybe Terry would give us a ride back into town. But when we got closer, the place was open, and no one was around."

Jax could buy the first part. Kids not thinking things through was commonplace. "And you decided to borrow the car?"

Dylan avoided his mother's scathing glare and nodded. "The VW is cherry, and the key was up under the wheel well. Hard to resist, you know."

No. Stealing had never been an impulse that moved through him. "How did you know where to find the key?"

"Scott found it."

Scott seemed to be more in charge of this joy ride than he'd first let on.

114

"Did you see anything suspicious? Hear anything? Did you look for Terry before you couldn't resist stealing the man's car?"

Dylan cleared his throat. "It sounds bad. I get it. But Scott was high, and I was...well, stupid. Honestly though, I didn't mean anything by it. I don't know Terry that well, but he's cool. If we only borrowed the car to get home, we were sure he'd understand. But..." He hesitated.

"But what?"

He shrugged.

"But you did more than just steal that car, didn't you?"

"No, I mean..."

"Then how'd your shoe get on the edge of the property?"

Dylan huffed. "Okay. We might have heard something. But I don't know what."

Jax shifted to the edge of the chair. "What did it sound like?"

"A scream." He looked at Jax. "And it scared the bejeezus out of us, as Mom would say." He glanced at her for approval, but she looked away.

Jax's chest tightened. "A scream for help?"

"That I don't know. We were amped. I was jumping at everything. Scott says it was a coyote and that I was being a chicken. Maybe, except I'd never heard anything like it before in my life. Like a war scream or something, you know. Piercing and from the gut. Like in those movies where someone is celebrating a kill. Predator. You ever see that movie? Scared the crap out of me."

"Dylan," Deanna said.

"Sorry, Mom. But it did."

The idea squeezed hard into Jax's stomach. Walter could have been screaming as he fell to his death. Or it could have been Chesney being murdered. Could Dylan have heard it from that distance? Sound carried, especially on a cold night. Unless... "You had to be further onto the property than just on the driveway."

Dylan swallowed.

Jax arched a brow.

"Okay, Scott might have been snooping around and that's when he found

Chesney's bike hanging in the garage."

Deanna put up her hand. "Jax, it might be best if Dylan had an attorney."

Dylan's eyes widened. "I didn't do anything wrong, Mom. We were just being stupid that night. I know it sounds bad and I'm sorry. But Scott grabbed the bike and took off into the forest and then the dumbass hit a knot in the road and flew off. He got so irritated he tossed the bike. That's when we heard the scream. He took off running without me. I listened for a minute and then took after him. There was still no sign of Terry when I made it to the garage, and then I just wanted to get out of there."

Jax met Deanna's eye, hopeful she wouldn't shut him down. She gave him a small nod. *Thank you.* "So, you ran past the garage?" he said.

"Yeah. To the road. I'd planned to sprint all the way home. Except my shoes weren't tied well and I tripped and lost one of them. I didn't know where it landed, and I didn't care. Scott was in the Bug and pulled up next to me. I hopped in and we were gone."

Jax waited a moment to let the information settle in. The night's events were unfolding, but he still didn't know what he had. Did Dylan do something to Terry? Did Scott?

"Where were you at eight o'clock that night?"

Deanna's eyes lit up. "That I can tell you. We were at the church for evening services. Didn't get home until nine. But Dylan sat next to me the whole time."

Dylan nodded. "Scott came over shortly after that."

Deanna nodded confirmation.

That only gave Dylan an alibi. "How was Scott at the time he came over?"

"Chill. We played video games until we decided not to." Dylan wouldn't meet his mother's eyes.

"Was there anything in the VW?"

"Like what?" Dylan said.

"Paperwork. Blueprints."

Dylan shook his head slowly.

"Dylan, are you sure there was nothing in that car? If I find out different after I leave here…." Jax held Dylan's eyes.

116

Dylan glanced at his mother, and that was all it took. Her effect on him was instantaneous.

Dylan frowned and walked out of the room. He returned with something wrapped in a bath towel and gave it to Jax, who unwrapped it. A Glock. Likely the one that went with the bullets in the glove compartment.

"Scott can be crazy sometimes," he said. "He doesn't even know about this. When we got home, he got out first and my knee hit the glove compartment. It popped open and I saw the gun. No way I was leaving it behind for him."

Jax pulled on black latex gloves before removing the gun from the towel. "He have a tendency to be violent?" he asked, as he checked the chamber. Unloaded. Didn't appear to have been recently fired.

"Impulsive might be a better word," Dylan said.

"Like you?"

He looked away and shrugged. "Anyway, he kept calling me a pussy because I yelled at him all the way back here, which ticked me off. I told him to go sleep somewhere else and get the car back on his own. Until you showed up, I didn't know what he did or where he went. He kept calling me yesterday, but I ignored him. I'm still ticked at him. But honest, he was supposed to return the car. Apparently, he didn't, huh?"

"Apparently," Jax said.

Deanna folded her arms over her chest. "In case there's any question Dylan, you're grounded for the next six months."

"I wish it were as simple as that," Jax said. "Dylan, you and Scott were at the scene of a crime."

Deanna closed her eyes, perhaps regretting not pushing for an attorney. "Are you arresting him?"

"Mom, help me." Dylan's eyes flitted like a scared rabbit.

Jax stood. He had every reason to take Dylan in for additional questions. But he sensed he could get more out of him with Deanna close by than he could in an interrogation room alone with him. Or worse, with Troy present. While Dylan had been at the scene later, Jax was convinced whatever happened to Terry stemmed from the disturbance around eight o'clock. Dylan had a verifiable alibi. Scott did not.

"I won't be taking you in at this time, but don't go anywhere."

"I can promise you that, Sheriff Turner," Deanna said.

He had nothing but respect for Deanna, but she could only do so much against Troy's arrogance, which clearly played a factor in Dylan's personality. Or perhaps it was youth. Teenagers could be dumb.

He wasn't sure yet if dumb equaled murder.

CHAPTER 22

Abby ignored Jax's call and pulled into the Children's Hospital for Hope. It had been her second home while Lulu was fighting leukemia, and the sight of it still made her muscles clench.

"You okay?" Olek said.

"I'm good." Even if she wasn't, they couldn't miss an opportunity to speak with Margot Coleman. A call en route confirmed she was on duty.

She rode the elevator in silence, old memories of previous visits all too fresh even after five years. Except for when she and Jax had delivered the doll house to the third floor, she hadn't come back. A good day. She could still see the smiles on the children's faces. She closed her eyes, holding onto that image as the elevator doors opened.

The nurse at the station paged Margot, who had moved to administration and was no longer on the floor. Maybe working directly with the young ones had become too hard on her. Abby certainly couldn't have continued to do it and a little pre-meeting digging had indicated Margot had lost her own child to cancer. She'd apparently lost her marriage too if Jonathan was sending her flowers.

Within a few minutes, the woman who'd held their hands at Lulu's last breath rounded the corner. Her eyes lit at the sight of Abby.

"Abigail." Her pace quickened as she approached. "How have you been?"

Abby had never seen her so chipper, or so friendly. To her anyway. "Good."

"So glad to hear it." Margot smiled and pulled her in for a hug, taking Abby by surprise.

Abby hesitated, and then hugged her back as Olek averted his eyes. He knew about Lulu, but it was not a subject she allowed him to drill her on. Even so, Margot's reaction to seeing her seemed off somehow. Forced? "Do you have a place we can talk?"

Margot's smile faded. "Of course. Sounds official."

Abby nodded and followed Margot into the spacious and well-lit nurse's lounge. A Keurig coffee machine and a plate of freshly baked muffins sat on the counter. A vending machine with an assortment of junk food was tucked in the corner.

They took a seat around one of the round tables scattered throughout as Abby introduced Olek. "He's my partner and as you might remember, I'm with the FBI. We're investigating a missing persons case." *Technically.* Abby had no doubt that it was only the body they sought, along with the answer to what happened and why.

"Oh dear," Margot said, leaning her forearms on the table. "Someone I know?"

"We believe so," Abby said. "Jonathan Lilly." She scanned Margot's face for recognition.

"He's Angel's uncle. Angel's an out-patient now, but when she was undergoing her chemo, he came by often. I was her nurse at the time." She frowned, her gaze on Abby. "He's missing?"

"Yes. And we have reason to believe that he sent you flowers," Olek said.

"I..." Margot looked at Olek then back at Abby. "He did?"

Olek pulled out a notepad. "According to the florist's recollection, the card indicated that you might be getting together? Is that not true?"

"Oh...," she said, recognition dawning. "That was a few weeks ago. And yes, you're right. He did. He sent a bouquet of lilies." She chuckled. "He's done that a couple of times over the last couple of years. He gets a kick out of it. You know, because of his last name."

Abby got it. Cute. She nodded.

Margot's face wrinkled. "But it's not what you think. The flowers were to say thank you for taking good care of his niece on the last chemo round. And the card was about getting together for a run. I'm planning on doing a charity event this summer and he's an avid runner, so he offered to train me. Which he did a couple of times. In fact, the week before I met him at his place, and he took me on the road." She frowned. "But I'm out of shape so he got a kick out of torturing me. That's why he could hardly wait to see me that weekend. He probably had some diabolical plan to take me up a steep hill."

Running would be torture. The amount required at the academy had been enough for a lifetime in Abby's book. "So did you go for that run?"

"I didn't." She shifted in her seat. "I bailed on him."

"Did the two of you speak?"

"No. I called, but he didn't answer." Her shoulders slumped. "When did he go missing?"

"The day after he sent you the flowers," Olek said.

Her lips pursed together. "Oh dear." Margot's gaze settled on a spot on the far wall behind Abby's head.

Abby cleared her throat. "You okay?"

"When he didn't answer, I figured he was mad at me for flaking on him. Now to think that all this time something might have happened to him."

Abby nodded. "Can you tell me anything else about him? When you went out for a run, did you notice anyone in the vicinity? Any interactions that seemed out of place?"

Margot shook her head. "Nothing. He was a good man."

"Did he confide in you about any concerns?"

"None."

"Was there any romantic notions between the two of you? Could he have had a former girlfriend take issue with the time you spent together?" Olek said.

"Oh gosh no. There was nothing between us. I showed up in my black baggy sweats and my hair like a mop on my head. No one would be jealous of that."

Olek smiled and Abby knew he was thinking the same thing. Margot was cute. Even in baggy clothes she'd be attractive.

"But you're divorced now."

"I'm definitely single—I suppose Jonathan could have thought there was something romantic… but I never gave him any signals. We were just friends."

"Of course," Olek said.

Some men took "single" as the only signal they needed. Abby scooted back the chair and pulled her card from her purse. "We won't take any more of your time, Ms. Coleman. But if you think of anything."

"Margot. Please. And absolutely. You'll be my first call."

"Thank you," Olek said.

Margot scanned the card. "Oh, it looks like we're neighbors. I moved to Misty Pines not long ago. I'm sorry about you and Jax."

Abby bristled. She and Jax hadn't made their divorce known to many. Certainly not to anyone at the hospital—it happened a few years after Lulu anyway. Margot hadn't been on duty the day they dropped off the dollhouse. "Thank you," Abby said, her head tilting. "How did you hear about that?"

Margot's face lit up. "I ran into him on my way home. Handsome as ever. And kind." She cleared her throat, maybe remembering who she was talking to. "I mean, it's a shame and all. You two seemed great together, but obviously the death of a child can weigh heavy on a relationship."

"Right." Had Margot always been keen on Jax? Yes, now that she thought back, she had. She just hadn't paid it much attention at the time. Lulu had been her only focus. Their daughter had been Jax's only focus as well. "Well, good to have you in the neighborhood. Call me if you think of anything."

As soon as the elevator door closed, Olek's eyebrow rose an inch. "What the heck was that?"

"Someone who likes my ex-husband, clearly."

"No, I meant that she didn't remember the flowers. Seemed like she only admitted that when I presented the evidence of it."

"That was odd. I also noticed another thing."

"What's that?"

"That muffin plate looked similar to the cookie plate in Jonathan's apartment."

"She said she'd gone running with him the week before."

Abby nodded. "True. But bringing baked goods to a fitness fanatic? Maybe

I'm old-fashioned, but the women I knew that started bringing out their baking skills around men were the ones trying to land a husband."

"You think she was lying about there being a romantic relationship?" Olek said.

Before she could answer, Abby's phone rang. Stonebridge Assisted Living scrolled across her cell. She braced for whatever it was *this* time.

CHAPTER 23

Jax had tried Abby as he pulled into the Meddle Beach parking lot, but she didn't pick up. And he didn't leave a message. He'd have to tiptoe into the request to speak with Dora. He didn't want to upset Abby—or the woman he'd called mom for ten years. Whether Dora had little affinity for him or not, he'd always liked her spunk and fire. And speaking with her would give him time with Abby...but just as importantly, if Dora had vital information, he couldn't let it lie for too long.

The tide was in, and the rain had picked up. Sand swirled like eddies across what remained of the long and narrow stretch of shore. There wouldn't be any surfers in these conditions, and beachcombers had long gone.

The conversation with Dylan replayed through his head as he watched the waves crash. Much as he wanted to see if he'd missed anything, it would be better to wait until the tide had receded or the weather improved. It might even be worth giving Koa a chance to earn her keep. See what she had in the way of skills. Rachel could be an asset too.

Being thrown into the Chesney case hadn't allowed him time to think on the future of his department. Troy Marks would insist that he did, and whether Jax wanted to admit it, he might have a point about expansion. If Jax had the larger, more experienced department, could he have already found Terry's body and tied up this case?

He drew in the brackish air, refocusing. He believed Dylan's story. But he'd also believed too much once, and it had cost him. Nearly everything. Self-respect most of all. And he wouldn't leave any clue or piece of evidence untouched.

He found himself driving out on Bull Mountain Road, his eyes searching the brush lining the narrow road. Dylan had said he and Scott had hidden the motor scooter off the road up from Terry's place. As he passed the house, he saw the butt end of Gerard's car in the driveway. He'd half expected Gerard to check in on the status of the case regularly, but he'd been silent. Maybe he was just allowing the investigation to breathe.

Either way, Jax would circle back to him when he had something to share. At this point, he was running in circles with Scott in custody. He'd tossed Terry's bike out in the forest—one mystery solved. But who had they heard screaming at midnight? Someone dying...or as Dylan had put it, someone celebrating a kill and cleaning up the evidence?

Jax traversed the winding strip with his eyes peeled for a break in the foliage. The weather front coming in from the ocean had hit land now and rain pelted the passenger windows, blurring visibility. But a glint of something metal in the bushes caught his eye.

He pulled to the side and slipped into rain gear and latex gloves before getting out. The wind lifted the brim of his hat as he strode the ten yards to the overgrown line of bushes. A red and chrome gas tank peeked through some of the limbs. The tilted scooter was about to fall out of the cradle of foliage. He grabbed the handlebars and rolled it onto the gravel embankment.

He unclasped his flashlight and directed the beam onto the bike and opened the gas tank, shining the beam inside. Empty, just as Dylan said.

He ran the light over the body of the newer Honda. He wouldn't expect anything less of the Marks family. But a blemish under the gas tank caught his eye.

He crouched and aimed the beam at a small hole in the tank. Dylan had been sure the tank had gas. It might have, but a hole that size and in that location would have leaked the fuel all the way out in a few miles.

Jax couldn't imagine too many ways a hole could have gotten there without intention. The symmetry and location suggested a pick or sharp metal object had been used.

According to Dylan, it was Scott's idea to come up here in the first place.

He might have sabotaged the scooter if it had been his plan all along to take Terry's VW and use Dylan as a pawn. This could be as simple as a burglary gone wrong. Except the timeline didn't match up for Dylan's involvement. Terry had gone missing at eight, but Dylan hadn't come onto the property until midnight. Maybe Scott had cased the place earlier, then decided he wanted to get someone else involved. Create a cover story of sorts. Scott might be able to answer that. But given his propensity for not telling the truth, Jax would continue to gather info until Scott had no ability to lie his way out.

A four-door sedan slowed, blurred by the pounding rain. *Rubberneckers.* They existed everywhere. Nothing to see here. He wasn't in the mood for small talk. But as the car rolled to a stop next to him, he recognized the driver.

Margot Coleman lowered her window, leaned out, and smiled. "Sheriff Turner. What brings you back here?" Her blonde curls framed her round face.

"Afternoon, Nurse Coleman. You should get along home. Weather like this, best place to be is inside. These roads can be treacherous if we get too much of this stuff."

"It's Margot, please. And I know my way around here well by now." She winked. "Did you get the goodies I left for you?"

Where were his manners? "I did. Thank you."

She inspected the scooter. "Everything okay around here? Sure has been more activity than I would've anticipated. A little scary."

He'd like to be more reassuring. Until he knew what happened to Terry, he wouldn't. Especially if people like Scott and possibly Dylan were out casing homes to burglarize. "I'm sure it's all good. But never a bad idea to keep your doors locked and outside lights on at night."

She smiled. "I feel safer knowing you're on patrol."

He smiled back. Trudy might be right that he didn't pick up signals well—but he was sure Margot was flirting. "Just doing my job, ma'am." He nearly winced. *Just doing my job.* Christ.

She blushed. "Well thank you for that. You know, you're a good man.

They're hard to come by. And I should know. I've had the worst luck since, well, you know. You start out dating, and then they stop calling. I think you're different though. Aren't you...?"

Margot was cute. Sweet. Had taken care of his Lulu. But he didn't have time for this. "Appreciate that. And sorry to hear. I need to get moving though and it's not safe for you to block traffic." Jax nodded to the pickup truck heading their way.

"Later, gator," she said, winking.

He lifted his chin and watched her go. Saved by the truck. He waved a hello and thank you at the driver he'd met before, Old McDonald, as he passed. He rolled the scooter to the back of his rig, popped the front wheel in, and slid it in on its side.

What didn't make sense about Scott's story and the VW was if he'd concocted some elaborate plot to get the car, why not get out of town fast, in the dark? Why wait until broad daylight, let alone wait for two days?

Scott was a dumb kid—a dumb crook. But something still bothered him about the situation: where were the blueprints? Had they ever been in the car? If so, where had they gone? If not, same question? They could have no relevance whatsoever and Brandon might be wrong that Terry took them home when he left two nights ago.

But Jax had yet to check all the possibilities. And while he'd questioned his own gut on his last case, it had come through for him in the past. He glanced at his watch. He'd drop off the scooter into evidence and if he got a move on, he could still make West Shore before dark.

His thoughts returned to Margot as he drove. He hadn't thought of any other women in his life since Abby. Or after. He'd been so walled off he was immune to advances and didn't see them coming. Margot was different. They had history.

Abby didn't seem to want to work on their marriage anymore. He held the steering wheel tighter. When was the last time she'd made him banana bread? Never. When was the last time she'd kissed him? Let him hold her? Shared coffee?

The milk he kept for her would expire tomorrow.

Whether he wanted to admit it or not, maybe their ship had sailed. His chest squeezed at the thought. Maybe you only got one chance and they'd blown theirs all to hell.

CHAPTER 24

Unlike Surfrider nestled on the outskirts of town, All About the Waves consumed a half block of West Shore smack in the middle of town. Surfboards of every variety and color were piled in racks outside, leaving no doubt what kind of business was behind the double doors. Like Surfrider, it was painted a bright and eye-catching ocean blue. Bluer than the waters found around the Bahamas, a place Jax would like to visit once in his life. In the Navy, he'd been stationed on a ship that traversed the Indian ocean. A far cry from any tropics or his own backyard.

Jax walked into the showroom. Surfrider was about craftsmanship and personalization. This shop was about selling merchandise—and lots of it.

To add that flair of authenticity and knowledge, Riley Higgins' surfing trophies were lined up in glass cases high on the wall behind the long counter and cash register. Above the cases were numerous medals and certificates and photos of him standing on a podium and receiving awards set in some location where sun and sandy beaches intermingled. Why Terry and Riley chose the Oregon coast after having a taste of those warm waves eluded Jax.

To the right of the entry, surfboards were sorted by manufacturer and in color schematics: Isle Surfboards, NSP, Bic, Avila, Riley Higgins Surfboards, Inc. An entire wall displayed wet suits, hoods, gloves, and boots. Shelves of waxes, special earplugs, and surfing watches took up another section. Who knew there were so many options?

Having taken to the waves only once in his life, Jax had used what was handy and borrowed. He preferred to ride the waves from on top of a sturdy boat with a fair distance between him and the ocean floor.

The man behind the counter was short and muscular, his hair the color of bark with a few gray strokes brushed on the sideburns—the aged version of the photos above his head.

"Riley Higgins?" Jax said.

Riley gave him a chin up greeting. "That would be me. How you doing, officer?"

"Good. Good. Nice set up you have here."

"Pays the bills." Riley glanced at Jax's uniform. "You're a little far from Misty Pines, aren't you?"

"It was a nice drive."

Riley smiled. "You looking to get into the sport? Because I have everything a beginner needs. Our selection of fiberglass boards is bar none the best, and I do some custom work. But for you, I'd go with foam core to start."

Jax shook his head.

"Don't worry. I've seen that deer in headlights look before. We give lessons. Perfect time of year to be starting. A little cold, but the waves are worth it."

Quite the salesman if he was in the market. "Not why I'm here, Mr. Higgins, but thank you."

Riley's shoulders inched towards his ears. "Has something happened to my dad?"

"Your dad lives in Misty Pines?"

"No. You're just a cop that's shown up not wanting to surf. So I…" He cleared his throat. "What do you need then?"

"I'm here to chat about Terry Chesney."

"I see." Riley met Jax's eyes briefly and looked away. Jax recognized the tactic of creating space. Distance.

A cell phone sounded from underneath the register. Riley reached to silence it without looking. "What's the son-of-a-bitch accusing me of now?"

Troy had been right about some bad blood between the two. "Nothing. I haven't spoken to him about you."

He sniffed. "Good. Because anything he says would be untrue."

"I'd like to find that out for myself. However, he's missing."

His eyes narrowed. "You think I had something to do with that?"

Jax shrugged.

He swallowed. "I don't know what you've heard, but Terry and I only had a friendly rivalry. Nothing more. We talk shit about each other, sure. What rivals don't? I still can't believe the lucky bastard bested me in that last heat and stole the trophy." His hand curled into a fist. "But that's ancient news and my wife tells me all the time to let it go. Anyway, last time I saw him was during the summer."

The way Riley held his body said the resentment was as fresh as the day it happened. "So you know nothing about a corporation interested in his designs? No competition between you two in that regard?"

"No. And for the record, they don't give a rat's ass about his designs. Even if they did, he isn't selling. There's nothing to be concerned about."

"Does that mean you have some designs for sale?"

"If I did, none of your business."

Jax nodded. "Because money can be strong motivation. Sounds like you have some history."

"Just because I'm a capitalist and want to make a living and provide for my family? That's thin, Sheriff, and a bullshit assessment of me. I certainly wouldn't cause anyone a problem regardless." The cell phone sounded, and Riley silenced it again. The phone on the counter rang. A 541 number crossed the screen. "Just a second."

"All about the Waves," he said. "Yes. Uh-huh. We carry that line." He walked over to the wall of wet suits. The cell phone under the counter came alive again, but only rang twice before stopping. "Yes, ma'am," Riley said. "We have plenty of smalls. Sounds good."

Jax waited until Riley had returned to the counter. "What's the issue between you and Terry anyway?"

"I told you. He took that last heat from me."

"No one ever beat you before that?"

His jaw twitched. "I have no problem losing when it's fair. But Chesney broke his ankle and got high sympathy scores. Like he was some kind of hero."

"Must have felt like déjà vu that he was about to best you again."

"He wasn't about to best me about anything."

Jax leaned on the countertop. "I'm having some trouble locating some blueprints that Terry might have had in his possession."

Riley's hands shot up. "Don't look at me."

Jax waited a beat. "Do you know a Scott Heffernan?"

"Never heard of him." He stared at Jax.

Riley hid emotions well, but Jax had detected the twitch under his right eye.

"He says he's familiar with you." Jax hadn't even asked Scott about Riley, but since he knew Terry, it didn't hurt to stir the pot and see what came to the surface.

"If he surfs, he might. I'm the best in town."

The landline lit up, scrolling another 541 number across the screen along with the name: Surfrider Surf Shop.

"You should answer that." Jax stared at Riley whose inaction spoke loud and clear. What didn't he want Jax to hear? "I insist."

Riley stretched his neck and answered. "All about the Waves," he said, but before the voice on the other end could say anything he added, "This isn't a good time. Can I call you back?" Riley turned his back on Jax and walked away.

But no amount of distance could dampen the panicked voice on the other end. "They're going to find…" Riley whipped around and pressed the off key at the same time.

"Wrong number."

Rachel and Brody would have been visiting Surfrider within the last couple of hours. They'd clearly done their own stirring of the pot. Enough so that Brandon was concerned about them finding something.

"Sure about that?" Jax said.

"Of course. And I don't have any more time to give you today, officer. I'm busy."

On cue, a young couple came through the door and Riley hustled to greet them, ushering them to the boards at the far left of the showroom.

Jax could push Riley, but Brandon was the domino that might be worth flicking first. He'd have Brody and Rachel bring him in and meet them at the station.

Jax walked out of the shop, the rain still pelting, as his own cell came to life. A text. Garrett was meeting Terry's girlfriend, the bartender, when she came on shift this evening. That worked.

But before he reached the car, the phone vibrated in his hand again. This time a call.

"What's up, Trudy?"

"Why weren't you answering your radio?" Trudy said, a tinge of alarm in her voice.

"I was in an interview. What's wrong?"

"It's Dora. She's been hurt."

CHAPTER 25

Olek Lasko was speaking with an orderly when Jax stormed through the entry of Stonebridge Assisted Living. They'd met a couple of times before, but Jax bypassed him and strode down the left hallway.

"I wouldn't go down there," Olek hollered after him.

"Thanks for the advice," he muttered, and kept walking. No one told him where he could and couldn't go in his jurisdiction. Certainly not some low rung FBI agent. Especially when Abby was involved. And Dora. Whether she liked it or not, they'd been family. Once.

White tufts of hair and wide-eyed faces peered out of the residents' rooms. Looking. Dora's door was closed, an EMT's gurney pushed up against the wall across from it. Whatever was happening behind the door, they hadn't decided to transport yet.

His hand was poised to knock when an old man grabbed him by the wrist. Startled, he stepped back, yanked free, and stared into the eyes of Dora's gray-haired neighbor.

"I tried to tell them." His voice shook. Abby had spoken of this former military man who seemed to fancy his redhaired housemate.

Jax softened. "Mr. Casey. What did you try to tell them?"

"That she'd gone. They wanted to tell her daughter that they couldn't find her that morning. But they couldn't find her the night before. She left after dinner. They made mushroom soup and Dora was not happy."

Mr. Casey's revelation supported Scott's contention that he'd seen a woman matching Dora's description wandering out on Meddle Road. The test results had yet to come back on the foot Dora had found, but it hadn't

134

been detached for too long and could potentially have belonged to Terry. If that were the case, had Dora witnessed the crime? He didn't believe in coincidences, and the break-in had occurred twenty-four hours after she made her find. Someone might be concerned that she could identify them.

"Thank you, Mr. Casey. I appreciate that information. And from one vet to another, thank you for your service."

The man stepped back and saluted, then shrank under the weight of his emotions before closing his door. They all suffered here from some battle, whether it was body or mind. Jax hoped age would be kinder to him. But he wouldn't count on it.

Jax knocked once on Dora's door and waited for an acknowledgement to enter. Only voices and scurrying came from the other side. He went in to find Dora on her bed. The two-man ambulance crew stood at the wall, along with a nurse whose name tag read "Bernice." A man and a woman EMT assisted Dora, who had a large angry gash over her right eye. But she was awake. Her eyes darted about in confusion.

Abby was at the other end of the room inspecting the screenless window with gloved hands. Staying out of Dora's line of sight, he came up behind Abby.

"What happened?" he asked.

Startled, she whipped around. "Jax." Her eyes wrinkled in pain, but maybe a bit of gratitude that he'd shown.

He placed his hand on her arm. "Is she going to be okay? Are you?"

She straightened, her professional side taking over. "I'm fine, but not sure about Mom yet. She says she hit her head and that Bernice saved her."

"Did the nurse see or hear anything?"

Abby shook her head. "I've only had a few minutes to chat with her, but she came in and found Mom on the floor bleeding and the window open."

"They wanted it back," Dora said, in a small voice.

"Why don't you stay here, and I'll see if Bernice can offer anything else. Then you and I need to talk."

Abby reached out her hand.

Jax took it and squeezed, his heart doing the same. "It'll be okay, Abby."

Abby drew in a breath and nodded. What had he been thinking when he contemplated Margot? Abby owned him. There had never been anyone else but her.

A few minutes later, Bernice led Jax into a small conference room and sat across from him. "I should wait for Mrs. Vernon, the administrator. She was out of the area visiting her sister today. It'll be a couple of hours, but she's on her way back."

"I appreciate that," Jax said, "but the sooner we determine what happened, the faster we all get out of your hair and let you get back to taking care of the residents."

She nodded, staring at her hands.

"Agent Turner—I mean, Kanekoa"—he'd never get used to that—"indicated you found Dora on the floor and the window open. Did you realize then someone had broken in?"

"No. In fact, I assumed she was trying to get out again. She does that."

"I'm aware. Don't you have alarms on the windows and doors here?"

"No. They've talked about them recently. Especially in light of Dora's disappearing acts. But we're a low-risk facility and..."

He didn't want to hear excuses. "Was she conscious when you entered the room?"

"Yes, and mumbling that they wanted it back, just like she did a bit ago."

"Any idea of what they want or who they are?"

She shook her head. "We do have security cameras outside the perimeter. We could check those."

A good place to start. He followed her to a small closet that housed a computer and cameras.

"We don't monitor them regularly," she said. "We're understaffed, but it records for twenty-four hours." Bernice sat down and whipped through a few keystrokes to back up the recording three hours ago and then set it to triple speed. Jax quickly reviewed the front cameras to find nothing out of the ordinary. He switched to the side building cameras. At about two hours in, the screen faded to black.

"I don't understand," Bernice said, twice.

But Jax had a hunch. He left her in the closet-office and walked outside to check his theory, ignoring Olek's raised finger to chat when he passed him in the entry. He didn't have the time or inclination to be friendly. He wanted answers.

He rounded the corner of the building and searched the eaves. One camera hung on the corner that monitored activity along the entire side. He looked up at the lens. Black. Someone had painted it. He scoured the ground and looked out over the open field that neighbored the care home. Someone could have approached from the corner. It was a blind spot to the building.

Whoever had come after Dora had known about the cameras, and had come prepared. Or at least knew what to look for before they breached the premises. A ballsy move regardless.

Back inside, he settled Bernice into the small conference room, his shoulders tight with urgency. "I understand that Abby was notified her mother walked off yesterday morning at some point."

Bernice looked away. "Uh-huh."

"But you and I both know that's a lie."

She stared at her lap. "I can't afford to lose my job."

"I understand your hesitation, but there's a man missing, and Dora might have seen something that has caused some concern. Or at the least, someone thinks she has."

Bernice stiffened. "Does that mean she's still in danger?" She put her hand on her chest. "Is everyone here in danger?" She slumped in the chair as the magnitude of protecting everyone in this building weighed on her.

"Since I'm not sure what we're dealing with yet, I can't say one way or another. I can tell you the faster we get the answers we need, the safer everyone will be."

She drew in a breath. "She didn't like what we served that night."

"I heard that much."

"And when she doesn't like something…"

Abby had come by her fiery side honestly. "What time did she go missing, Bernice? The truth."

She glanced at the door. Maybe wishing someone would save her. Or afraid Mrs. Vernon would storm in. The one time Jax had met the facility's administrator had been once too often. "Between eight and nine o'clock. She returned to her room after dinner, but we didn't see her during the turn down process."

"Why wasn't Abby called at that point?"

"Mrs. Vernon wanted us to do a thorough search first. Which I did. Me and another nurse took turns calling for her outside and walking the grounds."

"Why not call my office to assist?"

"Because she's done this before. She gets mad, goes for a walk, and she's back within a couple of hours. We try not to bother officials, or Ms. Kanekoa, until it's necessary."

"But she didn't come back this time."

"And we would have called except Mrs. Bartholomew, a resident whose room is on the other side, fell out of bed and urinated everywhere. She's over two hundred and fifty pounds and it took both me and the other nurse to get her cleaned and settled again. We were short-staffed that night and were running around, having to get medications for all the residents and…"

"You forgot."

Her lips pursed. "I've already been given a verbal warning. As lead nurse that night, I dropped the ball."

How many other balls had been dropped? This place was not safe for Dora. "When Abby got her mother back here, did Dora say anything about what she'd done or seen?"

"Nothing. She was in her own world and talking about ballet when she was a child. How important feet were. Honestly, the residents here talk so much, and I have so much to do, I…"

Bottomline, she shut them out. He didn't want to judge her. He was guilty of his own tunnel vision, but people paid for and expected their loved ones to be cared for here. And Stonebridge wasn't fulfilling that obligation.

Jax closed his eyes. While she confirmed the timeline, Bernice didn't offer anything more useful. What Dora had seen out on the beach, if anything, would need to come from Dora herself. With her mental walls rising and falling like shadows, finding the truth would be tricky.

Unless Scott Heffernan could shed some light. Or Brandon. While Scott could not have attacked Dora, if he was part of a bigger scheme he would have been able to identify Dora in some way to the perpetrator. Or could have. It was a reach. Speculation. All of it. At this point he didn't know what he had. And Brandon? Why had he called Riley? How loyal was Brandon to Terry?

"It's mine." A scream shredded the air. Bernice hopped out of her chair and Jax followed.

"Mom, I need to take that," Abby said as Jax entered the room.

He found Dora strapped to the gurney, gripping a piece of metal in her right hand.

Dora stopped and looked at him. Tilted her head. Remembering? Jax swayed with unease.

Her hand opened for just a second, revealing a surfboard belt buckle with a diamond fin. The kind that Terry had been wearing in that framed picture of him on the magazine in his office. The odds of there being more of those in this part of the state were slim to none.

Dora's grip tightened around the buckle and with her jaw clenched, she flung it straight at Jax's head.

"You son-of-a-bitch. You let my Lulu die."

CHAPTER 26

"She didn't mean it," Abby said, as the ambulance took off with Dora secured in the back.

"Yes, she did." And Jax didn't blame her. Not even therapy had truly shaken the belief out of his core that he was responsible. His own father would have seconded that blame—and not just about Lulu. Jax held out the bagged buckle to Abby. "You didn't notice she had this when you found her at the beach yesterday?"

Abby wrapped her arms around her body, her gray suit too thin to keep her warm from the night chill. Her breath hung in the air like the wall Jax felt between them. "No. But she could have easily slipped it into her pocket or into her bra. Bernice helped her undress, but my mother…"

"Can be sneaky," Jax said.

Abby grimaced as Olek appeared next to her and placed his hand on her arm, whispering in her ear.

Jax's chest pulled at their intimacy. It wasn't out of line. Next to a spouse, the relationship with a partner came close. But he held her arm a second too long. Leaned in a little too close.

Abby nodded and Olek went to the car they'd come in together.

"He likes you," Jax said, unable to keep the edge out of his voice.

Abby unclasped her arms long enough to wave Jax off. "Oh please. He just told me he'll get started on the reports for our SAC."

The never-ending onslaught of paper trails. "I wouldn't blame him if he did. You are a catch." He looked for signs they were still connecting. That she still wanted to. Everything was so tenuous between them. The focus had been on his faults for so long, it seemed Abby didn't want to look at her own stuff. Her own walls of protection.

She gave him a small smile. "This isn't the time or place."

Right. When would he be able to get her alone to talk again? If she'd come back to counseling...

"So why is the buckle important?" she asked, breaking his thought.

"It belonged to Terry Chesney. I've yet to hear back on the foot your mother found yesterday, but I'm afraid it will belong to him as well."

She nodded, her teeth clenching a little too tight.

He recognized that tick. "What do you know that I don't?"

"Nothing on that. But we were pulled in to assist on the foot found in West Shore earlier this month."

"And?"

"It belonged to a Jonathan Lilly who lived across the river. He'd been out for a run and hasn't been seen or heard from since. Like Terry, the body hasn't been found."

"You suspect foul play?"

"We're still waiting for confirmation, but my hunch is the foot was physically removed. Or maybe I'm seeing things. In the meantime, yes, we're treating it as a homicide."

"You think the killer dumped his body in the ocean then?"

"Perhaps. My vic's running route took him down toward the bay, which makes it convenient."

"He'd float right out with the tide and likely never be found."

"Exactly. But it might not be nefarious. If he was out on a long run, he could have gotten fatigued, slipped, hit his head. The foot was so badly decomposed...." Abby looked to the car where Olek waited. "I should drop Olek back at the field office and get to the hospital to make sure Mom's taken care of."

"Are you letting her come back here?"

She shook her head. "Hopefully they'll keep her a couple of days for observation until I can figure it out."

Jax agreed this was no longer the place for Dora. "It's a good-sized gash on her head."

"It is."

He might as well come out with it. "When she's able, I'd like to ask her about her time on the beach. I believe she saw something."

Abby bristled. "What makes you say that?"

"The nurse—Bernice. Dora went missing the same night Terry did, not in the morning like they'd told you. I have a kid in custody who I'm holding for unlawful use of a motor vehicle. He insists he found Terry's car on Meddle Road, decided to take it for a joy ride, and saw a woman matching your mom's description out wandering."

Abby drew in a deep breath, no doubt to keep her anger in check.

"Look, they're clearly not doing their job here. But I believe this kid was out on that road even though Marks' kid says they stole the vehicle from Terry's driveway."

"You think Dylan and that kid did something to Terry?"

Jax rubbed the skin between his eyes with his thumb. "I'm missing motive. Dylan is a pain in the ass and the kid, Scott, has petty crimes. But the amount of blood found in that forest...." He shook his head. "Not sure what I have yet." And with Abby in a hurry, there was no time to rehash what he did know.

She sighed. "I feel the same thing in my own case. But why didn't Scott call the police when he saw my mom? Who lets a woman in her nightgown roam a back road without having some concern?"

"He was high and supposedly sleeping it off. I buy some of that, but if Dora was out there, she might have seen something she doesn't realize was important."

Abby chewed her bottom lip. "She did say she wanted to give the foot back to the person it belonged to. It's a possibility." She shuddered. "God, if that's the case, we're lucky they didn't try to do something to her out there on the beach."

Jax reached out his hand and rested it in the same place Olek had, but she pulled away. His hand dropped to his side. "Let's not get ahead of ourselves."

"Are we? My mom's room was just broken into, and that belt buckle...."

"I agree, except we don't know how either the foot or the buckle got on that beach. The buckle could have been stolen from the house. The foot..." It had been removed too. Like Abby, he was waiting for confirmation, but his gut said he was right. He needed to get back out to the beach and do a more thorough search.

Jax's phone dinged with a text. The team had Brandon back at the precinct and ready for questioning. "I need to go. But if you want to come by the station later, I'd like to compare notes with your case—maybe over dinner?"

Her eyes narrowed. "You sure Margot won't be jealous?"

"Margot?"

She folded her arms over chest. "I ran into her today on my case."

"The one with the missing jogger?"

She nodded. "Apparently, his niece was treated for cancer at the children's hospital, and she was her nurse." She cleared her throat. "Anyway, she has a thing for you."

That's why Abby had pulled away. Did he detect jealousy? He'd be lying if he didn't admit to enjoying that some. But he'd already settled that matter in his head. "Doesn't matter. I only have eyes for you."

She smirked.

"Look, Trudy is good at problem solving. She could have a suggestion on Dora." Trudy was like a mother to them both. He also had his own selfish reasons for wanting to see Abby again and they didn't have anything to do with Dora. He was determined to have her see the light about them. For him to be the one she leaned on. Not Olek.

Abby closed her eyes. "Maybe tomorrow."

"I'll look forward to it."

Jax ducked into his patrol car. Dora was a dead-end for the moment, but the belt buckle suggested there could be more clues out on that beach. He'd look when the sun returned and after he found out what Brandon was hiding.

* * *

Jax stepped out of his cruiser at the station feeling like this had already been a long day when Troy Marks burst out of the front door like he'd been waiting for him.

"What the hell do you think you're doing, Turner?"

He'd known this would happen the minute he decided to question Dylan. He'd hoped Deanna would be the voice of reason. Clearly, Mr. Ego couldn't be reasoned with.

"Back it up, Troy," he said. "It could have been much worse for your boy."

"You coming to my house, after you'd spoken with me, is bullshit."

"I'm in the middle of an active investigation, buddy."

"And Dylan is part of that?"

"Did you know your boy snuck out with his friend Scott and they were up by Chesney's place the night he disappeared?"

"Bullshit."

"Have you gone home to speak with your family, or is this your usual kneejerk reaction to me asking questions?"

"Don't give me that crap."

"Dylan's already admitted it, Troy. I wouldn't have known about it otherwise, or that he and Scott stole Terry's vehicle."

"Damn him." His hands curled into fists. "I've told him to stay away from that juvenile delinquent."

"On that we agree. Dylan would do well to stay away from Scott."

Troy shook his head. "Having him in that youth program with people like Scott was a bad idea. That's where they met."

"I'm aware."

"Shaun Evans thinks he can save them all, but he can't. There are plenty in the program that are as bad as Scott, if not worse. And this is proof some are unsavable."

Jax had built an entire career on trying to solve the cases and fix the ills. He'd won some and failed too often. His short conversation with the youth program director had illuminated the same trait. But like it or not, he felt a pang of connection with Troy. Dylan wasn't easy to work with and having so many of his father's traits ensured he might never be.

"Look, I didn't arrest your son and I don't believe he's involved in Terry's disappearance. But he was at that property with Scott. His shoe was found near the road in front of Chesney's place. There's likely an explanation for all of it, but don't jump on my ass for doing my job."

Troy ground his teeth.

"You don't get to control the sheriff department, Troy. And get used to it. If that expansion you're gunning for comes about, many things will change. There will be more deputies on the street, but also more people, more crime. You'll lose more control than you're comfortable with, I'm sure."

"I'm ready for growth as long as there are no personal vendettas directed at me or my family. It's not my fault you were in a haze for several years after Lulu. Now that you're back in the game, don't get overzealous."

Jax balled his fists and opened them to dispel the tension. "I'm many things, but I'm not petty." Unlike Troy, who used every instance to bring up the past. His father and Troy would have gotten along well. The idea swirled like an eddy inside him.

He left Troy to stew in his own shortcomings as a father and was met by Trudy's glare and a plate of cookies when he walked into the station. "Last thing I need is food."

"Tell that to your new girlfriend."

Jesus. "Margot, again?"

Her eyes widened like Jax was holding out.

"I swear I'm not sending her any signals."

"M-hmmm. She actually wanted to leave you a thermos of hot chocolate because you looked so cold up on the mountain earlier today."

"Wanted to?"

"I told her you were allergic to chocolate," Trudy said, scowling.

He chuckled at her protectiveness. "She's just being nice." He handed the cookies back to her. "Take these home to Frank. He'll love them."

"Hmph," she said, thrusting another piece of paper at him. "Three things. Walter's former girlfriend is in Colorado. Lois left on that bus my church group put her on and hasn't been back. They're getting in touch with her to break the news about Walter."

145

That eliminated one potential witness to what happened out there. "Thank you for following up."

She sniffed. "The report on the foot is on your desk." She stared at him. "And three?"

She shoved another piece of paper at him. "Margot left her number."

With that, she turned and walked away.

CHAPTER 27

Jax read the report before he strode into the conference room. He had one question answered and his suspicion confirmed. Now for the rest of the story.

He sat across from Brandon, who ran his hands through his floppy hair over and over until Jax wanted to cuff him. Rachel stood at the door and Brody had gone home for the night.

Brandon shifted in his chair like he couldn't get comfortable.

"You seem nervous," Jax said, leaning back in his seat. He kept his arms open to be friendly. Brandon might be the weak link, but these situations required finesse.

"Nope. Just don't understand why I'm here."

"How do you know Riley Higgins?"

"I don't."

Jax eyed the young man.

He cleared his throat and squirmed some more. "I may have met him once I guess when he ran an ad for a counter guy. I applied."

"Ah. That explains everything."

Brandon nodded and stopped. "Wait, what's it explain?"

"Rachel, let's look up that ad. I'd like to see what they're offering. Hard to pass up more money, more benefits, right Brandon?"

"It was a long time ago," Brandon said, stammering. "You asked me how I might know him. That's how. That's all."

"Oh. So not recent. Wow, okay. Then why the urgency to call him this afternoon?"

Brandon's face wrinkled in confusion. "I didn't."

"That's funny because I was there, Brandon. Riley's cell lit up several times before you gave up and tried the land line."

"It wasn't…"

"Caller ID gave you away."

Brandon's face flushed. "I seriously don't know what you're talking about."

His physical response said different. "What are you afraid we'll find out?"

Brandon pressed his elbows onto the table and cradled his face in his hands.

"That is what you said on the phone, right? 'They're going to find out.' Your voice came through loud and clear."

He shook his head. "It wasn't me."

"Then perhaps we can try again in the morning and see if your memory returns. Rachel, go ahead and take him into custody."

"Yes, sir." Rachel took a step.

Brandon looked up quickly. "You can do that?"

Jax raised his hand to stop Rachel and focused on Brandon. "Your employer is missing, Brandon. His place of business was broken into. And you, his trusted employee, were talking with his rival and only competitor. You bet your ass I can detain you until I sort it out."

Brandon swallowed hard.

"By the way, how's your hand?"

Brandon glanced at his gauzed fingers. "Fine." Realization settled on his face. "You think I did something to Terry, don't you?"

"You tell me. Seems to be the consensus that he wasn't interested in selling his designs. But oddly, those blueprints you mentioned are nowhere to be found. Did they go home with Terry like you said, or are you negotiating with Riley Higgins to sell them to him?" Jax leaned back in his chair. It wasn't a reach to think that Riley, with his surf connection, would be a likely player. But could Brandon navigate all this on his own? "Whose idea was it to make it look like a burglary at the shop?"

"It's not what you think," Brandon mumbled, his hands shaking.

Jax reached into the paper bag and retrieved Terry's bagged belt buckle, setting it on the table.

Brandon closed his eyes, his reddened face fading to gray. "He's dead, isn't he? Terry's dead." Tears rimmed the young man's eyes.

"Why do you think that?"

"Because he was wearing that when he left. And you have it."

"It was found at the beach."

Brandon hung his head. Guilt? Or realization that Terry was gone?

"Whose fingerprints will I find on this buckle, Brandon?" He had no proof that Brandon had anything to do with Terry's disappearance. But he'd work every angle to find out what he *was* involved in.

"Not mine, I can promise you that. He wore it all the time though, and like I said, including the night he left work. He'd planned to meet Lisa and said something about dazzling her. She was mad at him about something. I don't know what."

"Lisa from the bar?" Jax said. Garrett should have seen her by now. He'd be curious to hear her version of events.

Brandon nodded.

"Well unfortunately, Terry was removed from this buckle in some way." Even more true now that the report on his desk indicated that the foot on the beach was Terry's, and it had not been naturally removed by being submerged in the ocean. There were knife marks.

"Maybe him and Lisa were at the beach and things got…"

"His foot was found there too, Brandon."

"His foot?"

Jax nodded.

Brandon's gray face turned ghostly white. "I feel sick."

Jax reached for a garbage can and nodded to Rachel who left and reappeared a few moments later with a bottle of water. She handed it to Brandon and Jax gave her the bag containing the buckle. "Get this processed. Trudy can show you how we do it around here if one of the men aren't out there to assist."

She secured the door behind her.

Jax waited as Brandon took a few gulps of water along with a few breaths.

"Let's start over," Jax said. "Who would have wanted to cause Terry harm?"

"Not me. I liked the dude. I worked for him for a few years, and he was good at what he did."

Fatigue had set in. Jax wanted answers. He wanted them yesterday, and he was convinced Brandon had some to give. Jax stood and leaned against the back wall, placing his foot flat against it. "Where are the blueprints you said Terry took with him?"

"How should I know?"

"They weren't at his house. They weren't in his van. They weren't in his VW Bug. Where else could they be? And why were you calling Riley Higgins?"

"I told you I didn't make that call."

"Then who did?"

Brandon closed his eyes.

Jax settled back in his chair and put his hands on the table. "If you liked Terry the way you say, then you'd want to help us find out what happened to him. Someone called Riley from the Surfrider. By your own admission, you're the only person who works for Terry. So, who—?"

"Gerry called," Brandon blurted out.

"Gerry? Terry's brother, Gerard?"

"Yeah," Brandon said, his voice low.

"You expect me to believe he called Riley?"

Brandon straightened. "Okay, I can't be a hundred percent, but he asked to use the phone."

Jax hadn't expected that. "Start from the beginning."

Brandon sank into the chair. "It was right after your officers came by the first time."

"Gerard just happened to come by to use the phone?" He didn't hold back the sarcasm.

"No. I called him." Brandon stared at his hands and shrank even further. "Look, I didn't want to get involved. But Gerry...he said it was the right thing to do."

"And what was that exactly?"

150

"He said Terry wasn't a good businessman. But that he'd thank us later."

"Terry didn't want to sell his designs to that corporation you mentioned, but Gerard had other ideas to the point of getting you involved?"

Brandon nodded.

Thinking back, Gerard had seemed cagey when Jax brought up the blueprints, but he'd dismissed it as being upset about his brother. "When did Gerard contact you?"

"Over a month ago. Terry was too stubborn, and Gerry said that as his big brother, he knew what was best. Terry couldn't expect to retire on what he made at the shop. He'd be angry at first, but he'd get over it."

"You didn't think for a second that as a grown man, Terry might know how to make his own decisions?"

"Sure, but he's a free spirit. Checks barely clear, you know. And..."

"Gerard offered you a sum of money for your assistance."

That white pallor on his cheeks had turned to crimson again.

"Who has the blueprints, Brandon?"

"See that's the thing. Terry did. But not because he took them home." Brandon returned to staring at his hands. Swallowed. "I put them in the back of his van."

The story just kept getting better. "And Gerard was supposed to get them?"

"No."

Jax leaned back in his chair. "Scott Heffernan."

"Yeah. He's a friend of mine and I offered to cut him in if he'd steal them out of the van."

He grimaced. "Why not just give them to Gerard directly? Why risk Terry finding them there? Or Scott screwing it up and getting caught?"

"Plausible deniability," he said. "You know, like they have on cop shows? I left Terry a message that I'd put the blueprints in his van because he'd mentioned working on them earlier in the day and I didn't want him to forget. That way he wouldn't think I was involved and that it would have been like a fluke that someone broke in that same night. But if they were just missing from the shop, then...you know..."

"You'd be the likely suspect."

"Right."

Convoluted, but Brandon was young, dumb, and watched too much TV. "So, Scott steals them."

"No, he planned to, but he called me panicked. He showed up to Terry's house, but everything was wide open. And he heard someone running out behind Terry's place."

"Terry?"

"He wasn't sure, but it scared Scott enough that he didn't stick around to find out."

"Except Scott went back later in the evening and stole the VW."

"I guess. I didn't hear about that part until your deputies mentioned it."

"Did you tell Gerard that Scott had failed?"

"Yes."

"And?"

"He wasn't happy." Brandon cleared his throat again. "Am I in trouble for this? Because it wasn't my idea. And I'm cooperating."

He'd probably seen that on TV too. "Keep talking. I'll let you know."

Brandon sighed. "Like I said, I told Gerard there might be a problem because Scott didn't get the prints, and he said it wasn't good enough. That Scott had to go back and get them."

"And he did?"

Brandon nodded. "We didn't want to make Gerard mad. He's intense. I mean, he wasn't happy I involved Scott at all. But I couldn't go up there and steal the blueprints myself."

And Scott decided he'd rope Dylan in. Might have even sabotaged that scooter to have a justifiable reason, at least to Dylan, why he wanted to steal that VW. More stupid decisions by a young person. Not that he'd never made a few of his own.

Jax tapped his foot, annoyed he'd been fooled by Gerard's *concerned big brother* act in the first place. He should have paid more attention to Koa's dismissal of him. "Do you think he'd be intense enough to cause Terry harm if he didn't get what he wanted?"

"Anything's possible. I watched this one episode...." He launched into a recap of a recent show where two brothers were after their father's inheritance and one of them left the other to drown in a river. "But to be honest, I never saw the two together. Maybe they got along fine. Anyway. Am I free to go?"

Jax didn't have a solid reason to hold him any longer. Being a punk wasn't a crime. Putting blueprints in the back of his boss's van wasn't a crime. Setting up a situation where they'd get stolen was, but he'd need more than an admission, or a lawyer would rip him to shreds.

But it made Jax more motivated to get back to what might have been a secondary crime scene now that he had some answers. "I'd like you to fill out a statement listing what you just told me and then yes, you can go. But I'd suggest you don't call Riley, Gerard, or anyone else. You hear me?"

"Yes, sir." He stood. "Thank you. I mean, it really was Gerard who called Riley. He grabbed the shop phone and disappeared outside with it."

He left Brandon to write the statement and found Trudy typing up a report at her desk. "I want a warrant pronto to ping Gerard Chesney's phone the night of Terry's disappearance, about a month before, and everything since. Where he was calling from and who he's been talking to."

"Will do," Trudy said without missing a key stroke.

No hon. No eye contact. He wondered how long he'd be in the doghouse this time. Seemed like he barely got out before he was right back in.

He turned to a friendlier face who'd been sitting at another desk making notes. "Tomorrow, bring Koa to work. Think she's in the mood for some action?"

Rachel looked up and smiled. "She was born ready."

CHAPTER 28

Garrett's attempt to meet with the bartender failed—she had some car trouble out of town but would be in the next day. He or Matt would try again tomorrow. There wasn't much more the team could do on the case until daylight, so Jax grabbed a burger and went home. He'd had no word from Abby. Dora likely hadn't said much, and he and Abby didn't call just to talk these days.

The next morning, Jax and Rachel headed out to Meddle Beach after meeting at the station. They'd foregone their normal briefing. Matt, having handled the night shift, went home to sleep until afternoon. Brody had his interview with Len's Auto. Not for the first time, Jax felt the smallness of his department. Troy was right. He would eventually have to decide about a hiring a full-time deputy.

That choice might be Rachel. As they stepped out of the cruiser, Jax noted the tide was out and the wind and rain had subsided.

Closer to the ocean, Koa danced at Rachel's feet, ready to go. Rachel had run by Terry's place to grab one of Terry's T-shirts, which Gerard had left out for her. She let Koa get a nose full of its scent before undoing the leash. "Find it."

Koa ran out ahead of Jax and Rachel in her red search-and-rescue vest. Jax had been around enough working dogs to know that the vest was crucial and signaled to the animal that it was time to work.

"Now what?" Jax said.

"We follow and watch. She's got a good track record in air scent. It'll be a challenge with the competing smells, but if she picks up Terry, or even

154

human, she'll come back to me."

"Even if it's a corpse?"

"Absolutely. You're convinced Terry's dead?"

Jax updated her on the report. "I don't see how he could be anything else."

"You think the brother did it?"

They kicked through a strand of washed-up seaweed and hopped over a small stream of water leading back to the ocean. "Money and jealousy can be strong motives for murder."

"Gerard has the jealousy thing for sure," Rachel said.

"And that surfboard design would be the money. With Terry not willing to give up the design, an argument could have gotten out of hand, or it could have been planned. Trudy's obtaining his phone records. They might shed some light." Jax kept his eyes peeled for anything that appeared out of the ordinary as they made their way to the scene where the foot and likely the belt buckle had been located. "By the way, I talked with your dad."

Rachel had her eyes glued to Koa, but her jaw twitched. "How'd that go?"

He wouldn't be telling Rachel anything she likely hadn't heard already. But how much was his place to share? "He has his concerns."

Rachel's eyebrow cocked. "And you?"

Jax shrugged. "I make my own decisions." Although he'd feel better with Jameson's blessing. "What I have learned is to proceed with caution. Which is why I'd like you to explain to me about getting heated with Scott yesterday?"

She sniffed. "Already told you, he ran."

"Right. Scared people do that sometimes."

"Guilty ones too."

"Also true. But it's part of the job. You must know that from your time in Portland."

"I do."

He gave her some room to expand. She didn't. "You'll need to give me more than that, Rachel."

She stretched her neck. "I was trying to impress you. Brody. All the guys, I guess. I saw how they looked at me during yesterday's meeting."

"I get it." And he did. Abby had long talked about the difficulties of being a capable woman among insecure men. It wasn't fair that a woman had to work harder to get half the respect. He'd never allow that in his department. "This is not a defense, but we were all burned in our last case, and trust is coming slow to all of us. No one said it would be easy to integrate into an existing team."

"Especially when Garrett wants the same deputy position."

Jax nodded. "He might, but he didn't apply. And I need someone who's confident in what they want enough to fill out the job application. If you don't, you're not the right person for the job. I need someone I can count on."

"I can be that person. I'm proactive. Assertive."

He knew that to be true. Jax recalled the cupboard of Girl Scout Cookies she'd talked him into buying when she was eleven. Top prize winners could choose between a karaoke machine or Go Pro camera. She wanted that camera. "I hear you loud and clear and I haven't made up my mind on the position. But getting along with the team will be crucial."

"I can do that too. They're not as bad as my other crew where the old boys' club ruled, and women belonged behind the desk."

He grimaced. "Didn't realize it was so bad."

"It's not blatant. I mean, everyone tries to act PC, but you know how it goes."

He nodded. "I appreciate that. But I'm most impressed by people who do their job and keep their emotions in check."

Her jaw set. "Are you able to do that? Was my dad?"

They'd both had their moments of failing miserably in that area. Wanting justice fueled many a fire. Feeling helpless in a situation added to frustration. "It's not always easy. You have to have healthy outlets, because that tension has to come out somewhere." His counseling sessions had hammered that lesson home and still he'd missed his morning run since the call came in on Terry. "But sometimes you have to fake it." Is that what Jameson had been doing all those years when it came to his prejudices? "Your dad's good at holding it back as well. But clearly, he has some opinions."

She huffed. "A few."

"Have you tried introducing him to your girlfriend?"

She stopped midstride. "Who told you I had one?"

Jax cocked his head. "You're willing to come to Misty Pines permanently. And you have a *friend* to stay with."

She started walking again. "Fine and no," she said quickly. Too quick.

"It might help."

"Not sure how. He thinks this is a phase, or that I'll snap out of being gay."

"He's like a few thick-headed people that don't understand it, but I do believe he's capable of getting there. What I am certain of is he loves you and would do anything for you."

"Funny way of showing it."

"I admit, his position surprised me, but he's a good man. He might just need some time to adjust."

"The world always wants time to adjust. Why is it that I need to wait for them?"

Good point. "You don't. But giving people we love some slack isn't a bad thing. If he doesn't come around, then that's his loss. But don't be too quick to slam the door closed behind you. And I suggested him meeting your friend, because it might help him understand that love is love."

She shrugged. "You're awfully progressive, Uncle. I wouldn't have thought that about you."

"It only takes losing your only daughter to realize that life is far too short for absolutes."

Before she could respond, her focus went to Koa who'd kept about twenty yards ahead, snout to the sand. Her nose lifted in full alert and she took off in a dead run. She cruised past the log where Dora had found the evidence and straight for the monolithic boulders a hundred yards further. She rounded the largest one nearest the water, skimming the surf. Spray flew up from her back paws.

Jax and Rachel jogged behind in the thick sand as Koa disappeared. They'd almost reached the rock when Koa returned and sat down in Rachel's path.

"She found something," Rachel said. "Show me," she said to Koa.

On command, Koa began to walk back around the rock, back through the surf. There was no other way around it as the other rocks blocked the beach at this end.

As they rounded the corner, it was obvious they were near the cliff line of what had to be Terry Chesney's bluff. The ravine where the climbers had come down to claim Walter's body would be another half-mile in. But that wasn't what had gotten Koa's attention.

In a small tidal pool, protected by rocks, floated a bloated body wearing running shorts and a sports watch. It was footless.

"Terry Chesney?" Rachel said.

Jax shook his head. "My guess is it's Jonathan Lilly."

CHAPTER 29

Jax called in Garrett from patrol to make sure beachcombers didn't come this far, and he made the appropriate calls to the medical examiner and Deputy DA. While they waited, he and Rachel ran crime scene tape around the perimeter.

His cursory search of the area indicated no need for Oregon crime to show. Whatever happened to Mr. Lilly hadn't occurred in that location. He'd washed in. Cause of death, undetermined.

Jax had waited to call Abby until the last minute. She had a lot going on with her mother and it wasn't customary to call the FBI in on a found body whether they were working the case or not. When he updated NCIC, it would trigger the call.

But Abby wasn't just *some* FBI agent. She was his ex-wife, and the woman he'd hoped to have back in his life…if they could get their differences ironed out. And she'd kill him if he left her out of this.

The ME and DDA were on scene by the time Abby leapt out of her Prius and joined Rachel, Koa, and Jax on the beach.

"You should have called me first," she said, her tone sharp and out of breath from the stretch of beach she'd traversed to get to them. The wind had picked up. At least she had a heavy coat on this time.

"Body is in my jurisdiction." Jax didn't want a fight, but even knowing normal procedure, she still questioned his motivations.

"You have a positive ID or just an assumption?" she said.

"See for yourself."

She headed for the boulders and disappeared.

"You two always that intense?" Rachel said.

"It's complicated," Jax said, ignoring Rachel's quizzical expression.

Within a minute, Abby reappeared. "Obviously bloated, but it does match the description we received."

"That was my assessment. And my delay in calling was to ensure you didn't have to stand around waiting for the ME to get here. But I figured we'd both want to know what he had to say." She was under stress on many levels, and he didn't want to add to it. They already had enough against them.

"Fair enough," she said.

"Where's your partner, stretch?" Jax said.

Abby frowned. "Agent Lasko is following up with Mr. Lilly's employer to make sure nothing was missed there."

"You think it's related to his job at the dam?" Jax said, having a hard time believing two victims with missing feet didn't have some type of connection.

"We haven't found a link yet, but one of Jonathan's main points of contact is back in the office today. Hoping he has something to share." She turned to Rachel, whose hand rested on top of Koa's head. "I'm Abby by the way."

Before Rachel could respond, Jax laughed. "You don't recognize her, do you?"

Abby's face scrunched. "Should I?"

"Jameson's girl."

Abby's eyes widened as she jutted her hand out in front of her waist. "Little Rachel?"

"I grew up," Rachel said, smiling.

"You sure did." Abby shook her head. "And you're working for Jax?"

"Well—"

"She's applied for the position," Jax said. "One of the notes I figured we'd exchange later."

"Your parents doing okay?" Abby said.

Rachel's smile tightened. "They're great."

"Good." Abby's attention went to Koa. "I didn't realize you had a K-9 officer in the budget. Commissioner Marks must be feeling generous."

160

Jax scoffed. "Koa's search and rescue."

"Police drop out. But she's got a great nose." Rachel ruffled Koa around the ears.

"May I?" Abby asked, nodding to Koa.

"Sure."

Abby smiled and bent down to pet Koa, who leaned into her strokes. Jax knew she'd always wanted a dog, but with their schedules and Lulu... It would be easier now if they lived together. He could take the pup to work. Trudy would love the company.

Abby stood. "Has the ME shared any thoughts on cause of death?" Her question broke through Jax's thoughts.

"Still waiting word," he said.

"I'll get Koa back in the car and see if Garrett needs an assist," Rachel said. "Good to see you, Abby."

"You too. We'll have to catch up so I can give you the low-down of working at the sheriff's office."

Jax caught the wink between them. *Great.*

The ME rounded the corner of the rocks a moment later and approached.

"What do we got?" Jax said.

"Homicide."

"Can you tell the cause of death?" Abby said.

"The hole in his chest and out his back is the probable cause."

"Gunshot?" Abby said.

The ME shook his head. "Not a knife, either."

"What are you thinking?" Jax said.

"Arrow. I had a similar case when I first started my career, and the wound looks similar. The post will tell us more of course. But at first glance, the wound is jagged as if it went in one way and yanked out another."

"Could he have survived the initial injury?" Abby said.

"I suspect not. Entry point was near the heart."

"Hell of an arrow," Jax said.

"Hell of a shot," the ME said. "You'd have to be a damn good marksman and within a decent range."

"Was he killed at this location?" Abby said.

Apprehension at the impending answer tweaked Jax. He'd determined that wasn't the case, but there was always that doubt. If the body had been there on the beach ever since Dora was out here, he and Abby had both missed it.

"Not likely," the ME said. "There's no blood in the water where he was located. Of course it could have washed away, but there are some items attached to the corpse that lead me to believe it floated in with the tide. Although he hasn't been dead for too long."

"Or the Dungeness and shrimp would have picked him clean," Jax said. He'd made a similar assumption earlier.

"Yes. Among a few other hitchhikers. The oxygen levels are unusually low in the ocean right now, too, which accounts for his body being somewhat intact as well."

"His foot was found in West Shore recently," Abby said. "Although he was reported missing before that."

"I saw the report just come across that foot today," the ME said. "It was not a natural release. It was cut off."

"We suspected so but hadn't seen test results yet," Abby said.

"Well, consider it conclusive. I'll get you the report on today's find when I have it," the ME said.

Jax nodded and he and Abby started back to their cars.

"You have time to compare those notes?" he said.

"Right behind you."

CHAPTER 30

It was mid-afternoon when Jax and Abby arrived at the station. Trudy jumped up the minute the front door opened, rounding her desk before they'd even crossed the threshold. Rachel and Koa stayed back with Garrett until Mr. Lilly's body had been removed and to search the beach after to make sure nothing had been missed.

"Abigail," Trudy said, embracing her. "Did everything turn out okay at the home?"

Abby returned the hug. "Mom was transported to the hospital last night. She's stable but had a concussion. Course the whole thing has her blood pressure up. They'll keep her for at least another day or two."

Trudy stepped back. "Don't you worry. I'm sure they're taking good care of her."

"It's just hospitals…"

"I know." Trudy reached for Abby's hand and squeezed it.

Abby cleared her throat. "How have you been?"

"I'm good. Frank is good. Work is busy."

"Okay you two," Jax said. "I know how this will go if I leave you together."

Trudy waved him off and gave Abby another hug. "If you ever need anything, I'm here."

Abby sighed. "I may take you up on that. Mom will need a new place. Somewhere focused on memory care, and close."

"Let me think about it." Trudy gave Abby a sympathetic smile.

"Anything on that ping?" Jax said, taking advantage of a break in the conversation.

"Just came in." Trudy returned to her desk and shuffled through some papers. "Gerard wasn't in Portland when he made that initial call. The ping came off West Shore's tower."

"That could be something." Or not. Gerard could have started to drive this direction out of concern—that's what a defense lawyer might offer. But after speaking with Brandon, Jax questioned whether that was the case. "Did Brody make it in?"

She nodded. "On patrol."

"Let's have him reach out to Gerard and ask him to stop by for a chat."

"Okay, and Matt did get in a while after you left with Rachel this morning."

"He supposed to be resting."

"He promises he had a few hours. But with Garrett busy at the beach, he took the lead on that bartender interview and got it. Said he called you, but it didn't go through."

"The beach can be hit or miss on reception."

"So Frank tells me when he doesn't respond to me while clam digging. I figured he wanted peace and quiet." She chuckled. "And I'd heard Koa was helpful. Told you Rachel would be a good hire." Trudy lifted her chin.

"Haven't offered her the job yet."

Trudy scoffed. "Why not?"

Maybe he wanted Jameson's approval, but it was more than that. He didn't want to screw it up and make a bad decision. "Have Matt find me when he's back."

"I'll leave him a note. Remember I'm out early to do some baking for the church sale. I'll bring you something special though. Not some plate of hockey pucks."

Jax noted the plate of Margot's cookies in Trudy's trashcan. Whatever made Trudy happy. At least she was talking to him. "I'll look forward to it."

He found Abby in his office. He'd stopped by the kitchen on his way and poured them a couple of coffees, adding some of the creamer Abby liked in hers. She was finishing off a bite of banana bread and texting when he set her cup on the desk.

"Bringing stretch up to date?"

"Just telling him where I'm at." She looked up from her phone. "Wish you'd quit calling him that. He's a good agent."

Jax's eye twitched. "He have anything new for you?"

"He's working on a few things, but his recent interviews have him convinced it has nothing to do with Mr. Lilly's job. Which means we didn't need to be called in, but now that we've got it, I'm not inclined to punt it back to local. Especially after finding out the foot was removed."

Jax dropped into his chair and took a sip of coffee. "I'm sure your SAC will appreciate the win when you get it."

Abby rolled her eyes. "Special Agent in Charge Carlisle is *always* about the win."

He sounded like Commissioner Marks. "Let's see if we can get it for him and us. We have two male victims, and two feet that appear to have been severed from their bodies. Based on that, I'd agree with Agent Lasko that it's not related to Mr. Lilly's work."

Abby set her phone down on her lap. "You think it's the same killer."

"Possibly, don't you?"

"Maybe, but what's the connection? The victims lived in different cities, had unrelated professions, ran in different circles. We're still working phone records, but preliminarily, there's no evidence that the two men knew each other."

"Was Jonathan involved in surfing or woodworking?"

"Nothing in his duplex indicated he dabbled in water sports or had any hobbies of that sort. He ran marathons. Worked for the BPA. Lived a quiet life. Loved his sister and his niece." She reached for another slice of bread. "How do you not gain weight with Trudy's treats around here?"

If he told her Margot made it, that would only bolster her belief that the woman had a thing for him. And they were working so well together. "I've been jogging like the counselor suggested." He gazed at her, hoping to spark another conversation.

She looked away instead. "Any other promising leads on your end besides that kid who stole the car? Scott, right? And Dylan?"

Jax brought her up to speed on Gerard's intent to steal Terry's surfboard designs and possibly sell them to a corporation.

"Sounds like the brother being involved has some merit."

He nodded. "He is a businessman with a jealous streak. Plenty of motive in that combination. I won't go so far as to say Gerard killed Terry, but he certainly could have arranged for it." He summarized Brandon's admission. "And Gerard apparently made the call to a competitor today. If it walks like a duck..."

"Maybe," Abby said. "But do you see either of those young men severing feet? Or breaking into my mother's room trying to steal back that belt buckle?"

She had a point. "I don't. Which makes me think it was someone else that had a lot to gain or lose. I need to revisit another surf shop owner, Riley Higgins, and find out where he was that night. I have zero proof of his involvement, other than the call he received allegedly from Gerard. But he'd have some motive on getting to that belt buckle if he was afraid prints would tie him in."

"Higgins. That last name sounds familiar."

"In connection to Jonathan?"

"I can't be sure. Do you think prints will pan out on the buckle?"

Jax steepled his fingers. "We could get lucky, but I'm not holding my breath with how many times it was handled."

Abby's face dimmed at that thought. "Let me know if you do."

He leaned back in his chair. He had one more link between the two cases he had to share. He'd put it off, unsure why. But if he'd learned anything this past year, things were best spread out on the table. "There might be one connection."

Abby leaned forward. "What's that?"

"Margot Coleman."

"*Our* nurse, Margot? The woman with the crush on you who's apparently a neighbor?" Abby said.

"Yeah, I think she meant 'neighbor' as in moving to Misty Pines in general. As I think I mentioned before, she lives up past Terry's place. When I spoke with her, she said that they'd only met in passing. But she is a common element in both our cases."

Abby bit into the bread. "It does seem strange that when she mentioned living here, she didn't bother to tell me that two men she knew had gone missing." Abby grabbed her cup and blew the steam off the top. "Seems that would be relevant."

"Except she might not be aware that Terry is still missing. We haven't made the identity of the foot or anything about the case public."

"True. It's possible she didn't put the two together. And even if she did, she might not tell me." Abby sipped her coffee.

"Why do you say that?"

"Women's intuition. I always felt she judged me, like Lulu being sick was my fault."

"You know that's a crazy thought, right? We were under a lot of stress. We did everything we could for Lulu. Maybe our perceptions were off at a certain point. Exhaustion and grief will do that. And she mentioned losing her own son to cancer. She might have been fighting her own battles at the same time."

"Perhaps." She waved it off. "You're right. Besides, if they were having a thing, she'd be baking him cookies. She denies the flowers my vic sent her were romantic, but Mr. Lilly had a plate full of goodies on his kitchen counter and in my experience—"

"How do you know they came from Margot?" he said, cutting her off.

"It was the same plate the homemade muffins she'd brought into the hospital were on."

Jax frowned. "What kind of plate?"

"Ceramic, white with blue flowers."

He rolled his chair to his computer and pulled up the Chesney case, clicking on the photographs taken of the interior of Terry's house. He clicked on the kitchen. The pie plate—a solid blue.

"What is it?" Abby said.

"Maybe nothing. It was a hunch, but this plate doesn't have flowers..."

Abby stood behind Jax and stared at the screen. "It's a similar blue though. She might wait to get to know the person better before bringing out the good stuff."

He glanced at the banana bread plate. White plastic. He hadn't rated fancy either. "Maybe. What I can confirm is she does bake for those she seems to like though." He nodded to the chunk of bread in Abby's hand.

"Seriously?" She dropped the slice into the trash and returned to the chair across from Jax's desk. "But I don't see her breaking into my mother's room. Or killing someone with a bow and arrow. Or severing their feet with a knife."

His eyebrow cocked. "And here I thought you believed women could do anything."

"I do. But…"

"It is a high level of violence, I hear you. And it's not a common method in which women kill," Jax said.

"Exactly. Especially if the motivation for the killings is emotional, like feeling jilted. I'd expect something much more up close and personal."

Jax smirked. "Doesn't get much more personal than cutting off someone's feet."

She rocked her head. "That's if it's related to the actual murders. But okay, you have a point."

He could spend the rest of his life going back and forth with Abby. Talking about work had always been easy for them. "Truth is though, until we have some certainty of how Terry died, we can't be conclusive."

"Was there a lot of blood?"

"There was, and I suppose an arrow could have caused it if it hit a major artery or vital organ, even the gut." And it would explain why there were no signs of bullet scars on the trees, and that the knife was there on the trail, unused. If the shot came from behind, Terry would've had no time to react. Like Mr. Lilly, he would have died instantly. And Walter…if he witnessed it, he could have run for his life—right off a cliff.

"Even if she were involved," he said, "there's the removal of Terry's body up on that trail. There were few to no signs of what happened to it. It's possible it was disposed of over a cliff. Closest one is out front of where we found the blood. Except Margot is small, and Terry, while not a big man, was dead weight. Even if she rolled him off—"

"Which could explain why the foot came ashore where it did."

"Right, but there's a lack of blood trail. And while we found the body of a homeless man who we believe could have witnessed what happened out there, there were no signs of Terry."

She nodded. "And with Jonathan, there are no obvious signs of motive. Margot doesn't appear to have been jilted by him. As I mentioned, he'd just sent her flowers," Abby said.

"Serial killers strike for less," Jax said.

Abby frowned, the skin between her eyes wrinkling. He'd always loved that. "You know the odds of that are slim," she said.

"But they exist."

"Sure, but at one percent of all homicides being tied to serial killing, and most of those committed by men—it's not probable."

"But women serial killers do often kill people they know, unlike their male counterparts."

She scoffed. "I don't buy it. You've got a disgruntled brother who wants to make money off his brother. You're familiar with Occam's Razor?" Abby said.

"Yes. That the simplest solution is most likely correct. But... what's yours?"

"We're working on a few things. At this point, it could be a disgruntled marathoner he beat."

"Could be Margot," Jax said.

Abby's phone lit up. She glanced at it and hopped up. "Occam's Razor. It's best you stick to your theories, and I'll work mine."

Just like that, she dropped into full FBI mode with every intention to stay in control of her case.

Jax stood, determined to pull her back. "I don't know about you, but I'm starving. How about we get a bite to eat and continue this conversation? An Italian diner just opened on the edge of town. I hear it's good."

Abby draped her coat over her shoulders. "Can't. I'm meeting Olek later to catch up and talk about our case."

Olek again. "You have to eat sometime."

"I need to do a couple of things before then. Thanks though."

Meeting up later would mean... "You're going out for dinner?"

"Didn't say that. But he is my partner, Jax."

Jax had no claims on Abby. He only wanted more time, something to eat—to keep talking. About the case, sure, but also about getting back to counseling. Together. "Then go meet him now and let's do dinner tonight. We're on a roll."

"Olek also has some ideas about getting my mother situated someplace in the next day or two. I'll catch up with you later."

"I can help you with that."

"I've got it."

Jax followed her out as far as the kitchen, his face flushed with being shut out. He wasn't sure who he was more annoyed with—Abby, or Olek Lasko. A good dose of both, he decided.

Matt appeared in the doorway. "Hey, Sheriff. Saw Abby leaving. Everything okay?"

Peachy. "Great. Tell me about the interview with the bartender." Jax refilled his coffee.

"It went good. The woman's name is Lisa LeRoux and she was cooperative, but didn't see Terry that night. In fact, according to her, they weren't dating anymore."

Had Brandon misunderstood? "Terry told his employee she was mad at him."

"She was mad alright. She stated that some other woman was in the picture, and she'd seen her at Terry's place, which was 'unacceptable.'" He air quoted Lisa's word.

"But Terry was trying to make amends?"

"Yeah, he said it was nothing and the woman was some neighbor being nice. But Ms. LeRoux said it didn't look that way to her and she told him to not bother coming over. Ever."

Huh. Two men. One sending flowers. One Margot might be pursuing? Abby didn't think it was possible Margot could be involved, and he wasn't entirely sure he bought that himself. He had a decent working theory of why Terry Chesney went missing, presumed dead. Even so, he couldn't discount people's capabilities when they were motivated.

He'd feel better if he questioned Margot himself. If nothing else, to eliminate her off any suspect list. "Okay, thanks Matt."

Jax headed back to his office. He could call Margot in. Or pay her a visit. He sat in his chair, knowing he'd get more information if he had her undivided attention in a non-threatening environment. Even if it sent the wrong signal to Abby.

He riffled through his stack of messages, found the slip of paper Trudy had handed him, and dialed.

"Margot, it's Sheriff Turner. Jax. Wondered if you were available for coffee?"

CHAPTER 31

Jax could be so annoying. Her mom stuff aside—which wasn't helping her mood—why did men jump to *the woman did it* when circumstances allowed? Always the woman. Although Abby wasn't naïve. She'd been in law enforcement long enough to witness women doing horrible things. But serial killer reached a different level of evil—and despite her and Margot not connecting during the time of Lulu's illness, she'd never seen signs that Margot could be ruthless.

While she wasn't a paid profiler in the Bureau—that position went to the agents in the Behavioral Analysis Unit—it had been part of Abby's training. Distracted or not, she wouldn't have missed it after all the time they'd spent around Margot at the hospital.

Abby had felt judged by Margot—as she'd told Jax—but being judgy didn't make one a serial killer either. Then to learn Margot had lost her own child to cancer... No. She didn't believe it.

What she did believe was that Margot liked Jax, and she'd sensed that early on when they first visited the hospital. For a long while, they thought Lulu would beat the cancer. They'd taken her in for infusion treatments and she'd responded well. Margot would be in the area and always came right over to give them encouraging words.

But even in Abby's haze, the long looks Margot gave Jax were too obvious to miss. Along with the lingering touches on his arm. The laughing at his not-so-funny jokes. Jokes she rarely, if ever, heard from him anymore.

Soon, Margot seemed to be everywhere, including with them during the treatments, just to check in. Then she was assigned as their nurse, greeting them with that same sympathetic smile every time they arrived.

Lulu loved her though and that's all Abby needed to ignore Margot's clear intention toward Jax. Abby ignored everything to see her little girl smile.

And if Lulu loved her...

For the next couple hours Abby researched centers for her mother, came up with a plan, and made a few phone calls. Then she met Olek at the office. The one man who didn't immediately jump to *the woman did it*. At least not yet.

With a plan for her mom in mind, and Jonathan Lilly's body with the medical examiner, she wanted to solve this case and get home early for a hot bath and snuggles on the couch with the only consistent and dependable man in her life, Murphy. Well. Dependable as long as the kibble bowl was full and the head scritches continuous.

"Productive meeting, I hope?" she said, settling at the conference table next to Olek. He had a manila folder laid out in front of him.

"Productive in that we can cross off the list anything work-related being the cause of Lilly's death. His main point of contact said Jonathan was a standup guy and did his job well. No one ever had a problem with him or vice versa."

"One down. How about that letter you were running down from the insurance company?"

"Now that was something. Looks like Mr. Lilly had a fender bender with a Riley Higgins."

"Higgins?"

"Yeah...name ring a bell?"

"It came up in Jax's case with Terry Chesney." She must have seen his name on the letter without realizing it. That's why it had sounded familiar. "What's he do for a living?"

"Owns a surf shop in West Shore."

"Chesney also owned a surf shop." Jax's theory about design plans for a corporation might hold merit and that made a lot more sense than Margot Coleman. "What kind of fender bender?"

"Mr. Higgins rides a hog, and Mr. Lilly backed over it."

"Seems like an open and shut insurance matter."

"Would have been had Mr. Lilly been good at paying his bills. He'd let his insurance lapse for sixty days."

"Let me guess. That lapse was during the time of the incident."

"Yup."

"Any indicators that Mr. Higgins tried to collect anyway?"

Olek pulled a call log from the folder. "He called Mr. Lilly's house several times. One being the day before he went missing."

"That call could have been the reason for the yelling the elderly neighbor heard," Abby said.

"Ms. Baka. Correct." Olek glanced at his watch. "How about we grab a bite and continue talking about the case there? I've done nothing but run around today and I'm hungry."

That wasn't at all in her plans. "I have a date with Murphy."

Olek grimaced. "You can see your cat later. C'mon. There's a new diner in Misty Pines I'm dying to try."

"I—"

Olek shot up out of his seat. "I'm not taking no for an answer."

Her eyebrow lifted, but she found herself standing. Her stomach grumbled. She hadn't eaten anything substantial today. She'd been so quick to turn Jax down, though. "I suppose this new place is Italian?"

"You've heard of it?"

She hesitated. Jax wouldn't appreciate her rejecting him only to go to the same place he'd suggested. But it wasn't like they were married anymore. They weren't. What were they? God, most of the time she had no idea. Whatever it was, she wasn't sure she wanted to blow it out of the water with a misunderstanding. "Only that it's good," she finally said.

"Look, I'm not asking you for a date," Olek said. "We have a case to discuss, and we'll think better with sustenance. Besides, you can't live on my grandmother's Kalochkes alone. Believe me. I've tried." Olek's innocent smile beamed.

She sighed, relenting. Jax had thought she'd end up having dinner with Olek, so what did it matter? If nothing else, she'd report back to Jax on whether the place was as good as he'd heard. "Fine."

Ten minutes later, they were about to pull into the lot when she spotted Jax climbing out of his patrol rig. She tensed as if she'd been caught doing something wrong. A ridiculous response. Olek was her partner. Nothing more. She shook off the *kid caught in the cookie jar* feeling. She was a grown woman. And a good investigator.

In fact, this would be a good time to chat with Jax about Riley Higgins as a connection to both of their cases. Jax should know about that.

She tracked her ex-husband as he slammed his car door and ran to the restaurant—where a smiling and waving Margot stood under the eaves. Her blonde curls rested on her shoulders, and she tossed her head back as he approached, laughing at something he'd said.

Abby's face grew hot. "I don't want to go here," she said. "Let's go to Mackie's instead."

"But the reviews...," Olek said, passing the restaurant.

"I don't care. I've lost my appetite for Italian."

CHAPTER 32

It wasn't quite five o'clock when Jax pulled into Little Italy's parking lot, still dressed in uniform. He'd invited Margot for coffee, but she was busy until dinnertime and insisted they check out "the new diner in town." If this was what it took to question her, he'd do it. Although he'd begged off when she suggested he pick her up. This wasn't a date.

Margot waited under the restaurant's awning, smiling and waving at him as he approached.

He jogged to the front door. "You're early."

"I was just excited to hear from you. You still on duty?" She nodded to his uniform.

"Technically, I'm never off." Changing might have given the wrong impression. This whole scenario could do that, but Margot had been so kind to him and Abby when Lulu was sick. He didn't want to scare her in the process of eliminating her from the potential suspect list.

"That has to get tiring—never getting a complete rest?"

"I knew what I signed up for when I applied," he said, chuckling. He opened the door and was met with the scent of tomato sauce and basil. His stomach rumbled. "After you."

The hostess greeted them and grabbed a couple of menus while Margot looked around at the décor.

"Very Italian," she said.

"Very." He searched for something else to say. He wasn't well-practiced at spending time with women, other than Abby. Marie Callender didn't count, even if she made a mean Salisbury steak. "And as you mentioned, new."

Margot nodded and looked out the windows overlooking the parking lot, her smile fading.

Great. He'd lost her before they'd begun. If he wanted her to talk openly, he'd better sharpen his game. "There's been some buzz about it, if you can call it that in our small town, and I've heard great things about the food. Speaking of which, thanks for the goodies at work. The boys appreciated them."

"Oh sure," she said, her tone flat. He'd probably screwed that up too by admitting he hadn't eaten the treats. She'd be even more upset if she learned what Trudy had done to the cookies. As soon as the hostess returned, she said, "Can we have a corner booth?"

"Absolutely," the young woman said.

Jax drew in a breath as they followed her. Corner booths were his and Abby's thing back in the day. Always facing the door.

The hostess placed the menus on the table and Margot slid into the corner. She got settled, her smile returning. "This is perfect."

The booth didn't have a view of the entrance, but when the door wasn't an option, facing the other tables worked fine. Jax slid in opposite Margot. "How are you liking Misty Pines so far?"

"It's good. Different. But people are so friendly here," she said.

"They weren't friendly in West Shore?"

"For the most part. It's just harder to meet people when an area is bigger. Or to get to know them well. Unless they're related to a patient." She grabbed the menu. "Downside of working all the time I guess."

The waitress appeared with two glasses of water, a breadbasket, and a rundown of the specials.

When she disappeared Margot said, "I'm sure you have no problem with that though."

"With working all the time?" Jax said, hoping to deflect what he knew she meant.

She batted her eyes, her voice soft. "No, finding women, silly."

He cleared his throat and started to peruse the menu. "Right. Well, as I mentioned, my job doesn't allow for much down time, and I enjoy the work."

That sounded lame. He should have jumped right into her relationship with Jonathan Lilly. He opened his mouth, but she beat him to it.

"So, then I should feel special that you've asked me out?"

Shit. He set the menu down. Why did he think this would go any other way? Not all women were like Abby apparently, where he had to work hard just to get her to have a cup of coffee with him. "I need to run to the men's room. Be right back."

"Sure," she said, her focus dropping to the menu.

Jax crossed through the restaurant, warmth creeping up under his collar. A couple more tables had filled since they entered. He headed straight for the bathroom to find an available sink where he could splash water on his face. He pushed open the door, and nearly ran over Shaun Evans coming out.

"Whoa, must be urgent," Shaun said.

"Sorry about that, Mr. Evans." Jax stepped back. "Hope I didn't get you with the door?"

"It's Shaun, please, and I'm good."

Margot had him flustered. Jax shook it off. "You're a little far from West Shore tonight, aren't you?"

"I was in town to see one of my boys, and heard this place makes a mean pizza."

West Shore had a few good pizza places itself, but nothing like the *new* to draw people in. "That's what they say. You here seeing Dylan?"

Shaun hesitated. "Yeah. You know, just checking in after…"

He probably didn't feel comfortable speaking about the kids he worked with. At least in front of a men's bathroom door in a restaurant. But it made sense that Troy would call Shaun back in if he thought Dylan was headed down the wrong path. "Hope you can make a difference."

"Always try. Anyway, just here for takeout. You?"

"Like you, checking out the new and shiny," Jax said, not planning to disclose he was here on a date. No, not a date. An interview. Even if Margot saw it different—which was his fault, and an assumption he needed to rectify immediately.

"Cool. How's Scott doing? You planning to release him anytime soon?" Shaun said.

"He's fine, but I can't talk about an active case. I'm sure you understand."

"Yeah. No worries." His head bobbed. "I'll see you around." Shaun sidestepped Jax on his way to the door.

"What about your pizza?" Jax said.

"Already got it. Just ran back in to…." He nodded at the men's room door.

"Gotcha. See you around."

When Jax returned to the table, Margot had placed her purse and coat where he'd been sitting. Instead of moving it, he slid in on her side, but stayed near the edge. She'd ordered an appetizer that was just arriving.

"I hope you don't mind," she said. "I was starved."

"Of course." They placed their dinner orders and when they had filled their plates with antipasto, Jax leaned back. "I appreciate your meeting with me because I was hoping we could chat about Terry Chesney."

She took a bite of breadstick. "Terry? Yeah, whatever happened with that? Everything turned out okay I hope?"

"No, it didn't. But we're investigating, and you'd mentioned that you'd made it a point to meet all your neighbors."

"Sure. There's more than I first believed up on that hill. Including that old man, McDonald. You know he lives in a shack on forty acres?"

"Yes. He's been around a while."

"Something weird about that."

"Some people like their privacy. Sounds like you visited Mr. McDonald then?" There'd be no way to know about his shack otherwise.

"I tried. His dog didn't let me get far. And not that I don't like dogs mind you. Before my dad left, I used to duck hunt with him and our retriever, Buddy, but…" Her gaze drifted away.

McDonald's old blood hound was a harmless bag of droopy skin and sad eyes. But if you weren't a dog person, he could be intimidating. Funny, he'd never thought of himself as a dog person. Koa had turned him around.

Hunting ducks was interesting, though. He would have never pegged her for that. "What do you use for bird hunting?" he said.

"Gosh, there's lots of options, I suppose. I was partial to the Browning Auto 5. You hunt?"

Not a bow. "Never found the time." Or inclination, but that wasn't how he wanted to lead this conversation. "How about Terry's place? Did you go to his house too?"

She wiped the edges of her mouth with her fingertip. "Not technically."

What did that mean? "The reason I ask is there was a home baked pie in his kitchen."

"Guilty as charged, Sheriff." She winked.

"So you brought it to him?"

"Well, he'd mentioned buying a store-bought one a few weeks back. You know they use filling from a can and their crust is always soggy. Anyway, I told him he hadn't tasted a good pie if that was his measuring stick."

"Then you did go up to his house?"

She shook her head. Taking a bite of salami. "No. That's what I mean by not technically. He'd just gotten home and was getting the mail, so I handed it to him right there on the road since I was on my way up the hill."

"I see."

"No law against being a good neighbor, is there officer?" She smiled.

"There's not."

The pizza they ordered arrived shortly after and they each slid a piece onto a plate.

"I ran into Abby recently. She looked pretty. As ever," Margot said.

"You don't say?" he said. "What caused you two to cross paths?"

She bit into the slice, pulling it away with the mozzarella stringing until it snapped. Her eyes never left his face. "She thought I might have some information on something she's working on. But I didn't. Don't you two talk anymore?"

He shrugged. "Not often."

She smiled again, seeming to like that.

"How about you? You mentioned getting divorced. I was sorry to hear that," Jax said, wanting the topic off him and Abby.

Her smile faded. He'd hit a sensitive point. "We weren't actually married,

180

but he was Joey's father." Her eyes softened. "He was devastated when the cancer took our little boy."

Jax understood that completely. "I'm sorry. I hope he's getting the help he needs."

Her face hardened. "Men don't always think they are the ones with the problem. They can't move on. They can't accept when other people move on either."

He'd take that as a no. Had Abby thought the same about him? She must have. "That must be… hurtful."

She pushed her pizza away. "Let's not talk about me. Tell me more about Misty Pines."

As they finished their pizza, he told her about the surfing, the fishing, the attributes of their small town. "If you're a reader, make sure to get to the bookstore. Emily Krueger has a great book selection," he said.

"Good to know."

What they didn't get back to was anything on the topic of Jonathan or Terry. She pelted him with so many questions about the area that they spoke of nothing else. The waitress slid the bill onto the table and walked away. Jax palmed it.

But despite that, he'd had enough. Margot was a nice woman, and it might be that her kindness to Terry had been misunderstood by his ex-girlfriend, Lisa. Margot had baked the man a pie to be neighborly. Perhaps Terry had given her a hug. It felt innocent enough.

What bothered him was that she didn't come fully clean about the details of running into Abby. Although the way she'd said Abby's name made him think Abby was right that she'd judged her when Lulu was sick. And that could mean she might not be prone to share information with her without a direct question.

"So, what now?" Margot said, inching her way more towards the edge of the bench. Closer to Jax. "Should we go to your place for a cocktail?"

"No," he said too quickly, as flush crept up his neck again.

She leaned back. "Oh. Did I read this wrong?"

He cleared his throat. "Perhaps. I just thought it would be nice to catch up, for old times' sake."

"I see. That's the way it is. And here I thought…huh." She nodded to the bench opening, a sign for Jax to move. "I'd like out."

He shifted. "Of course."

She grabbed her things, dug through her purse, and slapped a ten on the table. "I don't need you to buy me dinner for old times' sake. But thank you."

"I'm sorry if you misread my intentions," Jax said. "But I've got it."

"It's fine."

Before he could say another word, she marched through the restaurant and the clink of the exit bell followed.

Well, that went well.

He motioned the waitress over and handed her the bill and credit card.

A few minutes later he arrived at his cruiser to find its rear corner sagging. He circled around to find the back passenger tire flat from a slice in the sidewall. Something sharp had made that slice.

He looked around, but didn't see anyone suspicious. His eye twitched. It could have been someone with a grudge against cops in general, although that had never occurred here in Misty Pines. And the timing… Margot? Had she been that angry at him? Had he been the one to misread her?

He squatted under the car to grab the spare from the bracket underneath, but it too had a puncture to the sidewall.

His old feelings of appreciation for Margot's kindness towards him and Abby dissipated. If she was that easily triggered, his initial concerns about her might be justified. He certainly wouldn't take her off any suspect list. Not yet.

He stood, deciding which tire company could get there fastest from West Shore when his phone buzzed with a text from Matt.

"Gerard is here at the station and he's irate. Think you might want to get here fast."

CHAPTER 33

Jax entered the conference room where Gerard Chesney waited. He'd directed Matt to *make their visitor comfortable* until he could get there, which had taken a minute between waiting for Garrett to come get him and giving him directions to go back and get the tires changed.

With the time on his hands, he'd thought of Margot. She wasn't the sweet and even-keeled woman who had sat with Abby and him when Lulu took her last breath. Or who'd offered kind and encouraging words after, her gentle hand on their arms. Comforting them from their loss—an emotion she came to personally know herself when her son died.

His entire body tensed at the thought of that shared grief. How one event could alter everything. Could shatter a world. Margot hadn't mentioned her son, other than to say his father hadn't handled his passing well. Perhaps women just had an easier time of it…like Abby had appeared to. Or maybe they didn't. Margot's actions tonight could be a result of pent-up frustration.

By the time he reached the station, he'd shaken off his annoyance at Margot for leaving him stranded. If in fact she'd done the damage—he had no proof other than his gut and that didn't always serve him. But he hadn't shaken the idea of Margot's ability to kill. Was it possible? Under the right circumstances, it was possible for anyone to kill. But did her quick temper equate to doing something much more sinister to Terry? Or Jonathan Lilly, for that matter?

As Abby suggested, the simplest solution in his case included a scenario where Gerard, surfboard designs, and greed were involved. With motive, and lies rolling off his tongue, his perpetrator might have been waiting for

Jax right then.

"Where is he?" Gerard said before Jax's butt hit the chair.

Jax had taken a moment to leave his phone and jacket in his office and grab a couple of bottles of water from the kitchen before entering. "We haven't found his body, but the foot that washed ashore off Meddle beach two days ago belonged to him."

Gerard's face flushed and his gaze dropped to his hands.

"But I'm thinking you might know where he is better than me."

Gerard's eyes shot up and narrowed. "What's that supposed to mean?"

"You tell me. You're the one who was in Misty Pines when you made the call to him at eight o'clock."

"That's…"

"…what the phone records show," Jax finished. The ping on West Shore's tower hadn't been that exact, but Gerard didn't know that.

Gerard's mouth clamped closed.

Jax took a drink of his water. "It's time you come clean, Mr. Chesney. I'll find out your role soon enough. And evidence suggests you have one."

"What evidence?"

"A witness who says you coordinated with Brandon, and Scott Heffernen, to steal the surfboard blueprints so you could sell them off to the corporation interested in Terry's designs."

"I have no idea what ideas Brandon has filled your head with, but I'm not the bad guy here. I certainly don't know any Scott Heffernen. Nor do I have any blueprints."

Brandon had admitted that he was Scott's contact, but Jax didn't believe either capable of concocting a scheme like this on their own. "Semantics, don't you think?" Jax said. "With the corporate contact, you had everything to gain in this scenario."

Gerard's hands balled into fists. "Did Brandon tell you he agreed that Terry should be selling his designs? That my brother had a lot more potential than making boards for going-nowhere locals and tourists? That he was tired of holding his checks to make sure they'd clear?"

"A variation. He also mentioned you didn't mind how he got those blueprints for you. Only that he got them."

Gerard worked his jaw. "I told you. I don't have any blueprints."

"You seemed cagey when they were brought up, which suggests you knew about them. You just didn't think I did." Brandon mentioning them made sense though. He was trying to cover his ass. "So, if you don't have them, aren't you at least a little concerned about who might?" He had an idea of who Gerard was concerned about. Now to see if he'd admit it.

"Good question and yes, I am. But I keep coming back to the only other person around who'd know what to do with them—Riley Higgins. How about you talk to him and see what he knows about those prints. And while you're at it, what he was prepared to do to get them."

Jax folded his arms over his chest. "We've spoken. And while I was there, your call came through. You sounded concerned that someone would find out about what you were doing. Which leads me to believe you're in this together."

Gerard hesitated. Probably connecting the dots that Brandon had ratted him out. Finally, he slapped his hands on the desk. "God no." He squirmed before resting his elbows on the table. "I'm sure it doesn't look great, my holding back. But seriously, I didn't believe any of this had a bearing on the noise my brother heard, or I would have told you sooner."

"Then tell me now."

He shook his head. "I did call Riley. I was certain he'd taken those damn blueprints, which would be stupid. He might think he knows what to do with them, but the manufacturer would find out easily enough they were Terry's work. When I called, whatever you heard was me telling him to return them. That's all."

"Why would Riley steal them?"

"Because his game has always been to one-up Terry. To win. He's never gotten over losing to my brother on the circuit. I'm sure he thinks if he can pass off the designs that belonged to Terry, he'll get the accolades he believes he deserves." Gerard took a breath. "But he's wrong. No one will buy his story. I'd make sure of it."

Jax nodded, but his look said *bullshit*.

"Look, I'm not guilty of anything except for trying to get my stupid brother to think about the future for two seconds."

Jax retrieved the second bottle of water from the floor and set it on the table in front of Gerard, nodding to it.

Gerard sank into the chair and grabbed it, taking a long drink.

How true were Gerard's claims? All of them could be, but that didn't eliminate the other real possibility. "But you admit that you were at your brother's place that night, isn't that right?"

Gerard didn't answer.

"You were there, and things got heated. Did Terry know what you were up to? Did you fight?"

Gerard shook his head.

"Did you call him from out on the trail?" Brandon had said that Scott had seen Terry running into the woods. "Did you lead him out there to kill him?"

"No. No. No," Gerard said, each word gaining emphasis.

"Then set me straight," Jax said. "Because the way I see it, what better way to get what you wanted in this deal than to eliminate the only obstacle?"

Gerard squared his shoulders. "My brother was not an obstacle. He was a stubborn son-of-a-bitch, but this deal won't happen if he's gone. They want the design, along with the man, the legend. Don't you see, I had every reason for him to be alive. Not dead."

"When tempers flare, lines are crossed."

Gerard shook his head. "It wasn't like that." His eyes misted.

"Then what was it like?"

Gerard sniffed. "I wasn't even near Misty Pines when I called him. I was at a bar in West Shore. But that aside, Terry did hear a sound outside." He hung his head. "But I did lie. I figured what he heard was Scott, or whoever Brandon sent, outside stealing his blueprints. I tried to keep Terry on the phone, distracted, but he insisted he had to check it out. He said he'd call me back."

"Except he didn't call." Phone records confirmed that Terry didn't use his phone after eight. "And you didn't even attempt to get ahold of him again."

"You're right. I was afraid he was upset about the theft. It wasn't until an hour later that I learned that Scott hadn't gotten the blueprints yet. That's why I told Brandon to send him back. Then I was afraid to call. I didn't want my brother to put two and two together. Like my calls coincided with the burglary attempt." He cleared his throat. "Our relationship has never been one where I reach out late at night, and he would've thought that was odd. But when I didn't hear from him the next morning, I drove by his house. That's when I saw everything open and called your office. I should've gone the night before. Maybe I could've helped him."

"Helped him with what?"

"Don't you see? Riley must have taken the matter into his own hands. He beat us to it. He must have been who my brother heard that night."

Jax shook his head. "You want me to believe that on the same night you planned to steal the prints from your own brother, Riley Higgins had the same plan?"

"I know how it sounds," Gerard said, his voice tight. "But the corporation… they were wanting to make decisions on new designs and there was a time pressure to it. And I have no doubt that Riley Higgins did something to Terry. Brandon could have been double crossing me, feeding us both information. Who knows. My guess is Riley has those prints and intends to sell them off."

"You said he couldn't."

"I said it wouldn't work. That doesn't mean he won't try."

"Can you confirm one way or another with the corporation?"

"It doesn't work that way."

"You don't have a connection there?"

He huffed. "I've already told you they only wanted to work with the artist." His hands clenched. "And before you say it—they didn't like me much there, okay. I do push. Maybe they found that off-putting."

That part wasn't hard to believe. Jax leaned back in his chair. "This story has more turns and potholes than the road up to your brother's place."

"I'm telling you the truth. I was information gathering… for Terry to contact them."

The truth, or a diversion to get the attention away from himself? Gerard

187

had all but admitted orchestrating a B&E but fell short of an admission of attacking his brother. If he couldn't gain a contract without Terry, he'd be a complete idiot to alienate his brother, let alone kill him. But logic didn't always prevail in heated arguments.

Jax stood and waved Matt in, who'd been standing at the door. "Mr. Chesney, I'm going to hold you for a while longer."

"You can't..."

"I can. You'll give Matt here the name of that corporation interested in those surfboard designs. Once your story is confirmed about the design process, you'll be set free." Matt nodded that he understood what he needed to do. Jax turned back to Gerard. "If it's not confirmed, we'll talk about what's next. Either way, I'd like you to remain close until this is sorted out." If the DA decided to bring charges for Gerard's role, they'd want him close enough to be arrested.

Gerard's jaw clenched. "I have no problem with that. I didn't do anything to my brother, and I don't intend to leave town until he's found. So please figure it out. If something's happened to Terry, then Riley, or whoever is responsible, should pay for it. Do you hear me?"

Jax walked out without responding and headed for his office. The whir of the fax machine had just ended when he entered. Jax ripped the three pages from the tray.

Forensics had come back on the crime scene in the woods. The digital version was in his inbox, along with photographs.

He sat down and pulled up the computer copy. The weapon that had ended Terry had been recovered ninety-three yards from the pool of blood on the trail: a three-bladed broadhead arrow with Terry's blood covering the arrowhead.

Such a weapon, often used for larger game kills, would slice through a human with the right weighted bow. More importantly to his case, the injury would result in heavy blood loss—a fact he'd witnessed himself.

Bothersome, however, was the direction in which the arrow travelled. If Terry had taken the hit from behind, in a chase scenario, Jax would've expected the arrow to be out front. If attacked from ahead, the arrow behind.

But the arrow was west, toward ocean side, meaning it had travelled from the east. Given the trajectory of the blood on the trail, and where the arrow landed, Terry's killer was ahead and to the side. Waiting?

Arrows could fly three or four hundred yards if shot from a heavier bow. But how accurate were they at those distances? And if a smaller person was using it...the draw strength would take some muscle. But he'd never underestimate anyone's ability to do a task with the right motivation.

A crossbow could shoot even further. He was fairly sure a crossbow used a different kind of arrow and would be harder to load from the limited experience he'd had with one. Still—if the killer was waiting to strike, they'd have it locked and loaded in advance.

Jax might have entertained the idea of a bow hunting expedition gone terribly wrong and scared hunters covering their tracks—especially since sanctioned bow hunting ended over a month ago—except for one point. Jonathan Lilly's injuries had also been inflicted by an arrow.

That suggested both attacks were premeditated. In Terry's case, the killer would either have had the weapon on him or hidden in the forest. And he would've had to have enough time to get to it and zone in on Terry to make the shot. That didn't exclude Gerard, but it did eliminate a heat of the moment argument.

Where did that put Jax now? Was it Riley Higgins as Gerard suggested? If so, he'd have to find out if there was any connection to Jonathan Lilly. They both lived in West Shore, but so did a lot of people. Another thought came into his head. One he'd feel better about if he had a solid answer to.

Jax set down the report as the sound of fast footfalls headed in his direction. Garrett and Rachel burst into his doorway, out of breath.

"What's wrong?" Jax said.

"It's Trudy. Brody's at the scene of an accident. Car hit a tree. But there's two sets of tire marks... No witnesses," Garrett said.

Jax shot out of his desk. "Where is she now?"

"Brody had her transported to West Shore General. He said it's bad, boss. It's..."

Jax didn't wait to hear more. He grabbed his jacket and started out of his office.

"I didn't get a chance to get your tire fixed before we got the call," Garrett hollered after him.

"Then you're with me. And Rachel—" he said.

"I'll stay back and watch the phones. I'm here for you, Sheriff."

She had been there for him. For all of them. "Appreciate it. I need you to check one other thing. Margot Coleman. Tell me if she has any hunting licenses on record."

"Anything in particular?"

"Bow hunting. I have a report on my desk. It shows the model and design of the arrow used to kill Terry Chesney. I want to know who sells those arrows, and who bought them in the last year."

"Will do."

He nodded and turned to Garrett. "Throw me your keys," he said. "I'm driving."

CHAPTER 34

Jax and Abby arrived in the elevator lobby of West Shore General at the same time. He'd hesitated at first to call her. After their earlier conversation, she might think he had an ulterior motive to disrupt her dinner meeting with Olek.

Another time, she might be right to think him capable of that. Not now. This was Trudy. And he'd been wrong to waver. Abby viewed Trudy the same as he did: family.

"Appreciate your making the drive," he said. Jax punched the floor for ICU and they rode the elevator.

"Of course. The place is actually starting to feel like home."

Jax lifted his eyebrow questioning.

"Mom's on six," Abby said, her dark expression mirroring his own.

It had been a rough a week for them all.

"Glad you came," Trudy's husband Frank said the moment they'd stepped out of the elevator. His bushy gray brows formed a single line over his worried eyes. "She'd have all her feathers ruffled to think she was the center of attention."

Abby squeezed his forearm. "Yes, she would. How is she?"

"Holding her own," he said, his voice thick with emotion.

"Where was she headed at the time of the accident?" Jax said, feeling the sting of stress across his skin. Not only that Trudy was here, but the memories that being in a hospital dredged up in him. Tennis shoes squeaking on the linoleum floors. Antiseptics tingling his nostrils. Beeps of monitors and life-saving machines coming from the rooms. It had been a lifetime ago and only yesterday that he'd been in a place too similar with Lulu. Abby had to be feeling the same.

"She was adamant about getting to your place with some goodies she baked," Frank said, drawing Jax back. "Said something about showing you how a real baker made banana bread."

Jax shook his head. Trudy's actions had been motivated by Margot. She'd turned into a problem not only for him, but for his team. "Her car was found up on Rifle Road. Why would she be up that direction?"

Frank shrugged. "There's no reason I can think of. Isn't that fairly close to your place though?"

"Close, but only if you head straight out from my house. It dead ends a few miles in—elk hunters park out there before taking to those trails."

"Is she conscious?" Abby said.

Frank's face darkened. "She's in and out. She hit her head on the window. No side airbags." His eyes closed and he drew in a breath. Opened them again. Jax recognized the signs of trying to hold it together. "They took her for an MRI a bit ago."

"They're concerned about brain swelling?" Jax said.

Frank nodded.

Jax's gut bottomed out. Trudy was in dangerous territory.

"I'll touch base with Brody. See if I can get any more information," Jax said, digging his phone from his jacket pocket.

He stepped away, leaving Abby to comfort Frank. Just as he was about to punch in Brody's number, he saw a message had come in earlier while he was interrogating Gerard.

Jax clicked voicemail.

"Hon, it's Trudy." His assistant's voice was shaky over the whine of her car accelerating. "I..." He gripped the phone, increasing the volume to hear the garbled message more clearly. The reception would have been sketchy at best up where her car was found. But there was no hiding the fear in her tone. "...right behind me. You're in danger. It's..." A thud, like another car hitting the bumper. "...must be..." More garble. "If I don't make it..."

Another bang...a car impacting her again? A thunk. "Shit."

He'd never heard Trudy swear. She must have dropped the phone.

Tires squealed.

Another blow. This time, loud and shattering.

A loud pop like a gunshot. Possibly the airbag. Then nothing.

Jax's arm dropped to his side. Trudy had been chased and run off the road while trying to tell him he was in danger. What had she seen to make her believe that?

He motioned Abby over, who'd been watching him.

"Are you okay?" she said. "You look like you just stepped out of a sauna."

He cleared his throat and hit replay on the phone, pressing the phone to her ear.

As she listened, her features hardened. She nodded.

They returned to Frank who had resorted to pacing and rubbing the back of his neck.

"We need to check on a few things." Jax kept his tone level, even though every part of him felt taut as a guitar string, ready to snap. "But I want to speak with Trudy as soon as she's able. Please call me."

"I will," Frank said, his eyes on the floor.

Jax stood there, not moving. He knew what grief looked like. What hopelessness felt like. He grabbed Frank into a bear hug. "She's going to be fine. If love can bring someone through, she'll be back to us soon." It was a lie. Love didn't always have that power.

But he couldn't lose Trudy. Especially if she was lying in a hospital bed on account of trying to warn him.

He and Abby stepped into the elevator.

"What the hell happened?" Abby said.

"I don't know. But I intend to find out by retracing her steps. She clearly crossed paths with someone she was afraid would cause me harm."

"Agreed."

"Only problem is I'm without a car for the moment. You mind giving me a ride back to my place?"

"Or you could call Margot?" Abby lifted her chin.

"We've already been over this."

"You're right. And I believed you, until Olek and I, thinking we'd try that new diner in town, saw you and Margot walking in. Together."

"I wanted to ask her some questions of my own. I know you don't think she's involved, but I like to form my own conclusions." He folded his arms over his chest, unsure how he felt about her taking his suggestion for dinner with Olek instead. Or the need to answer questions about his investigation.

"M-hmmm. How'd that go?"

"Informational to a point. But in the end, like you, she misread my intentions and stormed out. Next thing I know, I have two slashed tires. And now Trudy..."

"You think Margot did this?"

His jaw tightened. It was a stretch, but he wouldn't discount it either. Things had headed south on him since their meeting. "I have to admit, it does concern me that both your mom and Trudy have been hurt since these cases started."

Any annoyance at Jax drained from Abby's face. "I was thinking that too."

They approached Garrett, where Jax gave him specific instructions to stay near the information desk until morning and monitor anyone who appeared to have any interest in the sixth floor or ICU. "Especially Margot Coleman." As a nurse, she'd know her way around the hospital, and that concerned him.

But Garrett was one deputy. It would be difficult for him to watch both women. Frank would call if anything suspicious occurred, but he was lost in worry and might not be clear-headed.

"I'll get Olek to watch for my mom, at least for a few hours," Abby said, as if she'd read Jax's mind. "I'll make sure he coordinates with your deputy."

"Touch base with Olek, then," Jax said to Garrett. "And call me."

Jax and Abby walked out of the hospital and approached her Prius. "I'll drive," he said, antsy to know what happened sooner than later.

"No, you won't," she said and dropped into the driver's seat.

He relented and checked in with Brody on the drive back, while Abby compared notes with Olek and heard the rest of the report that Jax's call had interrupted. Jax hadn't asked where they'd ended up eating. He didn't want to know.

They fell silent the rest of the way until Abby pulled to the curb in front of Jax's house. Even without the outside light on, he could see the outline of a basket that had fallen to its side on his stoop. He hopped out of the car before Abby could turn off the engine.

"Can you check your cameras?" Abby said coming up behind him. "Maybe they'll show something."

"Don't have any," Jax said, ignoring Abby's surprised expression. The blinds didn't look right. He pulled out his key.

"Why wouldn't the sheriff of Misty Pines have a security camera system? Especially after your last case."

"Keep wanting to believe in this town, I suppose." But he might be forced to rethink that belief after the latest events. He opened the screen to insert his key, but there was no need. The door creaked opened. The lock had been busted. Picked maybe, with a screwdriver.

He stepped into the living room, now certain that he'd be getting cameras installed. His lamps had toppled to the floor. The water glass from the coffee table lay in shards on the floor. The cushions on his couch had been tossed. And scrawled on his wall: a red heart with a black arrow through it.

"Think someone's sending you a message," Abby said.

"Looks like. My guess is Trudy saw who left it."

"That would make sense," Abby said. "And that message seems clear."

"Very." Two men. Killed with arrows likely straight through the heart. Except he had no intention of being next.

He did a cursory look through his house to make sure nothing was missing and no other clues had been left behind. Nothing, other than the message on the wall. He'd have his team help him go through the scene more thoroughly later. They were spread too thin for anything else.

"Well, you can't stay here tonight. It's a crime scene. And..."

He cocked his eyebrow. "You worried about me?"

"Just get your stuff. You can stay at my place."

He wasn't afraid—he could handle whoever had sent the message. But Abby wanted him with her.

He wasn't about to say no.

CHAPTER 35

On the twenty-minute drive to Abby's place, Jax's thoughts drifted to who would have left him that spray-painted message. It felt personal. He couldn't rule Margot out after their failed dinner. But he had no evidence to rule her in, either.

For all he knew, Gerard had left it before he came to the station. But would he have crossed paths with Trudy at that point? Not likely. It could be Riley. He rubbed his forehead. Or someone else he was missing.

He shook the thought and settled back in his seat. But he couldn't shake the ache in his gut wondering how long Trudy had been out there after her accident before they knew.

Abby lived in Cannon Beach, a small community fifteen miles south of Misty Pines off the 101. The bureau's satellite office was located halfway between there and Misty Pines, just like the assisted living facility where Dora had lived.

He didn't like that Abby had chosen a location so far from Misty Pines—from him. But he got it. They hadn't visited this area much as a family—with Lulu. Maybe it was easier to start over when memories weren't seared into every location.

If he'd done the same, he might have saved himself from the ensuing depression that followed. But like the sands on the ocean floor, those feelings had shifted. Now he took some comfort in the memories and places that had once caused him so much angst.

Abby pulled into her driveway and Jax grabbed his duffel out of the back of her car. "Nice place you got here."

Abby grabbed her purse. "You trying to tell me you've never seen it before?"

An impish grin crossed his face. After she'd left, he'd driven by once on a sleepless night and thoughts of what they'd had, and lost, consumed him. Not that he'd admit that to her.

They stepped inside her home. The outside might look fitting for a beach-lifestyle brochure, but inside the furnishings read *Architectural Digest*. Nothing like the home they'd shared together where a cabin vibe had dictated. Comfy couch, overstuffed chair. Chunky coffee table...it had worked well when he was carving. There'd be no setting his knife into the glass square that centered the sofa space here.

Abby moved through her home, flicking on lights. Murphy, once only Lulu's kitty, sauntered her way and rubbed against Abby's pantleg, a loud purr rattling his chest.

"Where do you want me?" Feeling every bit an outsider, he wasn't sure where he fit here.

Abby strode back and grabbed his bag. "I'll toss it in my office slash guest room. You want a glass of wine?"

"Since when do you drink?"

She arched her brow, like he should ask.

He got it. "Point me in the direction."

She nodded to the kitchen before disappearing into her bedroom.

Jax hunted for the wine in the metallic lacquered cabinets with pewter handles—a far cry from the oak cupboards in their...in his house. The backsplash, a thin striped glass tile, looked like a nightmare to keep clean. But the modern look did go with the rest of her space. He'd never known Abby to like modern. Had that happened after Lulu, or had she always liked it? He had strong preferences, but he didn't remember caring that much about décor.

The only homey thing he found was on the fridge—a dragonfly drawing clung to it by a lighthouse magnet. Jax had a similar picture in his glove compartment. Lulu had gone through an *infatuation with winged creatures* phase.

Abby compartmentalized far too much if that's all that remained of Lulu in this house. His jaw twitched.

Jax finally found a couple of stemless wine glasses and filled them with chardonnay. In the living room, Abby had curled into an overstuffed chair that Murphy, stretched next to her, blended into.

Abby's black hair, pulled back in a ponytail, reminded him of the first day they'd met at a Blazer's basketball game in Portland. They'd been ordering hot dogs, no less. Now the sight of her dressed in gray sweatpants and a blue sweatshirt, FBI emblazoned across the front, made his stomach flutter. This was the Abby he knew. He handed her the glass.

"Thanks," she said, her hand dropping to Murphy and stroking his head. "So, someone is targeting you."

"It's a possibility," Jax said, inching down to the edge of the gray leather couch.

"A possibility? First your tires. Then Trudy. Now your house. What part of that feels random?"

She was right. But as much as he needed to solve this case, he couldn't let this moment pass. The way things had gone down between them, this might be his only chance to talk with her like this.

"Not to go off subject...exactly," he said. She grimaced. Did she sense what was coming? "But what's happening with us?"

"What do you mean?"

"You were clearly jealous about seeing me with Margot."

"Was not."

"Please."

She lifted her chin and closed her eyes. When she reopened them, she took a long drink of wine. "It threw me off. But I wasn't jealous."

Did those walls ever come down? "Okay. If that's your story." He slid back into the couch.

"That's my story." She took a long drink. "The only thing I admit is that it surprised me. I expected a potential suspect would be brought into the station. Not..." She waved her hand. "...taken to dinner."

Sounded like jealousy to him. He hadn't consciously been hoping for it.

Or maybe he had. Why else had he agreed to have dinner with Margot when he'd only wanted coffee? And why even go down that road? It wasn't exactly protocol. "Like I said, I thought I'd get more info in a casual setting."

"Right, but you haven't said much more about what you found out."

"Because she's not who I want to talk about. You keep dodging the issue and it's important. You haven't come back to counseling. Even when you're there, you don't talk about the stuff that matters."

She looked at her hands. "I do the best I can."

"Do you?"

Her eyes met his. "Yes."

"Because I recall not so long ago you jumping on my ass about being checked out and not dealing with Lulu. I took your advice, and I dug deep. That's why I'm able to function. I'm not perfect, never will be…but I don't see you giving it your all in our sessions."

"It takes time. You can't snap your fingers just because you're feeling more grounded and expect me to follow suit."

"Maybe, but we can only fix *us* if we talk about why we're not together in the first place."

"You know why. You're better now, but how can I trust that you won't drop back into your old ways?"

The comment stung. "How about you? I have reasons not to trust you, as well. Hell, I have reasons not to trust myself. But I'm trying. And I admit my checking out was wrong. But I'm back." He looked at his hands. "We had something, didn't we? Ten years of something. Five of them in pure bliss with Lulu."

She took a drink of wine. "Yeah. We did."

"Did?"

"I don't know what you want from me."

"I want my Abby back." He looked around the room. "I don't even know who she is anymore. Sometimes I see glimpses. Other times, not so much."

She scoffed. "I wondered how long it would take until you said something about my house."

He hadn't wanted to put her on the defensive. "I mean it's nice enough."

"Gee thanks." She cleared her throat. "When I left you, I wanted my life to be different. I didn't want anything to feel like what we had."

He smiled. "So not even you like this stuff?"

"I didn't say that. But what I like most is that it's a new version of me. I had to create that for myself after Lulu. You should have done that too."

There were many things he should have done. Fought harder for his wife. Fought harder not to disconnect. But he was only human, and focusing on breathing to survive took all his effort. "I did my best too, Abby. But I couldn't let her go like you have."

"I haven't let her go."

She had. Lulu's artwork on the fridge hardly counted. He couldn't decide if he was angry at Abby for that—or heartbroken. He didn't want to be the only one keeping their little girl's memory alive. Hadn't she told him a few months ago that he was required to do that? Had that just been angry talk when Abby read that goodbye note?

"I don't have all the answers, Abby. All I know is I love you. I can't say sorry enough for going through my grieving process. I guess the question is whether we still have a shot."

She finished her drink and stood. "I love you, Jax. The problem is, like being surrounded by old furnishings, every time I look at you, I see Lulu. And it breaks me. I have no idea how not to be broken when I see you. You and Lulu had the same eyes. She had your chin. Your laugh."

A lump grew in Jax's throat. Lulu had taken after him—he couldn't fix that. "Only you can decide what you can deal with then. But I see her in you as well."

Abby's chin trembled.

"And despite that, I don't run from you. But emptying your house of Lulu because of the pain...I'll never understand that." His tone held more frustration than he'd intended.

She sighed. "Good night, Jax."

She disappeared into the hall and a moment later a door closed.

Shut out again. They had the same arguments every time they got close to the real stuff. He judged her process. How easy it was for her to move on.

Maybe she had the right idea, but he could never bring himself to not have Lulu in his life in some way.

He stared at his still-full glass of wine, his stomach souring.

In the kitchen, he dumped the glass and washed it down, returning it to the cupboard. He went into Abby's office and turned on the light. Her computer and desk were pushed up against a wall, and a futon had been pulled down to make a full-size bed—a set of sheets and blanket set on top.

But that's not what grabbed his attention. A collage of pictures had been framed on a corkboard above Abby's desk. He drew closer, staring at each one that reflected he and Abby's life together. Some were before when they lived in Portland. At the waterfront, their first apartment, the time he took her to the Space Needle in Seattle. The birth of Lulu. He'd filled the room with flowers and balloons that rainy day in March, and she had several of those with a dried rose pinned near them. And Lulu. So many pictures of their little girl.

A pull in his chest had him drawing in a sharp breath. He'd misjudged her. All along. She hadn't forgotten anything. It was all in a place where she saw it every day.

Maybe he needed to not be so quick to decide things about people. That had cost him in his last case when trying to find a missing girl.

Was it costing him now in finding Terry Chesney and bringing whoever did him harm to justice?

CHAPTER 36

This was the second time she found herself annoyed with Jax in less than twenty-four hours. She'd never invited him into her home since she moved out of theirs, and now she remembered why.

She yanked her toothbrush from the holder and squeezed the toothpaste too hard, pushing out double what she needed. What she'd told him was true. Why she had chosen to make everything about her life different. From every inch inside her home, to where she lived.

Cannon Beach was a haven. The bookstore there had the perfect mix of bestsellers and classics. The sweet smell of pastries wafted through the downtown area when Haystack Rock Bakery was in production mode. They always had a table for her at the Driftwood, and her order of clam chowder and garlic cheese bread followed. Her café latte always waited when they saw her walk in at Monks Coffee, too. She'd created a life in this town where no one knew her pain.

In Misty Pines, living with Jax, she saw their daughter on every street corner, and every time she looked at him. A lot of the time, that was okay. But there were moments, unbearable moments, when it wasn't. The memories of their little girl would flood back, and she couldn't move. He didn't understand her struggle, he was so lost in his own. And she had no energy to make him understand, because he was so quick to have an opinion about her.

She'd spoken of it in her private counseling sessions, yet the idea of sharing that in couple's counseling scared her.

She spit into the sink and cupped water into her mouth. All she wanted was to sleep. Maybe she did owe Jax more. But with Mom needing extra attention, and the demands of her position at the FBI, maybe the time wasn't right for them.

She settled under the bed covers still in her sweats and welcomed the pillow as it hit her head.

Then she remembered.

In all the distraction of Trudy's accident, Jax's house being trashed, her jealousy—yes, jealousy—about Margot, and being dragged into talking about their relationship, she hadn't mentioned the connection to their two cases. She stared at the ceiling. It could wait until morning.

She closed her eyes and flipped to her side. Uncomfortable, she flipped to the other. Then to her stomach. No, it couldn't wait if she didn't want to be up all night. She flung off the covers, marched to her office, and knocked.

When he answered, his face was ashen.

"What's wrong?" she said. "Is it Trudy?" She steeled herself for terrible news.

"I didn't realize…," he said, motioning his head to her collage.

That was it? She let out a breath. "Of course I have pictures, Jax. You aren't the only one who lost her."

"Let's get back to counseling. Let's…"

She could never resist his look. Sad eyes. Desperate to connect. She had walled herself off for so long…but that's not why she'd knocked on his door. She cleared her throat. "I will." She owed him that much. "But we have a connection in our cases that came up that you need to know about."

Jax stood straighter. "What is it?"

"Riley Higgins," she said, heading to the kitchen.

"What's he have to do with your case?" He followed.

She pulled a bottled of water out of the fridge and poured them both a glass. "Apparently he wasn't too happy with Mr. Lilly backing over his motorcycle."

"What motorcycle?" Jax asked.

Abby gave him the rundown of what Olek had found.

"Okay, maddening sure, but what's the proof that he killed him?"

"Calls to Mr. Lilly's house. At least one of them heated, if the neighbor is to be believed. Who unfortunately I'm starting to suspect is about as reliable as my mother."

"Not enough."

"True. Riley knew both victims, however, and was at odds with them."

"That part is compelling."

"Agreed. I'm heading back to chat with the neighbor. Olek has a way with our elderly witness, and we might get more confirmation. Truth is I got the information just before getting the call about Trudy, so…"

"No time to interview Riley yet."

"Correct. But tomorrow after I get my mom settled at her new place, Olek and I…"

"Like hell," Jax said. "Riley's been in the background of my case since the beginning. I intend to be there. I'll meet you at his surf shop."

She nodded. "Fair enough."

"That it?" Jax said.

Those eyes said he wanted more from her. More than she could give. She drained her water in one long drink and set her glass in the sink. "All for now."

CHAPTER 37

By the time Jax rolled out of bed the next morning, the only thing that remained of Abby was the half pot of coffee she left on. No note. She'd always been an early riser, but he suspected she'd hustled to avoid another conversation about their relationship. Or lack of one. Not that he blamed her. They had jobs to do. And he'd probably pushed too hard.

He winced, reflecting back on the night. There was no *probably* about it.

He'd have to rethink his approach if he expected them to find common ground. She'd changed. Time, circumstances, loss—it had changed them both. If he didn't adjust for that, he'd lose his chance. How many would Abby give him? Did he even have one now?

The saying *you can't go back* might be true in their situation. While he didn't want to admit it, law enforcement and a shared history might be the only things that bound them. He hadn't thought about who he was, what he liked, or his interests since Lulu. He'd ceased to exist, only going through the motions. His reality had been scarred with pain and depression for far too long and he'd only started to come back to life. Abby had experienced the same event, but she hadn't let herself dwell there, instead reinventing herself.

Might be about time he did too. Later.

Matt had texted. "Gerard was acting as Terry's agent. No Terry, no deal." So, the corporation had confirmed Gerard's story. Matt followed up with: "Gerard released. Report on the scooter's gas tank is on your desk."

Gerard might be free for the moment, but if it panned out that Terry's death occurred because the scheme to steal from him had simply gone wrong, he'd still be coming back in for conspiracy.

Jax drained the last of his coffee, rinsed the cup, and called a taxi. On the way to the station, he checked in with Frank.

"Any change with our girl?" Jax asked.

"She's stable, and there's no brain swelling," Frank said, his voice weary. "But she's still in and out of consciousness."

The smallest amount of tension eased from Jax's shoulders from the bit of good news. "We take what we can get, right?" But until she was fully awake and talking, he couldn't relax.

"You bet."

"Has the doctor given a prognosis?" Jax said.

"No. But one of your friends stopped by with a bouquet of flowers. According to her, Trudy not being alert is not a reason to be scared yet. The body needs time to heal."

Jax shifted in his seat. What friend of his would dole out medical opinions? His hands tightened on the phone. "Friend...you mean Margot Coleman?"

"Yes. Sweet lady. Knew her stuff."

How did she know Trudy had been admitted there? Unless... "What else did she say?"

"Not much. Just that she'd met Trudy a few times and enjoyed their conversations. Found them, what did she say...refreshing. And she was sorry to hear."

Margot held a different view of her interactions with Trudy than Trudy had reported. Unless *refreshing* meant she didn't sugar coat anything. Cordial or not, his long-time assistant never had been one to hide her feelings—and Trudy didn't think much of Margot Coleman. "Did she say how she heard about Trudy?"

"One of her nurse friends here mentioned it to her."

"Say who?" That person might have some useful insight on Margot.

"She didn't."

And finding that person might be like finding a black grain of sand on a white beach. What would it prove anyway? That theirs was a small coastal community and everyone knew people's business? The nurse community was even smaller and probably talked on the regular. It wouldn't have bothered him so much if he hadn't had a less than friendly parting from Margot last night. Slashed tires. Graffiti on his wall. Trudy in a hospital bed from an accident that could have been connected to what happened at his house.

He stretched his neck. One thing at a time. "This might sound strange," Jax said. "But don't let anyone in the room with Trudy except for close friends and official hospital staff."

Frank cleared his throat. "What aren't you telling me? Your boy, Garrett, he came up to check on me and I told him to get some shut eye. Was that a mistake? He didn't go far. Just said he'd close his eyes in the chapel and be back after he got a bite to eat."

Garrett had put in an all-day shift before the night watch and was directed to go home in the morning. The fact he'd stayed was above and beyond. But Margot must have come through the lobby when he'd stepped away. "No. No. It's all good. There are just a few things brewing on a couple of fronts. I'll feel better when we understand why Trudy was in that crash. Until then, I say we keep her visitor list small."

"Have to watch those storm fronts for sure," Frank said. "You know that Margot woman did say something else. Didn't seem so strange I suppose, but now that you've mentioned some concerns…"

"What's that?"

"I asked about her experience with head injury…specifically, if she thought Trudy would remember what happened."

"And?"

"She said sometimes it was better if people didn't remember things."

The comment could have been innocent enough—no one wanted to relive a trauma repeatedly. But if Margot had been involved in Trudy's accident… tension returned to every muscle in his body. "Thanks for letting me know. No one in the room you personally aren't friends with. Got it?"

"Got it. I'll call you the moment she's back with us."

The taxi pulled into the station's parking lot, and Jax's cruiser was waiting, tires intact. He climbed out of the backseat, determined to get to the bottom of this case. What he didn't look forward to was walking into that station without Trudy at her desk.

But the best he could do, what they all must do, was keep moving. Get the perpetrators behind bars. Keep Misty Pines safe. She wouldn't want it any other way.

Jax pushed open the door and nearly stopped in his tracks. Troy and Dylan Marks occupied two chairs in the waiting room; Dylan looking at his phone, Troy tapping his foot and rubbing his face.

Rachel sat at Trudy's desk, Koa near her feet. Matt was at his desk. His eyes went up in a *holy crap* expression, and then quickly back to the paperwork on his desk.

"Troy," Jax said, bracing himself. "What brings you two out this early in the morning?"

Troy shot out of his chair, yanking Dylan up with him. "Dylan has something to tell you."

This was a first. "I'm listening."

"You have somewhere more private we can talk?" Troy said.

Jax motioned them back to his office and sat at his desk, gesturing at the chairs in front of it. Dylan didn't pry his eyes off his phone until Troy snatched it out of his hands. "Dad."

"We don't have all day. Tell him."

"C'mon, son," Jax said, his voice even. "Let's hear it." He wouldn't push too hard. It spoke volumes that Troy, not Deanna, had brought Dylan down for a conversation. The information must be important. Or it implicated Dylan, and Troy wanted to stay ahead of it. Damage control. Either way, Troy's taut shoulders and clenched jaw meant being here was killing him, and keeping them in their chairs would be a tenuous process.

Dylan cleared his throat. "What would happen if I had those blueprints? You know, the ones you were asking about?"

Jax steepled his fingers. "I'd ask why you lied earlier."

Troy's face reddened, but his focus remained on the wall behind Jax's chair.

"Maybe I'd say it was because I wasn't sure what to do," Dylan said. "Like, I didn't want to be arrested. Bad enough I gave you the gun. I mean, what would you have thought if I'd handed you the prints then too." Boy had a point.

"It wouldn't have looked good, that's true. It's understandable you'd be scared."

Dylan nodded.

Jax did understand. Dylan was a kid. Impulsive, and prone to questionable decisions, but still a kid. "Then I'd say, you're doing the right thing by coming here and coming clean. So how about you start from the beginning?"

Dylan slumped in his chair. "It was Scott's idea. The reason I'm telling you any of this is because that jerk set me up. I was kicking his ass on Call of Duty and then he starts pacing. Looking at his watch. Says he wants to go out and we should take the scooter."

"Did he say specifically to Terry's place?"

"No. But he wanted to go up Bull Mountain. It's a cool ride down from the top, so I agreed. But then my damn scooter fails, and we're stuck."

"You said you felt set up?"

"Because we end up right by Terry's place and Scott starts changing his story."

"How?"

"He wants to go up the driveway and check out the house. I said no at first, but I didn't know what else to do. If I called my dad, he'd freak."

Troy's face remained red and stoic.

"Anyway, I said fine because maybe Terry would give us a ride home. Except then Scott starts talking about looking for some blueprints because he's doing a friend a favor."

Jax knew which friend. "Did he say who?"

"No."

"How about why he wanted them in the first place?"

"Just that they were valuable, and he had a plan to make more money on the deal."

Scott had a side hustle? Apparently, he was no one's friend. "Did he say how he planned to accomplish that?"

"At first, I was so annoyed I stopped listening to him. I mean, I heard screams up there. I was scared. And I don't know…" Dylan's eyes darted.

"Think," Jax said, leaning into the desk. "Who were those prints for? How was he planning to make more money?"

"I—"

"Now, Jax." Troy came to life. "If my boy says he doesn't know…"

Jax took a beat. Straightened in the chair. "But you do know, Dylan. Don't you?"

Dylan wouldn't meet Jax's eye.

"You said 'at first.' You must have started listening again at some point?"

Silence hung in the room. Jax grabbed the report on the scooter's gas tank and perused it to give Dylan a minute to do the right thing. As suspected, metal shavings had turned up inside the tank, put there by a screwdriver or pick-like tool.

Jax sat back in his chair. "Well, you're right about being set up. Your scooter didn't fail. The gas tank was punctured. Did Scott have any time alone with the scooter?"

Dylan drew in a loud breath. "Before we started the videogame he went out to the garage. Are you sure about the puncture?"

"Got the report. If the tank was full of gas…"

"It was," Troy said.

"Then getting to the top of Bull Mountain would have been about enough time to have a slow leak empty it out."

Dylan shook his head, his face hardening. "He planned it all. From the minute I let him in the house."

Finding out a friend was no friend was a hard lesson at any age. "Who was he getting those prints for?"

"Some guy named Brandon. But then Scott figured if they were so valuable, he could get more so he worked out a deal with someone else."

"Did Brandon have any idea this double-cross was happening?"

"I doubt it."

"Who did Scott approach to work a better deal?"

"No idea. He only said he'd give me some of the extra cash and make it worth my while. But to be honest, when we got back, I told him to eff off. I didn't want any part of it. He took off in Terry's VW all mad."

"And yet you had the prints?"

Dylan shrugged. "I always liked Terry and the more I thought about it, I wanted no part of screwing with him. I played along with Scott as he rambled on, but when I got out, I slid the prints out with my coat and ran inside. He didn't even notice."

The boy had done the right thing. Not only had he made sure the gun was out of Scott's possession, he'd taken the prints. Maybe to save Scott from himself, or to save his own ass. Regardless, even if Troy had every right to be mad, there was hope for Dylan Marks.

"Are you sure you don't know who he intended to sell them to?"

"You'd have to ask Scott. He made the calls."

"And I have the blueprints in the car," Troy said.

Jax walked them out and took possession of the blueprints. When he came back inside, he handed them to Rachel to check into evidence. "Did you stay in that chair all night?"

"No, boss. Koa needed a run and dinner. But I told you I'm here for you. I meant it."

Koa sauntered over and rubbed her head against his leg. Jax rested a hand on her head and gave her a few strokes down the ears. He could get use to this.

"Matt," Jax said. "Get Scott Heffernan into the interrogation room."

Matt jumped up and disappeared into the hall.

"Where's Brody?" Jax said to Rachel.

"On patrol. Matt worked all night, so Brody took his shift."

Jax nodded, approving. They were a team. They were working together, even without Jax's direction. Rachel had taken lead to make it happen.

He started back toward his office, then stopped. What was he waiting for in hiring her? He didn't need Jameson's permission, and it might never come anyway. She was doing a great job. He sniffed. In honor of Trudy, he'd take her advice. He turned back to Rachel. "You still like it here?"

She nodded. "Can't see myself anywhere else."

"Then you're officially hired."

Her face broke into a grin. "You won't regret it."

Koa barked and he left Rachel smiling and answering an incoming call.

For once, he'd made a couple of women in his life happy. Right now, he'd take it. Because there'd be a price to pay with his old friend and partner once he found out.

CHAPTER 38

"You can quit the bullshit any time," Jax said, having asked Scott Heffernan for the facts twice now. Their conversation had started with his Miranda rights.

"I already told you I'm fine talking to you, but I swear, I've told you nothing but the truth," Scott said.

Jax leaned forward. "Except you're not, and I'll list it out for you since you don't realize how much I know."

Scott shifted.

"First, you stole Terry Chesney's VW vehicle from his driveway."

"How do—?"

Jax lifted his index finger to shush him. "I'm only getting started."

Scott slumped in the chair.

"Second, you punctured the scooter's gas tank—I assume so Dylan would be stuck with you and you could implicate him in your crime."

"That's not true."

"Which part? Because your prints are all over the tank."

"I drove the scooter up the hill."

"Not according to Dylan."

"He might've forgot."

"That doesn't explain your prints underneath the tank. Or the fact that Dylan left you in the garage by yourself and that you specifically asked to take the scooter out."

Scott frowned. "Fine—but you make it sound like I planned for Dylan to take the fall. Dylan's a good guy. We're friends."

What did Scott do to people he didn't like? "But you needed his help, and you weren't above sabotage to get it, correct?"

Scott shrugged. "Mostly just for lookout. I mean I'd been up that hill earlier, and..."

"And you heard something? Saw something?" Brandon had said as much.

Scott gave a slight nod.

"What did you see at that earlier time?"

"Someone running."

"Terry?"

"Maybe. It was dark."

"So, if you were so scared, why'd you go back?"

He looked away.

"Let me make it easy on you, Scott. I already know that Brandon was paying you to steal some blueprints left in Terry's van."

Scott began flicking his thumb with his index finger as if it might ignite like a lighter.

A nervous tick, maybe. Jax had hit on something. "And I know that the blueprints were for Terry's brother, Gerard. So just confirm that's why you returned. How hard is that?"

Scott shifted back in his chair, his cuffs scraping the table. "Dylan tell you that too?"

Jax shrugged. "You tell me."

"He's really mad at me if he told you that."

"Setting people up tends to upset them."

"I didn't. But he wouldn't have helped otherwise."

Jax'd had shitty friends in his past—plenty in fact—but Scott was a new low. "Enlighten me then because it seems like a lot of trouble to go to for a little help. And why would you need it? You can steal a few prints yourself, can't you?"

"I was scared."

"We've established that. Of what? Or is it who?"

"Like I said, I'd gone to get them the first time and the place was open and

I saw someone running. It freaked me out. And then I called…" He stopped, clenching his jaw shut.

"Brandon, yes, I know. But that wasn't who you planned to sell the prints to."

"Look, I needed some cash. Brandon said he'd pay me part of his cut, which wasn't much. I mean, someone going to this much trouble means there's money tied to those prints. I watch stuff on TV." Another Brandon. If he started reciting *CSI* or *Hawaii Five-0* Jax might not be able to stop an eye roll. "It's always the guy taking the risks that gets nothing," Scott said. "And I wasn't gonna be that guy. Since I knew what those prints were for, I knew someone who might pay more for them."

"Who'd you call, Scott? It'll go much better for you if you start talking."

Scott jutted his chin.

"Or you can take the fall by yourself. Happy to start compiling the stack of charges immediately."

Scott seemed to think about that for a second and huffed. "Riley Higgins."

Bingo. "And he promised to pay you double?"

"Triple. And a couple of boards. My pick."

"Couldn't say no to that."

"No way."

Jax scooted back in his chair. "What I don't understand is how after all this, you didn't end up with the blueprints in your possession."

Scott scowled. "Yeah, talk about a setup. Dylan took them. Bet he didn't tell you that part."

Jax's face remained blank.

"Whatever, but I wanted them back. That's why I stuck around. Dylan's gate was closed, and he ignored my calls making me to stay an extra day. He can act innocent, but he's the one that doubled-crossed me." *Or he made sure he had an insurance policy.* "I'd waited long enough and was heading back to climb his fence. If I'd have just left the day before, your deputies would have never pulled me over. And I wouldn't be in this mess."

Finally, some truth. "I appreciate your honesty, Scott." Jax stood.

Scott lifted his hands from the table, the cuffs scraping the wood. "You letting me out of these now then? I'm good to go?"

Jax gave the kid a sad smile. He'd obviously not been watching the right television shows. "Sorry, son. Not this time."

"I didn't kill anyone."

"Maybe not. But theft is a crime."

Scott's face wrinkled in confusion. "So like, you're actually charging me? Does that mean I need a lawyer?"

"That would be best."

Jax returned to his office and shot off a text to Abby to coordinate timing to interrogate Riley Higgins, who he could now tie squarely to his own case. He could bring Riley in, but other than hearsay, there was no physical evidence tying him to the scene.

Shaun Evans had mentioned that he knew Higgins and didn't think much of his unwillingness to help with troubled youth. Shaun might be worth chatting with about Riley. If nothing else, he might have more insight into the man's character, and whether surfing was really the only skillset Riley had decided to mentor.

As he waited for Abby's response, he dropped into his chair. Normally, he had a rush of satisfaction when elements started to come together on a case, but he felt bad for Scott. He was a dumb kid that didn't have anyone, unlike Dylan who had Troy and Deanna to keep him in line. Shaun seemed like a good guy, but one person couldn't fix them all, no matter how much he tried.

Scott had been used on some level, and that bothered him. He might be a willing participant, based on his history, but what he also knew was greed on several people's parts had contributed. Brandon, Gerard, Riley Higgins: they were all part of that greed. But was one of them Terry's killer?

He couldn't dismiss Margot Coleman either.

He had the unsettling sense that he'd missed something. But what?

CHAPTER 39

Jax hadn't heard back from Abby after sending his text an hour earlier. Dora's transfer into her new digs must have her preoccupied, but his call to the hospital to confirm his ex-mother-in-law had in fact been moved went nowhere. They'd be happy to check—if he had a room number and was a family member.

Even identifying himself as the Misty Pines Sheriff hadn't gotten him closer. Olek had taken his duty to protect Dora seriously, putting in some safeguards. Jax wouldn't fault him or Abby for that.

But since he hadn't heard from Abby, she might also have hit a snag. Might even need an assist. He'd go to the hospital and check. If nothing else, being there for Abby might score him some points with her. After last night, he could use some on his side of the scoreboard.

Jax headed for the sixth floor where Abby had mentioned Dora was staying. He scanned the hall. A chair stationed outside one of the rooms down the hall was empty. No Abby or even Olek.

At the half-moon nurse's station Jax approached a nurse in pink scrubs, a metal patient chart tucked under her arm. "Excuse me, ma'am. I understood Dora Michaels was being transferred today. Did that happen?"

The harried nurse tapped the keys on the desk computer and her eyes scanned the monitor. "Her room wasn't ready at the receiving location. Transfer was delayed until later today. You family?"

"I am." Was. She didn't need details and the honest approach hadn't worked for him earlier. "Was her daughter by recently?"

She glanced at her watch as a light on a room behind her flashed and chimed. "Yes. She and her partner left together a few hours ago. I need to go. But Ms. Michaels is in 612. She was a little confused this morning when her daughter was here, but she's been doing great since lunch. I'm sure she'd enjoy the company."

"I…" He hadn't expected to speak with Dora. Abby might not appreciate it. More immediate, Dora might not be happy to see him. But if she was lucid, he couldn't pass up the opportunity. She might recall how she'd come across Terry's surfboard buckle, or who had been in her room or out on that beach. It could be the break he needed. And there'd been many times during his marriage where they'd gotten along well.

Abby would ask the questions if she was here, he was certain of that. And the way Dora could drift in and out of reality, he might not have another chance.

He nodded. "Thank you."

He tapped on 612's doorjamb and peeked in. Dora, her graying red hair pulled back in a ponytail, her face freshly washed, was elevated in the bed watching TV. *Wheel of Fortune* played on the screen, the sound muted.

"Up for a visitor?" he said with barely a toe inside her room.

Dora broke into a smile. "Jax." She waved him in. "Don't just stand there. Come in."

He resisted checking behind him to see if she was talking to someone else. She had said *Jax*. "Looks like you're feeling better."

"Much. You wouldn't think the food would be an improvement over Stonebridge, but you'd be wrong. The pudding is delightful, and they don't insist on me doing *any* activities."

It couldn't be easy having one's entire life directed. She needed the care, but thriving on independence himself, he couldn't live in that world. He hadn't seen Dora in such high spirits in too long. "Queen for a day."

She smiled. "I guess you could say that." She put a hand to her forehead where a bandage covered the gash Jax had seen just a couple of days ago, her smile fading. "Is Abby with you?"

"She's working." Jax sidled up to the bed, dragging the guest chair in the corner close. Her question could mean she wasn't as lucid as he'd hoped.

Only one way to find out. "Mind if I sit?"

Dora glanced up at the TV. "A chip on your shoulder."

"Excuse me?"

"The answer. As soon as the guy bought the 'O' I figured it out."

Jax glanced at the TV. "Appears you're right." She smiled with satisfaction. He hadn't known Dora to watch game shows, but things changed. People changed. She was distracted and her clarity, if she had it, might be short-lived. "I'm sure Abby has asked you this already, but you know how busy she gets. I was hoping you remembered more about what happened on that beach the night you found the buckle."

"Oh, it was cold." She crossed her arms over her chest, palms resting on her arms. "And I got turned around. Thought I was heading into town. I was craving one of those burgers from Grace's. They do make the best burgers there."

That restaurant had been closed for about a year. But Dora had been at the center for longer. She might not know. "The one smothered in fried onions?" he said.

"Yes, that one. It was Kaveka's favorite."

Kaveka—Abby's father. At least she knew that her husband had passed, a sad reality for both her and Abby. It could be a promising sign, except he'd died before they moved to the area. He and Dora must have visited there though. "They're good. But the beach. You'd found something out there by the log. A belt buckle that you brought back with you to the center."

"Right. Yes." She grabbed a white bag that had been sitting next to her on the end table. She reached in, grabbed a cookie and held it up to Jax. "Want one?"

They looked homemade. And Abby didn't bake. "Where'd you get those?"

"A lovely young woman came by with them early today."

His stomach tightened. "What was her name?"

Dora bit into the cookie, her forehead creased in thought. "I'm not sure. She's a nurse, though. Pretty blonde curls. A sweet face."

What was Margot doing here? "Did Olek speak with her?"

She shook her head, taking another bite, crumbs falling on her chest. "No.

That poor boy needed a rest and some breakfast. She visited right after he'd left."

I bet she did. Perhaps she'd waited for both he and Garrett to leave before swooping in for her visits since Frank had seen her on the fourth floor around the same time.

Jax lifted the bag of cookies from Dora's hand and set it back on the table. Then he slid into the chair, not wanting to alarm Dora. "Well, that was kind of her. Did she say anything special?"

Dora waved her hand. "You know, the usual stuff people say when you're in a hospital bed. Asked how I was feeling. What happened. I told her about getting turned around, and she was so nice to ask questions about what I remembered."

Exactly what he wanted to know. "What did you tell her?"

Dora grimaced, laid her hand with the cookie in her lap. "Just what I said."

"Do you remember who tried to hurt you in your room at the facility?"

Dora shook her head.

"Do you remember how you got that cut on your forehead?"

"No. It was dark in my room so I couldn't tell who came in. At first, I thought it was Bernice. Or that handsome Mr. Casey next door. He has a thing for me." She blushed.

Jax nodded. "I suspected."

"You did? Have you met him? Were you there?"

"I have, and yes." He knew better than to ask if she remembered his presence. She didn't, and it would only frustrate her to think otherwise. "You were preoccupied so you might not have seen me."

"Ah. Well, they wanted what I'd found on the beach. But I wouldn't give it to them."

"Man or woman."

"Not sure. The person didn't speak."

"Then how did you know that's what they wanted?"

"Because I was holding it and they tried to grab it."

"You were laying there holding the buckle?"

"Yes. It's pretty. Have you seen it? I can't find it anywhere. Maybe Abby packed it up with my things. I hope so. It sparkles so nice."

"But it was dark you said?"

"I kept it under my pillow for safekeeping. Those people at the center sometimes take things." Her face twisted in concentration. "But I don't know why I took it out that evening. Maybe I planned to look at it. I don't remember."

"It is nice," he said. Bernice and Mr. Casey were larger people. If she mistook the intruder for one of them, he might be looking at Riley as the perpetrator. Despite Gerard's claims of innocence, he couldn't discount him either. He was tall too. And something didn't make sense. "You said you thought it was your nurse at first, but didn't the individual come through the window? The screen was gone."

Her face reddened in a sheepish grin. "I punched that out a long time ago so I could get out one night. I kept the blinds down so no one saw."

Dora was sneakier than he'd given her credit for. "Then how...?"

"They came in the room through the door, but they hopped out the window after they realized I'd fallen and was hurt."

"You weren't attacked?"

"Oh no. The individual just tried to grab the buckle and I got out of bed and that's when I fell, hitting my head on the side table I guess...now that I'm thinking about it."

That was a whole new take on what happened that night in Dora's room. Regardless of the perpetrator's intention, security was far too lax there if people could waltz in. Abby had the right idea to get Dora out of there and someone regulating those types of facilities would be notified when this was over.

Dora's eyes fixed on the TV set again and she took a bite of cookie.

"Did you tell that nice lady who came with the cookies any of this?" Jax said.

She shook her head. "No. I didn't remember until now." She yawned. "I should have. I thought I recognized her, but I couldn't place her then."

He inched to the edge of the chair. "You remember now?"

"Oh yes. She was on the beach that night."

Margot had been on the beach? "You saw her?"

She nodded.

"What was she doing out there?"

"I have no idea. We didn't talk. In fact, I must have scared her because she ran off when she saw me. But those curls were what I remember. There's no hiding them, even under the stocking cap she wore." Dora smiled. "Abby's hair does that too. So cute. Are you two getting married soon? She sure loves you. Don't know why you're waiting. You're all she talks about."

Hearing how Abby had once felt stopped him. He'd love nothing more than to talk about those times, but Dora was slipping away, and he couldn't risk taking her off the subject. "I need you to think about that beach, Dora. What was Margot doing out there when you saw her?"

"She didn't say."

"Was she near anyone at the beach who appeared hurt?"

"I—I'm not sure."

"Did you get the belt buckle from her?"

Dora glanced at the cookie bag, her face slack. "When are you going to bring Lulu? She loves cookies. Why don't you bring her so I can share these with her?" Realization settled into her face. "You took her away, didn't you? Why would you do that to my Abby?"

A wedge of emotion lodged in his throat.

Dora squeezed the cookie, crumbling it. "Why, Jax?"

It was the illness, but the words dug in like a barb. "I'm sorry, Dora. I didn't mean to."

Her heart monitor shot up, beeps accelerating.

The nurse in pink scrubs marched into the room. "Going to have to ask you to leave," she said. Her stern expression left no room for argument.

"I was just heading out," Jax said.

"Why, Jax?" Dora's voice pleaded.

He walked out the door, his chest tight.

The comforting words of the nurse floated out of the room behind him. "It's okay, Ms. Michaels. Everything's just fine. Let's get you some more pudding. I know how much you like that."

"You can do that?" Dora said, her tone shifting. "You're such a nice girl. Your mother would be proud. Thank you."

The shift from reality to delusion had been like a switch. Although he'd sensed it coming. Abby wouldn't be happy that he'd riled Dora, but it had been worth it to learn that Margot Coleman had been out on that beach the same night as Dora.

Or had it? What did it prove? Dora didn't say Terry was out there being killed. It only proved that Margot enjoyed walking the beach at midnight. The moon had been full. A lot of clouds, but a good wind that night would have kept them moving. And he hadn't pinpointed what time she'd seen Margot. Early morning beachcombers were common in Misty Pines.

In truth, her presence didn't mean anything…there was no smoking gun here. Still, it was worth a conversation with the woman who'd seen them through their darkest days because she'd been showing up far too often in his world—and in this case. Cookies for Dora? Stopping to see Trudy? Nurse or not, she was too entwined. This time he'd make sure she didn't get the wrong impression about their meeting. But it would have to wait. She was likely on a shift, and he had a few more angles to work first.

He stepped into the elevator and hit four. Might as well check on Frank and Trudy to see if there'd been any change since their earlier conversation.

But Abby's text arrived the moment he'd hit the floor. "Heading to Riley's now."

Change of plans. He punched the button for ground and texted Abby back. "Be there in ten."

CHAPTER 40

Jax found Abby and Olek in the backroom of Riley's All About the Waves when he arrived. A young woman, just out of high school, worked the front desk. Her purple-streaked hair, stack of rope bracelets, Fibonacci tattoo revealed by a V-neck, and *what's up* tilt to her chin could have placed her on a warm beach catching waves. A lure to the young surfers who visited the shop, no doubt.

She used that chin to direct Jax to the back room, where Riley literally had his back against the wall: one foot planted against it, arms crossed, body language blaring defensiveness. Olek nodded to Jax when he entered the room.

Abby had taken lead. "You want to tell us that story again and see if it changes this time?"

"I told you the truth. It was no big deal. That guy hit my bike."

"Really?" Abby said, in a tone that Jax had grown familiar with over the years—the one she used to indicate you were full of it. "Because we found out you'd let your own insurance slide, and the repairs were over ten grand."

"Well…"

"And your shop has been struggling, hasn't it? You almost went bankrupt last year."

Riley's foot dropped to the floor. "That's because the mayor in this town added parking tolls to the beach. Parking tolls. You think young people are going to flock there and surf? You think they can afford it? The answer is no way. They head to Misty Pines. Or further south. Where it's free. That son-of-a-bitch nearly killed my business. But that has nothing to do with

225

this Lilly guy you're concerned about."

"We're more than concerned, Mr. Higgins," Olek said. "Mr. Lilly was murdered."

"What? When? How?" Realization appeared in the form of sweat on Riley's brow. "You don't think I had anything to do with that?" His eyes shot to Jax. "You again. Why's he here?" he said to Abby. And back to Jax: "You don't belong here."

Jax kept his expression even. Abby's questions had rattled Riley. Jax's presence had kept the quake going. Riley should be concerned. He'd admitted to financial difficulty. Frustration with people traveling to Misty Pines to surf. Even without the surfboard design angle, he could have other motivation for killing Terry. "We'll have our turn in a minute."

"Do I need a lawyer?"

"You tell us," Abby said. "We're just having a friendly conversation."

Riley scoffed. "You don't sound friendly." He grabbed a stepladder propped against a rack of life vests and plopped onto it. "But I didn't do anything to anyone."

"Except harass Mr. Lilly."

Riley didn't answer at first, perhaps calculating how much they already knew. His shoulders sagged. "I did. I was angry. I admit I called him."

"And threatened him?" Olek said.

"No. He agreed to pay. I was upset he had to do it in four installments. He said he didn't have that kind of money to pay all at once, but he realized he had put me in a bad place on it. We ended the call with him apologizing, and me saying—well, sorry I yelled at him."

Riley didn't seem the sorry type.

"You have any proof of that?" Abby said.

"Sure." Riley rushed to his desk on the other side of the room. The top was littered with paper. He shuffled through one pile, moved it aside, went to another. He needed a Trudy in his life to keep him organized.

Jax glanced at the wall of plaques and trophies on the wall above Riley's head. He wasn't only a champion surfer, he competed and won several skeet shooting competitions, and a few golf tournaments. The man's competitive streak ran deep.

A minute later, Riley whipped up a check stub and marched it back to Abby. "Here's his first payment. I cashed it the day it arrived."

Jax glanced over Abby's shoulder at the date. It had been written a few days before Mr. Lilly had gone missing. And Riley had scrawled the deposit date on it—two days later.

"Did it clear?" Jax said, ignoring Abby's pointed glance at his jumping in. It was a valid question. A check didn't mean payment.

"It did," Riley said. "You want proof of that too?"

"I will," Abby said. "When was he supposed to pay next?"

"Later in the month. So you see, I'd have absolutely no motivation to hurt Mr. Lilly. Unless I didn't want to get paid. And I do." He frowned. "I did."

He had a point there.

Abby knew it too. She nodded. "We'll be in touch." She turned her back on Riley and widened her eyes at Jax. "We'll catch you later."

"We should talk," he said. He wasn't looking forward to Abby's reaction when he told her about his conversation with Dora, but she should be brought up to speed on Margot's activities. Activities Jax hadn't had time to reconcile.

But something wasn't right about the Margot angle. Abby also needed to know that Dora had caused her own injury by falling. Which meant the person who'd entered her room didn't intend to cause her harm. They only wanted the buckle. That image didn't mesh with a cold-blooded killer that took out two men and removed their feet. Were they looking for two perpetrators?

"We'll wait outside."

Jax nodded as she and Olek strode out of the back room. He turned his attention to Riley. "Wish it was as easy when it came to Mr. Chesney," Jax said, although with the connection to Abby's case disintegrating, did he have his man? "You were angry at Terry. You said so yourself just moments ago."

Riley shook his head. "I didn't say anything about Terry. He's a jackass, but I've been mad at the mayor of this town. No one else."

"C'mon. It's public knowledge that Terry stole your thunder back in the day, right? And now he's taking your business."

"And what? You think no one else would open a surf shop in your town? You think eliminating him would matter?"

"Maybe not. But your desperation for money does. What were you willing to do to get those blueprints so you could sell the design?"

Riley slid his tongue across his teeth, his mouth closed. "I don't know what you think you know," he finally said. "But I'll tell you this. I didn't do anything to Terry or his blueprints. But I did get a call. Someone else had a plan. I didn't ask how, why, or where. But this whole night in question about Mr. Chesney, I wasn't available. I have an alibi."

"Really?" Jax utilized the same tone as Abby had. "You failed to mention that when we first spoke."

He huffed. "I didn't want to admit that I drank too much and ended up in the slammer that night."

"When did that call come in then?"

"Before I got drunk." He scoffed. "Maybe it's the reason I got drunk. I offered the caller a bunch of cash if he'd bring me the prints and they turned out legit. But..."

Terry's murder likely occurred at or around eight o'clock in the evening. Scott hadn't made it back until closer to midnight—when Terry was likely already dead. "You need to do better than that."

"Check with the Sea Hag bartender. I started drinking early in the evening and stayed until closing. Then the officer driving by saw me stumbling to my car. It's all in a report with West Shore's finest," he said, his voice bitter. "I'm sure you can check that out, Sheriff."

"Believe that I will," Jax said. "But I wouldn't be so smug. Sounds to me like you put out the hit on Terry and then created an alibi. Why else would Gerard call you at the shop the other day when I stopped by, so concerned they were going to find out?"

Riley blanched. "Did he tell you I did something? Because he's full of shit. He called accusing me of stealing those damn blueprints and telling me the corporation would find out and I might as well give them back to him. But I didn't steal them. That's why I hung up on the son-of-a-bitch."

That lined up almost exactly with Gerard's version.

Riley's jaw tensed. "You know, I'd appreciate it if you'd quit making stuff up to match with your elaborate theories. I did feel guilty. Like maybe it wasn't right to be involved. Contrary to popular belief, I got over losing to Terry. It took a while. But I don't hate the guy. I had no intention of accepting the blueprints. I'd changed my mind. Which ended up not mattering since I never heard from the caller again."

"And that's your story?"

"Yup. Like I said, I heard nada after that, and I was too busy making bail." Riley squared his shoulders. "If that's all, and you don't intend to arrest me, I've answered enough of your questions. I have a shipment coming in and work to do."

As much as he'd like this case to be solved, he didn't have enough to take Riley in. "That's all for now. I'll be in touch."

Riley huffed. "Yeah, you and that FBI chick. Things to look forward to."

Olek and Abby were nowhere in sight when Jax exited the shop. Before he opened his car door, he eyed Abby's card stuck in his wipers. He plucked it off and read the note as he slid into his cruiser. They wanted to check out one more thing before she had to get back to the hospital. She'd catch up with him later.

That works. He certainly didn't mind waiting a bit longer to tell her he'd spoken with Dora alone.

And checking on Riley's whereabouts the night of Terry's disappearance would be easy enough. But if Riley wasn't involved in Terry's murder, he had to go back and look at Scott, who fully admitted to being on the premises at the time. It was Scott who sabotaged Dylan's scooter. Scott that stole Terry's car.

But what was his connection to Lilly? Margot Coleman was a stronger suspect there. But had she murdered Terry and Jonathan? Trashed his place, leaving an ominous message indicating he was next? Run Trudy off the road? Wormed her way into Dora's room?

She was a piece of the puzzle that didn't quite fit. She'd demonstrated anger issues with him...and she'd been connected to both men. But there were factors that made it a hard sell to tie her fully. The archery factor being key. Of course, that could be said about all of his suspects.

What he did have for certain was Scott's admission to being on Terry's property on the night in question and to other dubious activities. A burglary gone wrong happened far too often. But the feet being detached... That was a different level of menace. Did Scott have it in him? There was one man who knew Scott better. Jax had planned to speak with him again anyway about Riley, and he lived in West Shore.

He pulled out Shaun Evan's number and dialed.

CHAPTER 41

Shaun Evans lived in a two-story cedar shake house with peeling white shutters and empty window boxes. The home had been cared for, once. He could tell by the pristine edging of the flower gardens that now contained blackened and long-dead flowers. Various overgrown fruit trees were scattered in the front.

That's where Jax found Shaun. Bundled up in an insulated wool jacket and stocking cap, pruners in hand, a pile of small branches at his feet.

"Was surprised to hear from you," Shaun said, lopping off one of the larger limbs of an old apple tree as Jax approached.

"This the right time to do that?" Jax nodded to the tree, never having spent much time in a yard himself.

"Perfect time. Got to nip those old branches when they're dormant. Catch them when they're sleeping, if you know what I mean."

He did, although it was an odd way to put it. "You have time to sit and chat?"

"I don't." He lopped off another branch. "Need to finish up and then have a few meetings to get to. What did you need?"

"Well, as I mentioned on the phone, was hoping you could tell me a bit more about what you know of Scott Heffernan."

"Told you about all I do know that day at the station."

"But you've been in his life awhile, enough so that when he had a police car on his tail, he called you."

"True enough," Shaun said.

"Have you known him to be violent?"

231

"Scott?"

Jax nodded.

Shaun cut through another thick limb in one motion. Those pruners were sharp. "I haven't. In fact, he never joined us on hunting expeditions."

"You took the boys hunting?"

"You bet. There's a lot of skills to be learned in that activity."

"You didn't find any concern putting guns into the hands of a troubled youth?"

Shaun's mouth turned in a half smile. "I don't invite just anyone to hunt. So, no—no worries."

"You'd mentioned knowing Terry well."

Shaun stepped off the ladder to face Jax. "I did. Good guy. Any more on what happened to him?"

"He's presumed dead under suspicious circumstances."

Shaun frowned. "Son-of-a-bitch. That's awful. Can't imagine anyone who would want to cause him harm…. Wait. Is that why you're asking about Scott?"

Jax nodded. "He now admits to being near Terry's place that night and involved in the theft of some documents."

Shaun shook his head. "I try, but sometimes I can't fix stupid."

Shaun's demeanor had changed a bit from the savior complex he'd presented when they'd first met. "Sounds like Scott didn't have much of a chance."

"Dad was a sperm donor. Single mother tried to find a replacement, but more like a revolving door of men. Abuse. Drugs. Scott took the brunt. Same story with a lot of them. But I had hopes for Scott when he got involved in the program. For a while it looked like he'd make better decisions. But if what you say is true, he didn't."

He'd hoped that for Scott too. "Clearly."

Shaun's face softened. "I apologize. I probably sound callous. It's frustration. You do this for as long as I have and you see enough success stories, you think you can change them all. Then when you can't, well… I take it personally. I like Scott. But he stopped listening to me after he got out of high school. And I can't help people who refuse to listen."

Jax nodded. Sometimes caring too much was hardest on the one who cared. "You'd mentioned knowing Riley Higgins. Did you actually work with him in the program at some point? I was unclear on that."

"No. Couldn't convince him. Which was a shame. Aside from his surfboard making skills, he's good with a bow and I thought the kids could get something out of that skillset. But he had no interest in sharing his knowledge. In his experience, 'once a thug, always a thug.' Wasn't willing to give the kids a chance."

Good with a bow? "As in bow and arrow?"

"Yeah. He competed at one point. After surfing, I think. Or at the same time. I don't recall exactly. But Riley likes to compete." He wiped the back of his arm across his forehead. "Let me put that another way. He likes to win."

Jax had seen proof of that on Riley's wall just an hour ago. He'd like to hear more about it. He rubbed his hands together, trying to warm them in the cool mist, and nodded towards the house. "Sure you don't have time to sit and chat?"

"I don't. And my house is under renovation. Barely have running water. It's nothing but dust. That's why I'm out here." He flashed a smile.

"Renovation can be a real pain. What are you having done?"

Shaun stepped back on the ladder and cleared his throat. "Would rather not say. Don't need the permit police hounding me."

"I'm not that kind of enforcement."

"Let's just say I needed a change."

Jax could understand that. "You married?"

"Nope. Never have been." He tensed.

Jax nodded, noting the shift. *No one likes to be alone.* Or was it something else? "Anything else you can tell me about Riley? Have you seen him recently?"

"You know as much as I do now. I don't think much of him. He's all about Riley. It's been at least a year since I ran into him, maybe more, and that's not long enough in my book." He lopped another limb. "Probably should get moving, Sheriff. Need to drag these to the back into a burn pile. Unless you want me to put you to work?"

"Appreciate your time," Jax said.

Scott didn't seem any more likely to have committed murder than when Jax arrived, but Riley's bow and arrow skills were an interesting twist. Confirming his whereabouts had just moved up in priority.

Jax pulled away from the curb as Shaun dragged his pile of limbs into the backyard through a gate that had been propped open with a kid's red Big Wheel. Shaun said he wasn't married. That didn't mean he didn't have children. A bad breakup could account for his short answer and attitude shift. *It certainly had that effect on me.*

Jax's cell rang. "Rachel," he answered. "What you got?"

"Two things. That report on Margot Coleman's hunting license just came through. She has a current bow hunting permit and has held one for several years. But it doesn't show the Misty Pines address. It's a West Shore location."

The license information made the hairs on the back of his neck stand up. The West Shore location made sense though. She'd lived there prior to moving to Misty Pines. The circumstantial evidence had begun to stack against Margot. Waiting until she was off work might not be an option.

But since he was in the area, it also might benefit him to meet some of her former neighbors ahead of that conversation. See what their perception was of Margot. "What's her former address?"

"2372 North Shore Drive."

He glanced up. He was on North Shore Drive. "Say again?"

"2372 North…"

"Shit." He'd just driven away from that very address. "What else?"

"Frank just called. Trudy's awake."

CHAPTER 42

When Abby and Olek arrived at Ms. Baka's house, a white moving pod sat out on the street, in front of Mr. Lilly's former residence.

That took her no time. "Motivated landlord," Abby said.

"Definitely all business," Olek said. "Wish I had more of my grandmother's treats to sweeten her."

"Ah, your charming personality will do that."

His brow arched. "Do I detect sarcasm?"

"None," Abby said, amused he'd taken it that way. "I told you before and meant it. You have a way with people. You're good."

"Appreciate that," he said, his hand on the door. "Do I have a way with you?"

Abby smiled. "I let you ride with me, don't I?"

"You do." He flashed a grin.

"There you go." Although they both knew she didn't have much choice. She liked Olek though. He was good company. More importantly, he was a smart investigator.

"So maybe we could resume our dinner that was interrupted the other night," he said.

He didn't say *interrupted when that ex-husband of yours called,* but she'd read his displeasure at the time, and it hadn't lessened. "Trudy is important to both of us. He had every right to call."

"But you're divorced."

That part was true. "In answer to your question, dinner works. We need to keep mulling over this case until it makes sense anyway. And if you're like Jax, you work well on a full stomach."

He frowned. "Jax, yeah." He cleared his throat. "I was actually thinking we could make our dinner more of a date."

Her cheeks warmed. She'd sensed his attraction, but she hadn't given him any signals that the sentiment was returned. Had she? "I'm not ready to date anyone." That wasn't the point. "Even if I were, I don't date my partners."

"Then I'll get reassigned."

"Where do you think you'd go in our small unit?"

He shrugged.

Other than being transferred out of the area, there wouldn't be any place. "Look, I don't want you upending your career on my account. You're a nice guy and..."

"Damn, stab me in the heart."

"Nice guy is a bad thing?"

"It's what women say to let a guy down easy."

She smiled again. At least he was being good-natured about it. "Let's just keep it business, okay? We make a good team. No sense complicating things. Can you live with that?"

"Always the rational one." He smirked. "You're probably right, so yes. I suppose I can do that. But your ex-husband was one stupid guy to let you go."

She hadn't spoken in depth about her and Jax's relationship. Olek had no idea that letting her go was the last thing Jax had wanted. And even now...

A woman came out of Jonathan Lilly's duplex, dressed in sweats and carrying a box. Abby recognized her immediately. "Let's go." She hopped out of the car. "Tabitha."

Jonathan's sister raised her hand in recognition. "Abby. You've been on my mind today. I was just getting the last of Johnny's stuff out of his place. Anything new in the investigation?"

Abby held back a grimace. West Shore police had notified Tabitha of Jonathan's body being found, but she should have contacted her sooner, personally, to give her details. They didn't have a lot more information to share, except for confirmation that Mr. Lilly had died by an injury to his heart—caused by an arrow, as the coroner had suspected. "No. Just here circling back on a few things with Ms. Baka, but if you've got a second...?"

"Sure," she said as Abby and Olek approached the house. "Come in."

They followed Tabitha into the empty living room, where she set the box at her feet.

Other than imprints on the carpet where furniture had once been, no other signs of Mr. Lilly having been here remained. The heat had been turned off and a chill filled the air. Abby pulled her jacket a little tighter. "I'm sorry there wasn't a better outcome."

The mask of coping slid from Tabitha's face, leaving grief. Tears glistened in the corners of her eyes. "Still no leads though on who did that to my brother?"

"We're working on a couple, but do you remember a Margot Coleman at the hospital?"

"Oh sure. Margot. She was Angel's nurse." Margot had said as much. "You don't think...?"

"We're exploring all angles." With the Riley Higgins lead not as viable as it originally appeared, she had to look at everything again. And Margot was an individual who knew both victims. "That's who your brother had sent the flowers to."

"Are you sure?"

"Positive. Ms. Coleman confirmed it." Barely.

Tabitha wrapped her arms around herself. "I can't believe that would have been the happy place he spoke to me about though. That wouldn't make sense."

"What makes you say that?"

"Because I found a note this morning when I was clearing Jonathan's drawers. More like a copy of a note, but it was written to Margot saying he was sorry if she misconstrued his intentions. He was only interested in being friends." She bent down and withdrew a sheet of paper from the box. "I saved it in case it was important."

"Are you talking about that young woman who brought him cookies?" The elderly voice came from behind them.

"Ms. Baka," Olek said, striding to her. "How are you today?"

"Good." Snuggled in her arms was the little yapper dog that had kept them on their toes their first visit. "Well, are you?"

"Yes. We believe they used to run together," Olek said.

"That's true. For a while."

"What happened?" Abby said.

"Don't know. But she came by the day before he went missing and brought him those goodies."

"Were there signs of a problem then?"

"I don't eavesdrop mind you, but…"

"Go on," Olek said.

"Well, he kept insisting he didn't want them. That he was sorry if she misread things. I think he'd sent her flowers and she rushed right over. A woman can be too forward, you know. I think she must have read something into it that he didn't intend."

"He'd written in the card accompanying the flowers that he could hardly wait for the weekend," Abby said. Hard to misconstrue that.

"Running," Tabitha said. "He always went for long runs on the weekend. He'd probably invited her to join him, and he used to be the captain of his college cross country team. He's a motivator. The flowers might have been sent to be encouraging. It was just his way."

"Was there anything more after that?" Abby asked Ms. Baka.

"I told you everything when you were here last. Except…"

"Yes?" Abby said, her voice and body tense. People holding out information wore on her. It was part of the gig, but still. She glanced at her watch. She needed to get back to Dora soon. Her room would be ready for the transfer. Her jaw set. It wasn't Ms. Baka that had her edgy. It was the nagging feeling that she couldn't get anything right.

"Well, I hadn't thought anything of it at the time. As I said before, I was rushing out for a bunko party and there are cats everywhere around this neighborhood."

"Cats?" Abby said.

"I guess I mean kids. That's more likely since they like to play pranks on us neighbors."

"What is it, Ms. Baka?" Olek stepped closer, taking on a gentler tone. He probably sensed Abby's annoyance. Abby had been right that he had a way with people; Ms. Baka smiled. "It's okay that you forgot to mention anything to us. It's easy to forget. But what do you remember now?"

She sighed. "It will be easier if I show you. It's around back."

Whatever it was, it had Ms. Baka concerned enough that she was trying to excuse not telling them. "Show us the way. Please, Ms. Baka," Abby said.

She nodded and they followed the older woman outside around the duplex. "I found it at Jonathan's front door. I didn't want him to come home and step on it. That would be horrible."

Ms. Baka set the dog down and opened the gate. "That's why I brought the whole thing back here." The little dog ran into the enclosed space, and they circled around the house to the backdoor. "You see, I wasn't sure what to do with it otherwise. When I got home from Bunko, I'd intended to ask him to dispose of it. But he never came back and…"

Abby's tension tightened into a sharp jab as she saw it.

A decomposing rat, nailed through the heart to a *WELCOME* mat, its two front feet cut off.

CHAPTER 43

Trudy was wide awake and shooing off a nurse trying to take her vitals when Jax walked through her hospital door. He'd received a call from Frank right after he'd hung up with Rachel. Their girl was back and feisty, as he was witnessing himself. Hopefully her memory was back with her attitude.

Still, before he'd rushed over, he'd run back to Shaun Evans' place. He wanted to know the connection between him and Margot Coleman. But both Shaun and his truck were gone, and the house locked.

"Give the young woman a break," Jax said, unable to keep the smile off his face. A bump on the head hadn't slowed Trudy down. She'd be just fine.

Trudy scowled at the nurse. "I don't know how many times someone needs to check a temperature, that's all. I told her I was fine. Everyone needs to quit fussing."

"Ma'am, I…" The nurse sighed and gave Jax a pleading look. "I'll come back." As she brushed past Jax, she lifted her eyes. "Maybe you can talk her down?" she whispered.

Jax winked. He'd do his best. "No guarantees."

"Don't know why everyone is scurrying around me like I'm the pope or something," Trudy said.

"Where's Frank?" Jax said. He had a way with Trudy that no one else did.

"I sent him to the cafeteria to find me a decent cup of coffee and a bagel. I'm starving. It feels like I haven't eaten in days."

Twenty-one hours, twenty-three minutes to be exact. At least since he'd gotten that call that Trudy had been in an accident. But who was counting? "I'm sure." He sat on the edge of her bed. "You up for some questions?"

"You bet. Although let me just tell you what I saw, because it'll probably answer everything already milling in that head of yours."

"Shoot."

She took a cup of ice chips from the tray in front of her and shook one into her mouth with a rustle. "I spent the afternoon baking, and I'd already swung by the church. Since you were close, I told Frank I'd planned to bring you some goodies, too. So, I did."

"What did you see when you arrived?"

"Nothing. At first. I got out of my car and took the basket of banana bread to your door. I set it down. That's when I heard something."

"What?"

"Cursing is what I thought at first. Or someone upset. But there were no cars in your driveway or even in front of your house, except mine. There was a white work van at the edge of the street, but not close enough to make me think they were at your home. I figured the noise must be from a TV you left on."

He hadn't. He rarely watched TV. "Is that when you saw someone in the house?"

"No. Your blinds were drawn. But I heard the cussing again and that's when I noticed your door ajar. I pushed it open and about had a heart attack right there when I saw that damn Margot Coleman standing in your living room staring at your desecrated wall."

"You caught her trashing my place?"

"No, but I'm assuming she's who did it. She was standing there inspecting her handiwork."

"But you said she was upset. Or cursing?"

Trudy started to nod, and then winced. "Yes. That's what it sounded like. But when I saw her, she saw me, and stopped whatever she'd been doing."

Even with his years in law enforcement, finding someone in his house would have rattled him. He could only imagine what had raced through Trudy's mind. He laid his hand on her forearm and detected a slight tremble. "What happened next?"

"I told her to skedaddle, but she just stared at the wall and said, 'it's not what you think.' 'Of course,' I said, and then told her it would be best if she didn't try to figure out what I was thinking and told her again to move her butt out of there."

That sounded like the Trudy he knew. "Did she go?"

Trudy shook her head. "And I didn't plan to stay and argue. I just told her fine, stay, and that you and your deputies would personally show her out. Or to a jail cell, but I didn't say that part out loud."

Margot would have assumed that, though. "But you didn't call right then?"

She frowned. "I didn't?"

"No. Because I heard your accident, Trudy." Even now the panic in Trudy's voice, followed by that bending of metal, had his nerves pinging.

She looked away. "That's right. I dialed, but I didn't hit send. I didn't have time. I'd just gotten into my car and she started to rush toward me." She waved her hand. "It all happened so fast. And I won't admit this to anyone else... but I was scared that she might try to attack me. It's why I didn't keep arguing with her. I'd seen what she'd done to your house, and someone angry enough to do that..." The tremble in Trudy's arms travelled to her hands. She balled them in fists and tucked them under the covers.

"You did the right thing, Trudy. You did the smart thing."

She gave him a faint smile.

"After that, I'm assuming you drove away without further incident?"

"Yes. I figured my best bet was to head to the station. If you weren't there, at least Matt or Garrett would be. Brody. Even Rachel. Anyone. I didn't care who. But a few minutes into my drive, a car came up from behind and started crowding me."

"Margot?"

"I don't know. Like I said, I didn't see the car she arrived at your house in, and I couldn't see anything but bright lights in my rearview. That's when I panicked." She looked away and cleared her throat. "I hit the gas pedal thinking I could outrun the person, but instead I drove past the street that would have taken me to the station. Next thing I knew I was heading out toward the country."

"On Rifle Road?"

She nodded.

It had to be Margot. That would explain how she knew Trudy was at the hospital, and why she'd be asking about her. She would have been concerned that Trudy would remember. "Do you recall anything else about that white van you saw?"

"No. Other than it had no windows. Like I said, it was parked at the end of the road. From your house I couldn't make anything out about it. And when I left, guess I wasn't paying attention."

Jax nodded. There couldn't be too many white work vans in Misty Pines, although no one on his suspect list drove one. Unless it was rented?

"I'm sorry. Guess I wouldn't make as good a detective as you thought," she said, snapping him back.

"You did just fine, Trudy. I'd still make you a detective over half the ones I know."

She smiled.

"But out on that road," Jax said. "That car that was following you, it hit you, didn't it?"

"It did. I lost my phone, and then I lost control. Next thing I know, I've got Frank hovering over me, all kinds of worry on his face that I haven't seen since my appendix was removed thirty years ago, and a slew of doctors and nurses poking and prodding at me." She jutted her chin out. "It's enough to make this old woman nuts."

Jax squeezed her arm. "Take advantage. Because the station is a mess without you. I've got Rachel manning the phones, and I've barely even seen my crew. Everyone is on auto pilot, but without you as the glue, it feels like we're scattered in the wind."

Trudy withdrew her hand from under the covers and rested it on Jax's. "I miss all of you too." She winked. "But don't you worry. As soon as they'll let me out of here..."

"Don't count on it," Frank said from the doorway. "I'm not letting them release you until you're running on all cylinders."

"You and your car analogies, Frank," Trudy said. "But don't you tell me..."

His hand whipped up in a stop gesture. "For once in your life you'll listen to me on this. You took a good hit to that hard head of yours, and I'm not taking any chances. You hear me?"

She melted into the bed and let out a huff.

Frank, the Trudy tamer.

Jax suppressed a smile as he stood. "I'll leave you two alone." He bent over and pecked Trudy on the cheek. "I've got some work to do."

Trudy blushed and shooed him away. "You go get that Margot Coleman, but you and the boys…and Rachel… you all be careful."

"Roger that."

For the second time Jax hit the elevator. Only he didn't have time to check on Dora.

Instead, he called Brody. "I want a search of Misty Pines and all surrounding areas for a white cargo van, checking rentals as well. Could have some frontend damage. And gather the team."

"Good to hear from you, boss. On it."

His next text went to Abby. "New development. Call ASAP."

She hadn't called by the time he'd hit the road back to Misty Pines.

CHAPTER 44

The day had gotten away from Abby. They'd bagged and secured the evidence of the impaled rat from Ms. Baka's home, and she'd dropped off Olek at the West Shore bureau office. Now, she rushed to get Dora from the hospital, who she should have had at the memory care home over an hour ago.

In her hurry to get back, she'd kept her conversation with Olek in the car brief, but specific.

"Margot Coleman?" Olek said. "You think so?"

"I believe it's possible. I want you to find out everything there is to know about her. She's a link in Jax's case as well."

Jax had tried to tell her, and she'd shut him down. But they could have that one percent chance of a serial killer in their area. Why she had the need to prove to Jax, to the world, that all her theories were right, was something to consider. Losing Lulu had shaken her confidence. It might be how she maintained some level of control. To avoid those feelings of failure or that she was wrong.

Like the ones that had come up around moving her mother to yet another care center. But she'd ticked off the reasons why it was necessary a million times—she couldn't care for her mother by herself. Maybe returning to counseling wasn't among Jax's worst ideas either.

"Let's meet up for coffee later and see what you've found," she'd said to Olek. Dinner might not be the best idea after their earlier conversation, and it'd be late by the time she got Dora settled anyway.

"You got it. In the meantime, I'll start with a search on Ms. Coleman's former places of residence. Could be there are some similar cases that are unsolved in those areas. More victims."

An unsettling thought by itself. "And former relationships. Didn't she say she was divorced?" She couldn't remember.

"You said she'd mentioned having broken up with someone. Maybe there's some information there too."

"Agreed."

She called the nurse's station on Dora's floor and let them know she was on her way. En route, her thoughts turned back to the case. There was no denying a theme. Both men had been murdered by arrows. The heart scrawled on Jax's wall, after Margot and his supposed "non-date." Now a poor rodent. Even a rat deserved better. Clearly, it was a warning.

Had Jonathan missed it before he went out for a run? Or had he ignored it, thinking he'd deal with it later? Did he know what was coming?

Had Abby received a warning like that, she would have called the police and canceled her run. But maybe he didn't realize how far gone Margot was. Their argument had only been the day before. Things had seemed okay right up until that point, enough that he'd sent her flowers. Most people didn't think a miscommunication would get them murdered.

Then again, he'd kept a copy of the note he sent to Margot. Perhaps he had sensed something.

The question was, Why would Margot snap? She'd lost her own child not that long ago. Had she not dealt with her grief around that? Jax hadn't for a long time, withdrawing and becoming a shell of the man she remembered.

In Margot's case, perhaps she coped by inserting herself into her patient's families. But there was no outrunning grief, and all its various stages. Maybe the attempt had pushed her over the edge.

Either that, or she used her grief as an excuse to control other people's lives.

Jax had tried outrunning his pain once and failed—he'd almost taken his life because of it. If Margot was outrunning hers, there'd been no signs of suicidal thoughts. Her rage had been turned outward instead. Did she blame her former partner for the death of their son?

246

If so, she might be killing him repeatedly, only in the form of men she felt had rejected her.

Her stomach tightened.

Jax.

She needed to warn him about what she'd found at Ms. Baka's place. She pulled around the hospital and spotted Jax's patrol car driving away. He must have been there checking on Trudy. She was too far away to get his attention. She'd park and then call him.

The lot was nearly full when Abby entered the parking structure, but she found a narrow space between two large trucks and squeezed the sedan in. She'd go up, fill out the myriad of paperwork necessary to release Dora, then run back down to retrieve the car and pick up her mom out front.

Before getting out, she tried Jax. The call didn't ring through. She waited a minute. Tried again. She shifted in her seat and looked around. The parking lot was all concrete and ten stories of building sat above her. Reception would be an issue.

She'd text him instead. Once she got into the building, it would likely send the minute a signal became available.

Margot Coleman is a problem. Watch yourself. Heading to my mom now. Let's meet tonight for a game plan. xoxo.

Where'd that come from? She backed over it, then typed it again. *Xo.*

No. Wanting him to be safe didn't mean she wanted to start over. Or did it? It had been nice having him at the house last night. And she'd made comments to Olek that she wasn't ready to date. She and Jax had had good times. The memories of how he hadn't wanted her to leave drifted in.

Then she remembered how irritated she'd gotten when he accused her of not keeping Lulu alive in her home. She backed out the *Xo.*

Call when you can. Urgent.

She hit send and placed her hand on the doorhandle.

A white cargo van pulled behind her, blocking her vehicle in. No good. She waited a beat. The driver might be waiting for another stall to open. She glanced out at the line of cars. No taillights to indicate a vehicle intended to leave. The lot was devoid of people.

She couldn't see the driver, but she waved her hand above her head: *Get moving.* Which they didn't. Maybe they had car issues.

She got out. "Going to need you to find another place to park." She raised her voice loud enough that unless they had the radio blasting, the driver would understand.

Still no response.

Guess she could go upstairs and take care of her mom first. If the van was there when she got back, deal with it then.

But she didn't like not getting a response. The back of her neck started to tingle.

Unsure of what the driver's story was, she put her hand on her waist, close to her gun. She stood to the side and rapped on the darkened window. "Excuse me. I'm Agent Kanekoa with the FBI. Please move your car to an appropriate parking spot."

The window started to roll down and she stepped back, glancing at the side view mirror to see inside. It was cracked, partially crumbled away. She couldn't make out who was in the vehicle.

She flicked her gaze back to the window and caught a blast of burning liquid square in the eyes.

She gasped and staggered backwards, her butt hitting the trunk of her own car. Her eyes clamped closed. *Run.* She started toward the elevator bays—her training directed her to get away from these vehicles—but without sight, she had no idea where to go.

Before she could figure it out someone grabbed her from behind, started dragging her backwards. Another blast of spray, and she couldn't breathe. She dug back anyway. Stomped her attacker's foot. Elbowed. Hit ribs. Turned and sent a random thrust upward with the heel of her hand. She connected with a face. Enough to cause a grunt.

But another shot of mace sent her reeling. Her attacker took her down, slammed her head to the concrete. Fastened zip ties around her hands and feet while she lay there stunned. Then they yanked her from the ground, threw her over their shoulder, and tossed her in the van.

As she lay writhing in pain, her only thought was, *Who will tell my mother?*

CHAPTER 45

Jax hit the New Youngs Bay Bridge that connected West Shore to Misty Pines, among other coastal towns along the 101. Thoughts on next moves in the case flipped like an old-fashioned Rolodex in his mind. He had his crew working different angles, one being that white cargo van that Trudy had seen at the edge of his street. It might mean nothing, or everything. The individual—Margot?—who'd left him a message on the wall of his house had to have gotten there somehow.

And there was the arrow. If they got lucky, the sporting goods shop would have a list of purchasers. But all this info would take time to gather. Being spread thin didn't help. Normally Trudy would hustle information on the phone. Instead, he'd needed one of his deputies to do her job. And somewhere in there, they all had to eat and sleep and handle the rest of whatever else arose in the daily life of Misty Pines.

But he wouldn't complain—not with Trudy awake and talking. They were getting through. He couldn't ask for more.

The drive gave him a moment to think about other angles as well. Like the fact that Margot's former address had been the same as Shaun Evans'. That had been a surprise, and those were never good in a case.

Shaun had never married—his tone had been adamant on that fact. Margot had said she'd had a recent break up. Neither had mentioned their involvement with each other to him—did that mean anything? Not necessarily. Either way, based on the timing and the children's toys in Shaun's backyard, it looked like the son Margot lost to cancer had been Shaun's as well.

Shaun and Margot's lives ran parallel to Abby's and his, although the death of their son had been more recent. It spoke volumes as to why Shaun's house had looked neglected. Loss could also have contributed to Margot's odd and obsessive behavior.

With Shaun's background, it also made sense that Margot had a hunting license. Shaun had made it a point to mention Riley's abilities with a bow and arrow. Did Shaun suspect something? Was it a diversion and Shaun had the same skill? Had he taught Margot, or did she pick up the ability later?

Maybe she'd taken an interest because of Shaun's youth program. Perhaps she'd been involved with that as well...she'd said right from the beginning the coast and forest called her name which was why she'd moved to Misty Pines in the first place.

But that was supposition. He'd ask these direct questions to Margot for real answers.

As he cleared the bridge, he veered to the right onto the road leading to Misty Pines. His phone rang—Jameson.

He could avoid his former partner for a bit longer. But evading conversations never made them easier to deal with. Besides, he should be the one to tell Jameson of his decision to hire Rachel before he heard it elsewhere. Unless he'd already heard and that's why he was calling.

Jax hit the green *ANSWER* button flashing on his phone. "Hey, Buddy."

"Oh, is that what we are?" Jameson said, his tone a notch below chilly.

So much for delivering the news first. "Rachel call you?"

"She did. But that's not why I'm calling you. Because you and I at this point have little to talk about."

There'd been a few times over their years as partners when Jameson had been miffed at Jax. More recently, when Jax had iced him out of his life after Lulu died. He hated that hiring Rachel had caused a fresh rift. "Look, Rachel is more than qualified to be a deputy of Misty Pines. Like it or not, she wants the job. And I need a good deputy." She might not stay forever, but until she decided to move elsewhere, he'd take full advantage.

"Despite what I said? No, despite what I *asked*? As a friend by the way. As a favor."

Maybe Jax had hired Rachel *because* of Jameson's unreasonable ask—his unacceptable reasons. No. That wasn't true. Jax had meant every word out of his mouth. Rachel's qualifications made her the best fit. He'd promised to be objective, and he had been.

"I figure you'd understand after my last situation that having someone with investigative experience and that I could trust with my life was high priority. Ever think maybe you're the son-of-a-bitch on this one?"

"You and Grace seem to be singing the same tune on that."

"Always liked Grace best." That usually got a response. This time, silence hung between them. Jax cleared his throat. "You said you weren't calling for that anyway. What's up?"

Jameson huffed. "Rachel needed an assist about some arrow involved in your case."

At least he hadn't shut out his daughter. He could live with Jameson's anger—Rachel shouldn't have to pay that price. "You know something about arrows?"

"Not much, but apparently the sporting goods store that sells this particular arrow is in Portland. She figured it would be easiest for me to check it out and lean on them if they argued."

"See, she's smart. She didn't ask me about doing that. Like I said…"

"Damn straight. You're lucky to have her. Anyway, it took a bit for the store manager to get through the rewards program—that's how they track history on their merchandise—but he eventually managed to get a list of purchasers of that item."

Jax flicked his blinker and swung right onto Main, leading to the station. "Happen to see a Margot Coleman on that list?"

"Sounds familiar. The arrow's more popular than you'd think though, and it's also specialized and a bit pricy. Not one you'd use for target practice."

"Any of those arrows purchased in the last couple of months?"

"As soon as last month, I believe. But there's something else."

"Yeah?"

"That arrow is also known as the Queen. It's used specifically for hunters who shoot bows under fifty-five pounds. Meaning smaller people, often women, because it's easier for them to manage."

But would it have the same range? "They didn't happen to mention distance on that?"

"No. But Rachel's been doing the research so she'll have more for you."

Jax parked in his designated spot. "Appreciate the assist."

"Did it for Rachel."

"Good enough for me."

Jameson clicked off before Jax could say goodbye. They'd have to agree to disagree.

Inside, Matt manned the phones, and Brody and Rachel were at Brody's desk perusing what Jax assumed was the list Jameson had sent over.

"Just got off the phone with your dad," Jax said to Rachel. "Good thinking on that."

"Thanks. And I did a little more digging. You mentioned early on that you thought the shot would've had to have been taken a couple of hundred yards out, and then you decided closer to a hundred yards for accuracy. But those arrows, based on weight and bow draw of course, would be most accurate in the fifty-yard range."

"Good to know," he said, liking how she had answers to questions he hadn't even asked yet.

"Anything on the white cargo van?" He headed to the conference room, Brody and Rachel following, and took a seat at the head of the table. His deputies pulled out chairs from the sides.

Matt strode in wearing Trudy's headset. "I don't know how Trudy does it. I hope she's coming back soon."

Jax chuckled. "Frazzled?"

"A bit."

"She makes it look easy, but she'll be back in no time." They hadn't broached that subject—Frank might insist she retire. She was long past that age. But he hoped she'd be back. He relied on her. They all did. "I spoke with her earlier anyway. Feisty and full of fire."

Brody smiled. "Just the way we like her."

True that. "Anyway—the white van?"

Brody had brought in a file folder with him. "There doesn't appear to be any white cargo vans that have been rented in the past week, but I started a search of vehicles owned by all the people connected one way or another with this case and bingo."

"Bingo?"

"Yup. There is a 2018 Ford white cargo van registered to All About the Waves."

Jax's jaw twitched. "Riley Higgins?"

"Yeah, but it's not that simple. Appears the van was reported stolen last night."

Riley hadn't mentioned that. But why would he? Jax had been there interviewing him as a potential suspect. There'd be no reason to disclose the stolen vehicle at that point. But had it actually been stolen? Or was Riley covering his tracks?

"Sounds like another visit to Mr. Higgins is in order. Matt, call West Shore and see if we can get a confirmation that he was arrested for DUI on the night Chesney disappeared."

"Will do." Matt hustled out of the room.

Jax's phone lit up. He didn't recognize the number. "Sheriff Turner."

"Mr. Turner, this is Agatha from HomeTouch Memory Center."

He scooted to the edge of his chair. Abby hadn't mentioned the name of Dora's new home, but HomeTouch must be it. "Yes, Agatha. What can I do for you?"

"Normally we wouldn't bother an emergency contact, but Ms. Michaels was supposed to be here a couple hours ago now and we haven't seen her."

Emergency contact? He took the call into the hallway. "Does that mean you've already tried to call her daughter?"

"Yes, sir. Several times. She's not answering. We thought perhaps you'd heard from Ms. Kanekoa or knew what was happening."

"I saw her earlier in the day, but haven't spoken to her since. Did you call the hospital?"

"Yes. Ms. Kanekoa had called to let the staff know she was on her way so they could have her mother ready. She said she'd be up to fill out the necessary release papers. Ms. Michaels has been waiting for some time now. Ms. Kanekoa is not answering their calls either."

Jax rubbed his forehead, trying to stave off a tension headache. "I'll see if I can find something out and call you back when I know."

"Thank you, sir."

He disconnected and immediately tried Abby's number. It went straight to voicemail. Something had happened. Abby wouldn't leave Dora waiting.

Rachel joined Jax in the hall. "What's wrong, boss? You look like you saw a ghost."

"Abby's missing."

CHAPTER 46

Jax dug around on his desk to find a business card he'd put—where the hell was it?—somewhere. He moved a few files before he found it in his top drawer; he must've tossed it there after returning from Stonebridge the night Dora had been hurt in her room.

He punched in the listed cell number and waited for Abby's partner, Olek Lasko, to answer. He barely let him get his name out when he did.

"Olek, this is Jax."

"Jax? Turner?"

"Yeah. Abby with you?"

"No. Why?"

"When did you last see her?"

"She dropped me off at our West Shore office and went to pick up her mom. That must have been…" He paused. "Gosh, over an hour ago now. We're supposed to meet up for coffee later tonight to talk about the case."

West Shore wasn't so big, or traffic so bad, that it would take an hour to get anywhere in that city. "Do me a favor?"

"Sure—as long as you fill me in on what the problem is."

"Her phone might not be working, or she might be having car trouble. All I know is I got a call from the new memory center that she never showed with Dora. And the hospital said she never came for her."

"Which would not be like her," Olek said.

"No, it wouldn't. If you'd check out the route to the hospital or the grounds—"

"I'm ten minutes away. Hold tight and I'll be back in touch."

Jax disconnected and jumped out of his chair, heading for the kitchen. Ten minutes. He glanced at his watch and at the sink, letting the water run cold. Bending over the basin, he splashed water on his face.

Being an FBI agent had its sketchy moments, and yet he'd never worried about Abby to a large extent. She was always smart—smarter than he'd ever been—and took care of herself. And FBI, while not devoid of risk, didn't have that daily interaction with the public that boiled down to continuous threats to their lives. Pulling a vehicle over for speeding could be the last thing an officer ever did. Domestic disputes turned ugly fast.

But while Abby hadn't been missing for hours, it was still out of her norm. And nothing short of a problem would make Abby not be there for her mother.

The click of nails on the floor came from behind him. Jax yanked a paper towel from the holder and dried his face, then looked down to find Koa leaning against his leg.

He bent down, coming nose to nose with Rachel's black lab. Jax looked into her brown eyes and caressed her head. "I'm fine, girl. But thanks."

Rachel appeared in the doorway. "She sensed you."

"From the other room?"

"I told you she was good at search and rescue."

Jax stood, his hand remaining on her head. "That you did. Anything on Riley yet?"

"Matt just confirmed Mr. Higgins spent the entire night in custody. I also went ahead and called his shop and confirmed that he's there now and they close at six."

Jax nodded. Until he knew where Abby was, Riley dropped to second priority.

"How'd the conversation go with my dad?" Rachel asked.

"As well as could be expected. He didn't want me to hire you. I was surprised you'd broken the news to him already. Half expected I'd do that."

She shrugged. "I thought you might think that and I'm not running from my dad on this. Better it come from me."

It was her story to tell, not his. "Did your conversation go any better than mine?"

"Probably not. But I love Brittany and I see how you and Abby dance around your feelings. I don't want that for me and Brit. I'm announcing it loud and proud, even if it rankles my pop."

"He still wanting to convert you?"

She attempted a smile. "Yeah, well, as we talked about, it might take more time to get him to understand that this is who I am. Whether he does or not is on him. I'm willing to at least try. But as far as coming aboard here, I'm excited to be on the team."

"I haven't had time to bring them up to speed yet."

"I took care of that." She winked.

Jax arched an eyebrow.

"Don't worry. They weren't surprised. Even Garrett congratulated me."

"Garrett's a good guy and a good deputy."

"They all are."

She was right about that. He'd relied on his team to keep the department running during this case and they'd performed flawlessly. But things were changing here. Commissioner Marks would owe him after this case. Jax could have taken Dylan in a couple of times but hadn't. Sure, Troy had also done him a solid by forcing Dylan to come clean, but all the same, Troy's desires for expansion could start with the sheriff's department.

He glanced at his watch. Six minutes.

"I'm sure Abby's fine. Maybe her cell battery died."

That idea had come and gone in his mind. Abby didn't let things like that happen. "I'm sure she's fine, too." Koa leaned in closer. He'd read that dogs came equipped with a keen sixth sense. Koa had erased any doubt he might've had on the subject. He stroked her ears. "You want to tell her I'll be okay? No sense in the two of us worrying here."

Rachel clicked her tongue. Koa hesitated a beat before she trotted to her side, did a half-turn, and rested on her haunches next to Rachel's shin. Her dark, knowing eyes never left Jax.

It was a little unnerving to have his mental health cared about so deeply. Oh hell. Her attention was helping. "Come here, girl."

Koa looked up at Rachel, who nodded, and resumed her position at Jax's feet. "What do you think the odds are that that van was actually stolen from Riley Higgins?" If they were to be a successful team, he'd need to lean on her for her opinions.

"Fifty-fifty. Seems like a good diversion tactic. The guys and I were talking, and they agreed. He didn't mention it when you saw him?"

Jax shook his head. "Which is why I'm thinking it might have been stolen. Seems like being pre-emptive would have been smart if he had something else in mind."

"Makes sense."

Jax held his cell a little tighter. Three more minutes. *Hurry up, Olek.* Not knowing, being out of control, wondering—the combination gnawed away at his remaining nerves.

The phone vibrated in his hand, startling him. "Turner here."

"Sheriff, it's Gerard Chesney."

Not the call he wanted. "Yes, Mr. Chesney. What do you need?"

"It's more what I think you need to see."

Jax glanced at his watch again. Two more minutes. "What's that?"

"I decided to go through Terry's stuff. Couldn't bring myself to leave, and well, it needed to be done anyway."

"Yes, Mr. Chesney. I'm sorry to rush you but I'm expecting another call."

"Yeah, right. Remember when I told you Terry had said that varmints had been bothering him, but not the animal kind?"

"Yes, I remember that." Where was Olek?

"Well, I'm texting you a picture I found on his phone. It's not good. Riley Higgins might have been playing some sick game with my brother… But honestly, I'm not even sure he did this."

"What is—?" Jax's phone vibrated. Olek. "I need to go. Send that picture."

"On its way."

Jax clicked over. "What you got?"

"Route there was clear so I went straight to the hospital. Abby's car is still in the parking lot," Olek said, sounding winded.

"She made it that far. Good." A small flicker of good news. No car accident.

Maybe reception had been the issue. She might be upstairs right now. But the knot in his stomach said it wouldn't be that easy.

"She did, but there's something else."

"Out with it."

"Her phone was under a neighboring car and the screen was cracked."

Broken and not with her. Only one way that would have occurred and that's if Abby had been taken. That stomach knot twisted tighter. "Check the security footage?"

"Already on it and I've notified the Bureau. But Jax, security said not thirty minutes ago a visitor had come in and complained that they'd nearly been run over by a white van on its way out of the parking structure. Driver didn't stop, just sped out of here like they were on fire. And there was some damage to the front end."

Heat crept up Jax's face. "As soon as you got something on that footage—"

"I'll be back in touch," Olek said. "I also just sent you a picture we took at Mr. Lilly's house a couple hours ago. Abby tried to send you a message earlier that failed, so I know she'd want you to be brought up to date. Bottom line, she believes Margot Coleman is dangerous."

His phone dinged with Olek's incoming text and Jax immediately clicked on it. The image of a rat missing two feet, nailed through the heart to a WELCOME mat. His stomach turned in on itself. "What's this?"

"It was left on our victim's doorstep the day he disappeared. Neighbor had moved it thinking she was doing a good deed and then failed to remember it during our initial interview."

"Jesus. And Abby believes Margot left it?"

"It's a theory."

Jax concurred. It was a good one, and the message couldn't be clearer. It also lined up with the other messages throughout this entire case. Jax no longer believed they were dealing with a jaded businessman.

They had a serial killer on their hands. Someone whose own heart might have been pierced straight through from—what? Life? Maybe. A relationship gone bad? More likely. He wasn't a profiler, but it didn't take one to know that rage and emotion could drive these actions.

He already sensed that the white van seen in the hospital's parking structure and on his street were one and the same. The person inside must be their perpetrator. But could Margot have overtaken Abby? Killed Terry leaving little trace? Killed Mr. Lilly? She was a hunter, which took skill…and strength to haul out the kills. Whoever it was, he prayed the cameras would ID the sick individual they were dealing with.

The front door slammed open and Jax heard voices rising from the reception area.

"If you don't do something about it, I will," a man said.

Jax didn't recognize the voice as he marched down the hall. People should know better than to burst into a sheriff's office.

"What's going on here?" Jax said, his eyes landing on the old man he'd met days before.

"It's Mr. McDonald," Matt said.

"He knows who I am," McDonald said. "He stopped me and my old boy, Hank, on our way home the other day. I told you then, I'm telling you again. Those kids on my street are going to get us law-abiding citizens killed if you don't do something about them. I was nearly run off the road not twenty minutes ago."

Jax drew in a breath. Everything was hitting the fan at once, but he didn't have time to deal with reckless teenagers right now. "Calm down Mr. McDonald. Brody here will take your report and we'll—"

"I will not calm down." The man's face reddened. "And I'm certainly not going to sit around and waste my time while your flunky scribbles some notes, and you do nothing about them. That van nearly ran me off the road."

Jax stopped cold. "Van? What kind of van?"

"What difference does it make?"

"Think, Mr. McDonald," Jax said.

He huffed. "If I had to venture a guess, I suppose someone might use it for work. White. No windows."

"Did you get a look at the driver?"

He looked away. "No. Hank dropped his ball on the floorboard, and I'd leaned over to get it for him so I didn't get a good look at that maniac." He stared at Jax. "But don't you go thinking it's my fault. I was on my side of the line."

"Where was the van headed?"

"How am I supposed to know? I didn't follow it."

"Who else lives up past your place?" Brody said.

Jax knew exactly who lived above him.

McDonald sniffed. "Not a lot up further 'cept for that new woman who just moved in. Nothing but a nuisance, always trying to be friendly."

"Thank you for coming in, Mr. McDonald," Jax said. "We'll take care of it, I assure you."

The old man sniffed again and left, slamming the door behind him.

Jax pulled his keys from his pocket. "Matt, you stay here and be our point of contact. Rachel and Koa, with me. Brody, pick up Garrett. We'll reconvene at the bottom of the Coleman property."

He could wait for Olek and have the FBI back him up. Abby was a federal agent. They had the resources. They had manpower.

But that would take time—time Abby might not have.

"Margot Coleman?" Rachel said.

He nodded. While he didn't have confirmation of who was driving that van, they were headed in the direction of Margot Coleman's place. After what Olek had shared, he had to go with the assumption that she might be driving.

Jax couldn't imagine a scenario in which she could've taken Abby. Unless... A wave of nausea rolled through him. Unless she'd already made the kill shot with her arrow before removing Abby's body.

No. Olek hadn't mentioned blood. There would have been blood.

But the messages of the broken heart... It made sense that Margot's grief over her lost child had consumed her—turned her. Who he hadn't had time to check on was Shaun Evans. He'd like to know where he was right now.

CHAPTER 47

Abby had participated in numerous abduction drills over the years with the Bureau. How the she'd let herself get drawn in and taken, was something she'd have to dissect later. Right now her head pounded, breathing seemed to set her sinuses ablaze, and her eyes stung like they were getting pricked by a thousand needles, but she had to shut that all out.

She had to figure a way out of this mess.

Her training was all she had.

She knew how to negotiate. *Personalize yourself.* "My name's Abby. I was at the hospital to pick up my mother who was waiting for me. She's elderly." She waited. Nothing. "What's your name?" Silence. "Did I upset you when I asked you to move your van? It was not my intention."

The driver still didn't respond.

"I haven't seen your face so I can't identify you. You can just drop me off and drive away."

Although she'd hunt this asshole down if it was the last thing she did.

It would help to understand who she'd be hunting. Whoever it was, the reason had to be connected to the Lilly case. Which meant it was likely connected to Jax's homicide investigation as well. Her abductor was not a large person. She flicked through the small list of suspects. Riley Higgins maybe. The attacker's arms had felt bulky, so not Margot Coleman. Terry's brother? They hadn't established that he knew Lilly. The kid who'd been involved with Dylan. Scott. She didn't know if Jax still had him in custody.

Olek had been looking into Margot's past relationships—information he would have shared with her over coffee tonight.

262

So he'd realize then that she was missing. Jax might realize sooner…but if not them, Mom. She'd put up a fuss if she had to wait too long. There were some things in her life that Abby could depend on. Mom's impatience was one of them.

But Abby didn't have her phone. It had gotten knocked out of her hand during the attack. So even if they discovered her missing, they wouldn't be able to track her.

She pushed through the sinking feeling of being on her own and tried a couple more times to start a conversation. With no response, she focused on listening to where they were going. She recognized the woosh of wind against the van as they crossed the New Youngs Bay Bridge. The vehicle veered right shortly after crossing. Misty Pines perhaps? She lost track after that. She only knew they were climbing, and as she rolled to the left, then the right, they were clearly on a curvy road.

With the number of hills and trails throughout the coastal range, she could be anywhere. Her chest tightened. Even if Olek or Jax figured out she was missing, how would they ever find her?

The van went up a bumpy road, then rolled to a stop. The driver hopped out, covered in head-to-toe camo, but otherwise she couldn't discern anything recognizable or noteworthy. She readied herself for one of the doors to open. She'd put up a fight. She wouldn't make this easy for him.

Instead she heard voices. Low, angry. Accusing. "What were you thinking?"

She strained to listen over her ragged breath and crashing heart, but she couldn't make out anything else about the speaker. Her head was fuzzy, still pounding from the blow she'd taken.

A door slammed. A moment later, a scream.

Piercing.

Definitely female.

Not good. Abby might not have much time. She inched herself into a sitting position against the van's side. With her hands still behind her, she drew her knees close enough to press her pant legs against her eyes, wiping away as much of the residual spray and tears as possible.

Blinking several times to clear her sight, she got a better visual of her situation. She couldn't open the van from the inside here, but if she could crawl through the front, she could get out the driver's door. The passenger side of the van faced the house, and she couldn't risk being seen.

She shuffled on her knees to the front, unsteady. Being upright sent a wave of dizziness through her, followed by nausea. The smack her head took on the concrete must have left her with a mild concussion.

She peered through the passenger window and refocused. They were parked in front of a brown cabin. A lump formed in her throat. It looked like the pictures she'd pulled up of Margot Coleman's place. Abby hadn't told Jax that she'd done more digging on her or that he was right about her being messed up.

But a woman had just screamed. Had it been Margot? Or had Abby been too quick to dismiss the possibility that it was Margot who abducted her? Camo coats were thick and bulky.

She didn't have any time to analyze it. She stumbled to one knee, then shifted her hip onto the driver's side. Her back now to the door, she gripped the handle and lifted, easing the door open. She swung her body out and slid onto her trembling legs.

She eased the door partially closed, not wanting the sound to echo, and crouched by the front tire. The long driveway behind her would lead to the road. But they were up on Bull Mountain, and it would be a long open trek down before she could reach help.

The forest loomed straight ahead.

A crash came from inside, followed by more yelling.

She dropped to her knees. Whichever way she chose, she wouldn't get far with her hands tied. Her first tactical class had gone over the technique of getting out of zip ties. No matter what the instructor said, or the various videos they'd been forced to watch, the move wasn't as easy when your hands were strapped behind you. It would hurt. She knew that from the few times she'd practiced it. But pain was better than death.

Using her butt as a wedge, she slammed her hands down against her body. The plastic dug in, forcing a small yip to escape her mouth.

She froze, afraid she'd been heard, listening for footsteps or an opening door.

Instead, more yelling and crashing came from inside the house.

Gritting her teeth, she tried again. Nothing. Tears formed in her eyes from the plastic ripping into the meat and bone of her wrists. Pure refusal to fail rushed through her. The third time, she whipped her hands against her, triggering a razor-sharp jolt to her shoulder—but the tie popped, and her hands flew free.

She found a rock in the driveway and dug it into the locking mechanism of the tie to free her feet.

The house had grown quiet. Out of time. She had to move.

The ominous forest ahead sent a skitter of fear through her, but at least its vastness guaranteed a place to hide.

Staying low, she crept into the trees. Once she was far enough in, she took off running.

CHAPTER 48

En route with Rachel and Koa, Jax called Shaun Evans. Any insight he might offer on Margot could be helpful. He didn't answer.

Next he called Margot, and left her a careful message. She didn't know what he knew.

"Margot, Sheriff... Jax here. I didn't like the way we left off at the restaurant, and I'd like a do-over. How about a cup of coffee? Give me a call."

He set his phone near the gear shift.

"You think Margot could have Abby?" Rachel said.

"I'm not sure. I've run through a few scenarios, none of them good. They all involve taking Abby by surprise." Not an easy feat. Abby was seasoned. Professional. Always wary. But even the best of them could get distracted, miss something right in front of them. He'd been guilty of that himself.

Was he missing something now? Gerard's text. Had it come through? "Will you check my phone? Gerard Chesney was going through Terry's things and found a photo of something disturbing. He was supposed to have sent me a picture of it. But Olek's call distracted me."

Rachel grabbed Jax's phone swiped up. Within a few seconds she said, "Whoa."

"What is it?"

"A photo of a rat with a knife through its heart."

"You must be looking at what Olek sent."

She swiped right and then left. "No. This one is from Gerard. Although it's similar to the one Abby's partner sent."

Jax frowned and glanced over. Sure enough, the picture was of a knifed rat lying next to a sheet of paper. "What's the note say?"

"'I won't tell you again,'" Rachel said.

That could mean too many things. But something about the image bothered him. "Is that a leather handle on that knife?"

Rachel's eyes narrowed as she widened the image. "Yeah. Kind of weathered. Knife looks like a Ka-Bar. Saw one similar in my dad's stuff once when I was a kid." She zoomed in further. "The initials near the hilt are USMC."

USMC? Jax glanced at the photo again, then focused on the road as it wound up Bull Mountain. "US Marine Corps."

"Yep," Rachel said.

Shit. Shaun Evans had been wearing a similarly engraved knife on his belt that first day. They'd found no signs of that knife in Terry's possessions. Had the person issuing the threat come back for it? Might explain the tools on the garage floor that night. And where was the knife now? Had he been looking at the wrong person all along?

Margot hadn't called by the time they reached the base of her property. He and Rachel hopped out of the rig and joined the team. Brody and Garret pulled in behind them minutes later.

They had no line of sight to Margot's house, but the white cargo van was parked straight ahead, about a hundred yards, next to a line of towering firs. Several downed birch trees had been pulled across the drive. They couldn't pull in even if they wanted to. But it also meant that whoever had driven that van had no intention of trying to leave, at least not down Bull Mountain Road.

"Rachel, I'll have you walk the perimeter for any exit points and then stand guard at the end of the property."

"Yes, sir," she said.

"Brody, I'll have you stationed halfway up, close to that log. If things go south, you make quick work getting the word to Rachel." Jax didn't wait for confirmation. He knew Brody would like to be in the thick of it. Rachel would too. But they were a small team. Everyone had to be somewhere.

"Garrett, you're with me."

"I'm ready," Garrett said. He went to the back of Jax's rig and started pulling out bulletproof vests, handing them to the team.

There was a time when vests were optional in this small town. Jax would have to rethink that for the future. Times had changed.

In this instance, guns might not be at play since arrows seemed to be the weapon of choice. But the vest would give some protection from an arrow. Better to make sure they kept their eyes open and ears perked so that they didn't have to test it.

His phone buzzed with a text. Olek again. "No visual on the driver's identity, but they were wearing camouflage."

"Call Olek back," he directed Rachel. "Let him know where we are. This thing goes sideways, it won't hurt to have the FBI on their way."

"Got it. Let's not need them," she said.

"Sounds good to me."

He motioned Garrett and Brody over and they began their walk up the driveway, silent but for the crunch of gravel underfoot, mist expelled with every breath. They left Brody at the halfway point and approached the two-story house with their hands on their gun holsters.

The house sat on a ravine and had a clear shot down the mountain. He circled his finger in the air, an indicator to Garrett to cover the back.

Garrett, expression solemn and eyes focused, gave a tight nod and disappeared behind the cabin, drawing his gun.

Jax drew his and approached the house, watching for movement from the four windows. Not even a curtain stirred. The dead calm around him left only the pounding of his heartbeat in his ears.

He climbed the two steps to the front door and tried the handle. It turned. He stepped to the side and pushed it open. Waited.

Nothing.

"Sheriff Turner here. Margot, are you inside?"

Silence.

"Shaun?"

Still nothing.

He almost yelled out Abby's name. But if she were in the house, she'd be making noise. He didn't let his mind drift to the possibility that she couldn't.

He strained to listen. A small thump. Upstairs?

He wasn't sure. He stepped inside and inspected the living room. A lamp base had toppled off the end table, leaving its shade on the sofa. Papers and books were scattered on the floor. Area rugs flipped up at the edges. A struggle had taken place here.

Another thump.

He fought the impulse to race up the stairs. It could be a trap. He cleared each room downstairs first. All empty. Garrett was stationed at the back, watching every angle. Jax tapped on the glass and gave the signal that he was headed upstairs.

Garrett gave another curt nod. His young deputy was running on pure adrenaline. They both were.

Jax ascended the stairs sideways, eyes pinned upward for a potential ambush, ears straining to hear the slightest movement. He was only met with more silence.

He found most of the doors on the upper level open. He secured those rooms, then approached the single closed door at the end of the hall. He drew in a breath and stood to the side. Tried the handle. Locked.

Another thump. This time, muffled sounds followed. "Abby?" he said.

Enough. He took one step back and gave a single sharp kick, slamming the door open. But it wasn't Abby he found bound and gagged, tears streaking her face.

It was Margot.

CHAPTER 49

Jax pulled Margot off the floor and eased off the duct tape from over her mouth.

Margot sucked in air and shook her head. "That son-of-a-bitch. I'll kill him."

He guided Margot to a chair. "Who are you talking about? Shaun Evans?"

"Yes, of course. He's my ex."

Jax's thoughts spun at how he'd missed the clues that Shaun was a killer. Except the arrow found at Chesney's scene was designed for a woman. And his slashed tires at the diner after Margot stormed out...although Shaun had shown up there that night too.

But he'd sort that out later. Abby was still in danger. "What happened?" Jax said. "Where's Abby?"

"I'm not sure," she said, holding up her bound hands to Jax.

He'd been duped before. "Not until I know more."

Margot huffed. "You're wasting time. Abby got away, but she won't get far with Shaun on her trail."

Away? "When? What makes you think that?"

"I—" She closed her eyes, maybe trying to rein in her emotions at being tied and gagged.

"Now, Margot! What's going on?

"Shaun told me he had Abby in the van, and I tried to get her. But we argued. Then he said he needed a place to hide her for a while and he went outside."

Shaun's actions made no sense. Abby wasn't even working this case. "Why would he take her?"

"He changed after our Joey died." She swallowed hard like something bitter had filled her mouth. "He walked away from me. From us. He was a good man before that, but something about losing our son..."

"What about Abby?"

"I tried to keep an eye on him," Margot said, seeming not to hear Jax. "But then I started dating. And it was like he wouldn't let me go. I sensed he was threatening the men I was interested in because one minute they wanted to see me, then they stopped calling. Like they were afraid of me. I moved here to start over. Thinking it would be different."

"Margot. Please. Focus." He didn't have time for this.

"I don't know why he took Abby, other than he made some comment that if you were after me, he'd take Abby from you."

Any attraction had been on Margot's part, but she could have been feeding lies to Shaun. She had seemed jealous of Abby. Shaun could have his own reasons too, though. The sick game getting played right now could have any combination of rules.

Margot turned red. "Look, I tried to help Abby. When he came back inside, he was angrier than I'd ever seen him because she'd gotten away. I told him the best thing he could do was turn himself in and he freaked out that I'd turn him in. That's when he chased me up the stairs and locked me in this room. I assume he's trying to find her."

Which was what Jax needed to be doing.

He barked into his radio. "Rachel, Brody, any signs of movement or Abby down by you?"

"Negative," both came back. If she wasn't on the road, then she must have gone into the forest. That thought turned his mouth dry.

"FBI is on its way," Rachel added.

Jax couldn't wait. Abby was in unfamiliar territory, likely unarmed, and up against a skilled outdoorsman. A killer.

"Garrett, I have Ms. Coleman upstairs. I need you in here with her."

"Roger that."

Jax clicked off and turned to Margot. "My deputy will stay with you until this is sorted out."

"You seriously think I did something?"

"Until I get Abby back…" Margot looked away and he didn't feel inclined to explain further. "You'll be safe with Garrett." He led her downstairs and settled her into another chair.

As he waited for Garrett, he noted a telescope at the wall of windows overlooking the ravine. If he could spot Abby, or any movement in the trees, it could give him a direction.

Jax squinted through the lens with one eye, closing the other.

"It belonged to Shaun," Margot said. "In fact, he was up here that next day…after Terry had gone missing. He kept looking through the telescope trying to find him."

"Find him?" Jax focused on a mound of dirt in a clearing, near where they'd found Terry's blood, and noted the location before shifting the telescope to the left toward the trees on Margot's side of the canyon.

"Yeah, he liked Terry and it bothered him that he'd gone missing," Margot continued. Her tone flat. "Now I think he had something to do with that. He asked me about whether I liked him. And I did. That's all he would've needed for motivation to go after him."

Jax shut out Margot as he scanned the area where the trail started and Abby might have gone. It took a minute of searching, but movement maybe a quarter mile in caught his attention.

Without another word, Jax marched to the front door, passing Garrett on his way out.

Margot hollered after him. "Be careful. He took his bow."

CHAPTER 50

Jax radioed his team just as he entered the trail.

"I should go with you," Brody said.

"I need you where you're at. Everyone is to hold their position."

Silence met him in response.

"Confirm," Jax said.

"Yes, sir," came back three different times, with little enthusiasm.

Right or wrong—smart or just plain stupid—Jax had to do this alone. Shaun's expertise with a bow would put his team at risk of being plucked off one by one. It would be hard enough to keep himself alive and hone into any sound that didn't belong out there.

Besides, his deputies needed to keep Margot safe and be available if Shaun circled back.

Jax drew his gun and started up the trail, surrounded by towering pines, moss-laden oaks, and cool dampness. He came to a fork, but several different footprints littered the trail, giving him no guidance as to which direction Shaun or Abby might have gone. He had to go by what he'd seen through the telescope. He veered right.

The further he went, the more tall grasses and ferns covered the dirt trail. He came upon a patch of mud, a single large print embedded in it. Shaun's. Had to be.

It was the last sure clue he got. Still, he kept to the right. He could only go through what felt like the clearest path.

Trying to stay quiet as his feet tangled in ferns and stringy grasses, he spotted a clearing up ahead. Could've been the one he'd seen from Margot's living room, although the terrain had all started to look the same.

Staying low in case Shaun tried to draw a bead on him from the far tree line, Jax crept through the meadow, struggling to hear anything out of place. Watching for any sign that Abby had come through here.

He made it through the open area and entered the forest again. It was cold, his puffs of breath dissipating in front of him, but adrenaline had him overheating. He hadn't hiked this far in too long. Sweat trickled down his temple.

He ignored the fatigue, driven by his desire to find Abby. She had no idea he was out here looking for her, and he had no way to tell her. He tried not to think about whether Shaun had found her first.

That was another reason he didn't want his team nearby, although he'd never admit it to them and could barely admit it to himself. He couldn't be sure what he would do if he found Abby dead or injured at the hands of Shaun Evans.

Jax believed in law. Justice. Doing the right thing. But a man could only bear so much, and he loved Abby. He couldn't guarantee he wouldn't react in all the wrong ways if—

A branch snapped and he froze. The noise had come from somewhere in front of him, on the far side of a clump of bushes blocking his direct route.

Staying low, he crept around the knot of tangled vines and leaves, hoping he'd find Abby hiding. Praying for it.

Instead, Shaun Evans stood alone, his back to Jax and his hands on his hips, scanning out ahead.

No bow and arrow though. Shaun had a gun tucked in the back of his waistband.

Jax leveled his own gun at the man. "Hold it right there."

Shaun whipped around. "Sheriff," he said. "What are you doing out here?"

"More to the point, what are you doing out here?"

"No, I mean, how did you know…?" His face slackened. "You didn't… Oh shit."

"Yeah, oh shit. Turn around, get on your knees, hands above your head." Normally he'd want him on the ground, arms spread like an airplane, but there wasn't enough room. He'd improvise, and hope Shaun didn't go for that gun. "I know you're armed. No sudden moves."

"It's not what you think, Jax. I had nothing to do with Abby. I'm out here trying to find her."

"With a gun?"

"That was just for protection from—"

"Turn around and get on your knees," Jax ordered. He didn't have time for lies.

Shaun dropped, hands high, shaking his head. "Let me explain."

"Once you're in handcuffs. Now cross your legs and interlace your fingers. I intend to secure your gun. If you make any sudden moves, I will shoot you. Do you understand?"

"Fine, but…"

"Fingers interlaced and put your hands on your head, Shaun. I won't ask you again."

Shaun complied. Jax strode behind him and cuffed him.

He heard the whir of the arrow an instant before it embedded itself in Shaun's chest.

The man let out a howl that echoed through the trees and crumpled to the ground, leaving Jax exposed.

Jax dove to the dirt, scoured his surroundings for the shot's origin. Out ahead. To the left. He grabbed Shaun by his jacket and dragged him back towards the clump of bushes for protection.

Jax inspected Shaun's chest. Blood spread from the wound, soaking into Shaun's denim jacket.

With the arrow embedded, he couldn't put enough pressure on the entry point to stop the bleeding. If he removed it, Shaun might bleed out right there.

"You'll be okay," Jax said, uncertain whether that was true. "Who did this?"

"Margot." Shaun's breaths came in short gasps. "Only one person could make that shot. She killed Terry. She took Abby. Was trying to find her. Bring her in. But…" His words came in spurts between breaths. "She killed others."

Jax scanned the trees and clearings, desperate to find Margot. What had she done to get away from Garrett? If she was out here with a weapon, he'd been incapacitated.

Jax was supposed to make sure his team went home safe at night. The weight of having failed at that nearly toppled him. As did the thought that he'd been duped. He'd known it was Margot, sensed it, and he'd let himself be distracted by her lies—her well-recited version of events—and other people's doubts.

He couldn't let Margot harm anyone else. He had to concentrate.

He focused like a laser for any movement around him, but was met with stillness and silence.

A shiver ran up his spine. Whether he could hear or see her, Margot was out there.

He covered Shaun as best he could to hide him in case Margot came back, and sent off a text to Rachel that it wasn't Shaun, that the man had been shot, and to check on Garrett. But the message just spun. He'd silenced his radio the moment he entered the forest; he couldn't risk turning it back on.

He secured Shaun's gun in his waistband but removed his cuffs. "Stay out of sight and I'll come back for you as soon as I can."

Shaun only nodded, the loss of blood clearly taking its toll.

Jax crouched and peeked out from behind his little wall of bushes. He shook them to draw Margot out but got nothing.

She might be on the move.

Jax stood and sprinted toward the tree line. He drew no fire, which told him one thing—Margot, an expert marksman, had stopped hunting Jax and Shaun, and was now heading for Abby.

He had to find her before Margot did.

CHAPTER 51

Abby had been moving. West, she thought. She could barely make out the faint thrum that reverberated through the trees, indicating the ocean was out there...somewhere. But the forest had never been her friend. She might have gotten turned around.

She stopped, glanced back, tried to place the ocean. No *might* about it. She was lost.

She'd run and kept running—had tripped over a jutting rock and crashed face-first to the ground. She'd found a clear stream to rinse her eyes, but it hadn't been enough to clear them completely. Her sight still blurred.

Now her clothes, drenched with grime and sweat, clung to her skin. The coppery taste of blood trickled into her mouth, and the cold air stung as a constant reminder of her injuries.

The dense brush and trees made it hard to know which direction she'd started from. If she continued west toward the ocean, there'd be cliffs. Hopefully they wouldn't be too steep to climb, because if she fell into the ocean, she wouldn't escape. She'd end up dead like Jonathan Lilly.

She'd never loved the coast, not like Jax, but he'd convinced her to move. He'd wanted out of Portland, and she'd go anywhere with him back then. It didn't matter that the perpetual mist frizzed her coarse hair. Or that five minutes on a boat would leave her hanging over the side in misery. Jax had been here, and that's all she'd needed.

But it had brought them nothing but one tragedy after another. The worst of them, Lulu. Then the divorce. The major stall in her career after her last case. Now this. Abduction. Had she lost focus, or had she just thought she was a better agent than she was?

Anger pushed her to keep walking as the terrain climbed higher. But anger could only take her so far. Exhaustion had moved into her muscles. Ache and burn made each step an effort. Then she saw it—a break in the trees. Only a few more minutes of walking to reach it. She shivered, hypothermia starting to set in.

Her legs felt weighted, but she forced herself into a jog to that clearing. Maybe from there she could see where she was and where she needed to go.

She'd seen no signs of anyone since she entered the forest, but she'd heard branches breaking behind her. Someone following, maybe. But that had been several minutes ago, and since then, there'd been a deadly calm around her. No animals but for one scurrying rabbit; even the birds had stopped chatting in the canopy.

Then she heard a scream.

Guttural, primal, male. Behind her.

She whipped toward it, exposed on the open ridge. Was her abductor out there, frustrated? Or had someone been hurt?

It seemed an eternity before she tracked movement below. A man running through a clearing. Khaki clothing. Broad shoulders. Tall. She'd recognize that form, that stride, anywhere.

Jax.

He'd come for her. The thought pulled in her chest. She almost yelled for him...then stopped herself.

If he was running, he couldn't have made that scream. He wouldn't anyway. Ever. Even in his darkest moment—their darkest moment. She knew what his pain looked like, sounded like. So if not him, who?

Had he taken down her abductor?

Sudden movement off to the left of Jax. A woman. In bulky camo coat and pants, she looked large and menacing—the same camo Abby had seen the van driver wearing. But with her stocking cap off, her blonde curls flipped in the wind.

Abby's stomach caved in on itself. Margot Coleman.

A thick strap looped her shoulder, and as she turned, Abby could make out a long cylinder on her back. A quiver?

Margot's line of sight seemed to be directed toward Jax—watching him run across the clearing, just as Abby had.

She was tracking him. Jax had no idea.

Margot started to move toward the trees where Jax had now disappeared, giving Abby a clear view of the object in her hands—a bow.

Weaponless, Abby only had the element of surprise on her side. But she wouldn't let Jax get killed.

She hurried back down the way she'd come and disappeared into the safety of the trees. She would have to get around behind Margot somehow. She'd worry about how to disarm her later.

Abby went wide in the opposite direction from Margot and Jax. She moved as fast as her legs would take her, keeping her eyes on the ground to avoid any branches. If she were to have any chance at all, she couldn't let Margot hear her coming.

No one would take Jax away from her if she had anything to say about it. Certainly not Margot Coleman.

Abby came up on the other side and stayed low as she crept in the direction Margot had gone. She'd lost sight of her and Jax at this point, but she only had to find Margot. The thought of that woman having eyes on her ex-husband made her face flush with anger.

She pulled that anger back. Anger made for cloudy thinking. There was no room for error out here.

She was just about to step out of the forest when she heard voices.

"Margot, I know you're out here. It's no use," Jax called.

He did know Margot was tracking him. But where was she? Did he see her?

"FBI agents are on their way," he continued. "My entire team is outside this forest. There's no place for you to go."

His voice echoed from up ahead but there was no response to his words. Had Abby gone past Margot?

She stopped, listening, her heart ricocheting against her ribs. She had to find Margot first.

"You'd never understand." The voice came from Abby's right. Close. Too close.

Margot must be so transfixed on Jax that she wasn't paying attention. That could change at any moment.

Abby held her breath and ducked, inching her way toward Margot's voice.

"Try me," Jax said.

"People always leave," Margot said.

"Sometimes they do, Margot. We can't control everything." Abby heard the hurt in his voice. "It's completely out of our control. But you can't go around killing people because you're hurting."

"Like I said, you'd never understand."

Abby edged closer, eyes peeled, and—

There. Margot was well hidden in the bushes. Only her blonde curls gave her away.

Jax had to be out ahead, but she couldn't see him from here. And he couldn't see Margot. The camo and the leaves made her nearly invisible.

Margot's head was down, but she had her bow ready, arrow nocked.

"I lost Lulu," Jax said. His voice had grown louder. *No, Jax. Don't come back this way.* "You know that's true, Margot. You were there the day Abby and I lost our little girl."

Abby's breath caught.

"And then I lost Abby. I thought we'd have a chance again. I tried, I wanted to try more. But I can't want it for both of us. I've had to let her go." Abby's chest squeezed. "So, I do understand how devastating it can be. But it's no excuse. It's your responsibility to move on—to heal. No one else."

"My daddy left all those years ago. He never came back. Then Shaun. But I couldn't hurt Shaun. He loved our little Joey and I wouldn't take him away from our boy. You know, he left before Joey died. He moved out." Her voice was cold. "When I needed him most." The coolness disintegrated into a whimper.

Abby's heart ached at Margot's pain.

"But I still couldn't kill him because I saw my little boy in him. Do you know what that's like?" Abby did. "And then Jonathan and Terry. But they didn't have children. No one would miss them. They were easy."

"And Walter?" Jax said.

"He wasn't supposed to be there."

"Well, I'm sorry, Margot. That's rough, your dad. And Shaun. He shouldn't have left. But you can't stop people from leaving."

Her laugh sounded more like a cackle. "Unless you make it so they can't walk away."

The feet. That was why the feet had been removed off the two men. Any sympathy that had seeped into Abby vanished. Grief or not, this woman was a cold-blooded killer.

Margot lifted her bow. "And you," she said. "You're no better. You're like the others."

Abby saw Jax now. He'd drawn his gun, but his eyes were everywhere except where Margot was hidden. He stood about thirty yards away. Close enough that a well-placed arrow would kill him.

Margot began to draw the bowstring.

Abby stepped into Jax's view. "FBI, Margot—put down your weapon and step out of the brush."

Margot's eyes glanced Abby's direction, a crooked smile on her lips. "You don't have a gun to stop me."

She didn't. But Jax did. Margot had clearly seen that, but she spun her arrow Abby's direction as she pulled the bow taut.

"Drop your weapon," Jax yelled.

"Bye-bye, Abby."

The crack of a gunshot ripped through the trees, and Margot hit the ground.

CHAPTER 52

The team had found Garrett handcuffed to the refrigerator with a bump on his head. When the EMTs arrived, they cleared him shortly.

Over the next several hours, the FBI took over the scene. Not only because Margot had been involved in their Jonathan Lilly case, but because they didn't take kindly to abduction of their federal agents. Jax was happy to share the show. He decided to assign Rachel and Garrett to work in tandem with them, as evidence was secured for both cases and the Oregon State Police crime lab did the heavy lifting.

In the meantime, there'd be an investigation into what happened out in those woods. Justified or not, he knew he'd be taken off duty while the shooting was reviewed. He was okay with that. Taking a life wasn't easy, even when there was no choice, and he wouldn't turn down some time to process it.

The medical team brought Shaun in on a gurney. Before they hustled him away to the hospital, Jax had a few minutes with him. As the ambulance drove away, Jax huddled with his team at the back of his cruiser.

He was thankful all of them were unharmed. Still, he had to know.

"How'd Margot get the best of you?" he asked Garrett, who had yet to make eye contact with him.

"I turned my back on her. She got me talking about that telescope, and insisted I check out how great it was. I had one when I was a kid…and anyway next thing I know I was hit over the head, and she had herself out of the cuffs and me in them." His face darkened. "Maybe I'm not cut out to be a cop after all."

"Nonsense. There's no crew I'd rather work with than all of you. And you worked together."

"We all did, boss," Brody said. "After we didn't get Garrett back on his radio, we found him and realized what happened. We looked everywhere for Margot. We figured she must have gone into the forest, but we couldn't get ahold of you. Rachel and I followed anyway, but it was Koa that found Shaun bleeding out. We acted accordingly." Rachel and Koa had been the right choice.

"I'd silenced my radio," Jax said. "But you did the right things." He squeezed Garrett's shoulder. "All of you." They were a young crew, with much to learn, but they'd acted with heart and unity. Troy Marks would be getting a call about expanding this force to more full-time deputies. "It was a good learning exercise, regardless, even if some mistakes were made...by all of us." *Especially me, for not trusting my gut sooner.*

"Yes, sir," Garrett said.

The coroner had taken custody of Margot's body and the crunch of the wagon's tires as it left the driveway caught their attention.

"Tragic ending," Rachel said, Koa at her side. For the next half-hour they chatted about what had driven Margot. Grief. Rage. Rejection. In Jax's brief time with Shaun before he'd gone to the hospital, Shaun spoke of Margot's simmering anger that her father had left. It had marred her whole life. Rotted her from the inside out. So much so that he had to get away, even though he hated to leave while their son was sick.

"How did you know to be here?" Jax had asked him before the ambulance doors closed.

"After you left my place, I called Margot but couldn't get ahold of her. I'd been trying to keep an eye on her since our breakup last year. That day you saw me at the restaurant...I wasn't in town to see one of my kids. I didn't want to be with Margot anymore, but I loved her and sensed she wasn't right. Not for a long time. Anyway, when I checked her work, they said she'd never showed. Didn't even call. Not like her at all. I came up here to wait and see if she was okay. I was as surprised as anyone that Abby was in that van."

Jax could never know for sure why Margot had targeted Abby. But Margot had felt he'd rejected her like all the others had. So instead of coming after him directly, she went after the one person she knew had his heart.

It was beyond Jax's comprehension how someone could be so caring for others in their moment of pain and torment, yet so murderous when triggered. There could be others who had crossed Margot Coleman. The FBI would have plenty of time and resources to delve into that.

Jax released his team, sending Brody back to the station to work and update Matt, who was probably wondering what had happened to everyone. Abby approached, a thin blanket draped around her. He nodded to her. "In case I haven't mentioned it, thanks for the save back there."

She shrugged. "I think you might have saved me."

"How about we saved each other?"

She gazed at him for a long moment and then leaned into him. "I like that."

His chest swelled as he embraced her and set his chin on top of her head, soaking in their closeness.

"But let's face it," she said as she pulled away, "you're the one that came in all Rambo to find me."

Jax let out a belly laugh at the image. "That I did."

She smiled and then grew serious. "Besides, I owed you one because I didn't believe you. But your instincts, they were spot on. You're a good cop, Jax. I'm sorry if my doubting your theories made you think otherwise."

He arched an eyebrow. "I have a few other instincts I'd like to talk about."

"You do?" There was that tone Jax was so familiar with.

He bumped her shoulder. "Yeah, like, that we make a good team."

"Maybe." She wrapped the blanket around her tighter. "What does that mean for us though, Jax?"

"I'm not sure. How about we take it one step at a time." He paused. "Or we can take it in stride."

She chortled. "Are you serious with the feet puns?"

He grinned. "It's what you love about me."

"I do love you, Jax."

He'd known she did the moment she risked her life for him, but he wouldn't scare her away by getting too sentimental. Instead, he grabbed her hand and squeezed. He'd take the advice he'd given Margot. Sometimes you had to let go. A little, anyway. Now wasn't the time to push his desire for them to be back together. He'd planted the notion—that was enough for now.

"Need a lift?" he said. Olek was standing nearby, waiting. Jax waved at him and got a lifted chin. "You've got a good partner there."

Abby turned and held up a finger. "He is," Abby said. "And his grandmother is quite the baker." She winced. "Mom. I need to get to her."

"Already taken care of. The hospital was gracious enough to hold onto her until you can get there tomorrow. In the meantime, Frank is working double-duty keeping her and Trudy company."

"Thanks. That will give me time to update my team and give a statement."

It was more than that. "And you wouldn't want to miss out on the action."

"You do know me," she said. "This was personal. I just want to make sure nothing's missed."

Jax nodded and gave her another hug, then watched her join her partner, who placed his arm around her. He wouldn't begrudge Olek that. When he'd thought Margot was about to shoot that arrow and kill Abby, it had nearly gutted him.

He imagined Olek had felt something similar while he didn't know where Abby was, or if she was okay. Partners were family. He thought of Jameson. No matter how long it took, he'd make things right with him.

But he wasn't done yet with this case. Jax dropped into his car and shot off a text. There was one last thing to check before he could go home.

* * *

Gerard met him outside by Terry's garage dressed in a warm jacket and carrying two shovels over his shoulder.

"You up for this?" Jax said, bundling himself.

"Are you ever?"

"I could be wrong," Jax said.

"I hope you're not."

He understood. Not knowing the fate of a loved one was always the worst. Closure, even if it ripped out the heart, was far better.

Jax led the way through the forest trail. It was twenty minutes of navigating the root-gnarled pathway until they reached the area where Terry's blood had been located. Another ten before they reached the clearing that Jax had seen from the other side of the ravine.

The large mound of dirt lay before them, freshly churned and damp from the forest mist. Sensing he had a crime scene on his hands, he radioed Garrett to alert the ME and give them the coordinates. Gerard stood guard as Jax dug, using small shovel loads to avoid disturbing anything. It didn't take long for a Surfrider T-shirt to show through.

Terry Chesney had been found.

Gerard's face fell and his shoulders shook in...Grief? Shame? The DA would likely make him pay the price for orchestrating the theft of the blueprints. It hadn't contributed to Terry's murder, but how could Gerard reconcile betraying his brother with his claim of looking out for him?

Gerard had only cared about himself. That wouldn't be easy to live with.

EPILOGUE

Jax walked into the department. He'd had less than a week off while the FBI conducted their investigation into the shooting, and with Abby as the key witness, he'd been cleared quickly. Rachel had taken lead in the meantime. Garrett was answering the phones, she and Matt were on patrol, and Brody was off for the day.

Jax's stomach tightened at the fact that Trudy still wasn't at her post.

Garrett took an incoming call. "Yes, ma'am," he said. "No ma'am."

Jax grimaced, trying to decipher who he was talking to or what about.

Garrett leaned back in his chair. "I'm sure there's a perfectly good explanation for the dog barking. Uh-huh. I'll be sure to have the sheriff check it out on his rounds." He rubbed his eyes. "Yes, Sheriff Turner is back on duty. Yes, we're happy about that too. Have a good day."

Small town problems. The way Jax liked it. He didn't mind that someone was happy to hear he was back on duty either.

Garrett whipped off the headset. "How in the heck does Trudy handle this job?"

The door opened in answer, and Trudy came in on a walker. "What, I get a little hurt and you replace me?"

"No, ma'am." Garrett jumped out of the chair, flinging it backwards.

Jax couldn't hold back a full laugh. God, it was good to see her. He took long strides in her direction and encased her in a hug.

"Hon, hon," she said, patting his back. "In this instance, I may be made of glass. Step it back a bit."

He released her. "Doc and Frank said you'd be lying low for a few more days."

She frowned. "Since when do I do what I'm told?"

"Thankfully, not often."

She nodded sharply and leveled her gaze at Garrett. "Put that chair upright please and let me get to work."

"Yes, ma'am," he said.

And that's all she wanted to say about it. It's all that would be said. Trudy's resilience reflected Misty Pines. They'd all be fine. It might take a while, but their community would rebuild trust again.

He'd be there to make sure they did.

* * *

A few days later, Jax looked out at the surf crashing into shore. A bonfire built in Terry's honor filled the air with the brackish scent of smoke and seaweed. Dressed in a borrowed wet suit, Jax stood with one of Terry's surfboards under his arm. On the other arm hung three wreaths: one for Terry, one for Jonathan, and one for Walter, the homeless man who had simply been in the wrong place at the wrong time.

Gerard gazed out at the surf next to him, along with Dylan and a dozen people from the local surfing community. Absent were Brandon and Scott, who would likely have charges brought against them by the DA. Riley was simply too embarrassed to be involved.

But those people were beside the point. Those who had cared for Terry or brought him justice had one task left to honor the surf legend. And Jax was determined to honor all who had encountered Margot.

The waves reminded him, as they often did, of the men he'd served with in the Navy. Of the father he could never please. Of the betrayals in his past. Of his strained relationship with his former partner. If you weren't careful, waves could pull you under. Or at least knock you off your feet.

Some memories might never die. Some he didn't want to. Like Lulu's warm breath on his neck when she nuzzled him as he put her to bed. The smell of strawberry bubble bath when he came into the house after work.

The giggles of Abby and Lulu that had once filled his home.

Death had a way of reminding him of things lost.

Shaun Evans had lost too. He'd lost his son, and he'd lost Margot, who'd let rage and bitterness sit in her like acid. It ate a hole in her psyche and her soul. To such an extent that she couldn't bear any more loss of her own.

The idea of it sent a shudder through Jax. He could have been Margot. Hadn't he nearly been, when he let the grief of losing his own daughter consume him? But he'd come a long way since.

He looked up on the hill behind them. The sun coming up from the east drew a silhouette of the figures watching there. Abby, with Jonathan's sister and niece. Trudy sitting on her walker. Rachel, with Koa by her side.

He'd also gained much. He lifted his arm in salute.

"Let's do this," Gerard said, with Terry's ashes tied in a container on his waist.

Jax swallowed the lump in his throat, a mixture of sadness and fear. He'd only been on a surfboard a few times in his life, but as they entered the frigid water, Jax laid on the board and paddled in rhythm with the rest of them.

He'd been doing it his whole life, paddling fast so as not to sink. He wasn't sure what lay ahead for him with his department, or with Abby. He'd begun this case not trusting anyone. Now he felt like he had a team he could trust. A deputy he could rely on.

There'd be wounds to mend with his former partner. More training for his team. And Abby. They had a ravine to cross themselves. There'd be no easy path. At least she wanted to get back into counseling. In time, maybe they could learn to trust each other again.

They'd certainly been there for each other in that forest.

There was hope. For the moment, that was enough.

About the Author

Mary Keliikoa is the author of HIDDEN PIECES, the first book in the Misty Pines mystery series, and the multi-award nominated PI Kelly Pruett mystery series. Her short stories have appeared in Woman's World and in the anthology Peace, Love and Crime: Crime Fiction Inspired by Music of the '60s.

A Pacific NW native, she spent many years working around lawyers. When not in Washington, you can find Mary with toes in the sand on a Hawaiian beach. But even under the palm trees and blazing sun, she's plotting her next murder—novel that is.

You can connect with me on:

https://www.facebook.com/Mary.Keliikoa.Author

https://twitter.com/mary_keliikoa

https://www.facebook.com/Mary.Keliikoa.Author

https://www.goodreads.com/author/show/20038534.Mary_Keliikoa

https://www.bookbub.com/authors/mary-keliikoa

Also by Mary Keliikoa

HIDDEN PIECES, A Misty Pines Mystery, Book 1

DERAILED, A Kelly Pruett Mystery, Book 1
  DENIED, A Kelly Pruett Mystery, Book 2
  DECEIVED, A Kelly Pruett Mystery, Book 3

PEACE, LOVE AND CRIME (anthology)

Made in the USA
Columbia, SC
02 March 2023